The Same Earth

Also by Kei Miller

Fear of Stones and Other Stories
There Is an Anger that Moves (poems)
New Caribbean Poetry: An Anthology (ed.)

The Same Earth

For Pat,
Hope this
makes you
smile!

Kei Miller

[signature]
30/05/08

Weidenfeld & Nicolson
LONDON

First published in Great Britain in 2008
by Weidenfeld & Nicolson

1 3 5 7 9 10 8 6 4 2

© Kei Miller 2008

A CIP catalogue record for this book is
available from the British Library

ISBN-978 0 297 84479 2 (HDBK)
ISBN-978 0 297 84480 8 (TPB)

Typeset by Input Data Services Ltd, Frome

Printed in Great Britain by
Clays Ltd, St Ives plc

The Orion Publishing Group's Policy is to use papers that
are natural, renewable and recyclable products and made
from wood grown in sustainable forests. The logging and
manufacturing processes are expected to conform to the
environmental regulations of the country of origin.

Weidenfeld & Nicolson

An imprint of the Orion Publishing Group
Orion House, 5 Upper St Martin's Lane,
London WC2H 9EA

www.orionbooks.co.uk

De river ben come down
de river ben come down
de river ben come down
mi couldn't get over

why-o, why-o, why-o
then is how you come over?

Jamaican folk song

Me alone, me alone inna de wilderness
forty days and forty nights inna de wilderness

Jamaican spiritual

For
Michael Schmidt,
Michael Moineau
&
Michael Andrew

Contents

Acknowledgements

A novel, I've found, takes time to grow, and it does so in many countries, in cafés where you stay for hours after buying the cheapest thing on the menu. Also on trains, and in in-transit lounges, and in so many rooms which the unemployed writer could not possibly afford to pay for. So – to Dad and Mom: thank you for your faith and (y)our house where I never had to pay rent (even though you might have needed it!) and where I completed over ten drafts of this novel. To the Gergis family who provided a little bit of West Indian warmth in Wales one Christmas and the room where I completed the very first draft of this. And to the Yaddo Arts Colony in New York where I stayed for a month in a grand room with a grand piano, and completed yet another draft.

The Same Earth began while I was a student at Manchester Metropolitan – so to all my classmates who read the early parts and were helpful, but especially Emma Lynden, who read more than any classmate was required to, and even more especially to Michael Moineau, who read more than any classmate or friend or healthy human being ever should!

To old and constant friends: Richard Graham – if only I could return the favour and pass my eye over a couple hundred pages of your work but, alas, I know nothing of investment or finance. Heart-bless, ute! And Ronald Cummings – the villagers in Watersgate would have been a lot less colourful if you hadn't grown up where you did. Thanks for telling me stories and letting me pilfer. Much of you is in this.

Every writer thinks his agent is the best, and I do! Alice, you've been so wonderful. And Kirsty, my editor at Weidenfeld – this novel became so much better because of your eyes!

House in the
Middle of the River

September 1983

Imelda Agnes Richardson learned something important on the morning of 29 September 1983; she found out things could change overnight. On that morning she walked out of Watersgate, a single suitcase dragging behind her; in it all the clothes and bed things she could manage to rescue. She could not have known that her favourite piece of clothing, a bright red cardigan bought in England and never worn in Jamaica, was even then ruining all the other damp clothes surrounding it, its dye spreading generously to all corners of the suitcase so that for months afterwards Imelda would be forced to wear the colour red like some kind of Revivalist Mother warding off ghosts and duppies.

Even if Imelda had known about the sweater and its ruining effect, she would not have cared, for it was with an angry heart that she was leaving Watersgate. No one was there to say goodbye. All the windows and doors were shut tight. The only sounds that could be heard were a few birds, the steady roar of the river, and Imelda taking muddy footstep after muddy footstep towards the bridge, then towards the good road, and then (it was generally assumed) onto a bus that would take her to Alexander Town Square. It seemed that it was she alone, she alone in the wilderness.

Of course such appearances were deceptive. In a village like

Watersgate everything is seen, every movement known. There were at least a dozen people who had witnessed Imelda's exodus, but they each felt that the woman deserved this, that it was punishment from God himself, so to call out to her at that moment would be to cohort with the devil and who would want that? For destruction to fall on their houses overnight, as it had on Imelda's?

One week earlier Tessa Walcott had been walking up from the river, and if someone from outside had been watching they might have been amazed or even concerned that a woman of such considerable girth could carry all that weight (not to mention the bundle of clothes atop her head) on such thin ankles. Being an outsider, they would not have witnessed this weekly march before – every Monday to be exact – and would not know that of all the women coming up from the river with wash bundles, Tessa often carried the largest. She not only washed for herself but also for various people in Alexander Town Square, including her eldest son who drove up each Sunday to deliver onto his mother's porch the week's laundry. Under their breath many people accused the boy (indeed, he was now a grown man) of being plain 'wutliss' and lazy. But it was Tessa herself who had made him promise to bring his laundry to her, for in this way he would remain in her sight, and she could continue to look after him. In any case, washing was the closest thing to heaven that Tessa Walcott could imagine. To hear her talk of her younger days working for a magistrate in the town – fifteen years straight without him ever finding fault, and him indeed loving her for her honest ways, because if Tessa found money in any of the magistrate's pockets she would always return it to him in full – to hear Tessa tell these stories you would think that washing was the most honourable profession in the world.

On that Monday, one week ago, as the woman neared Imelda's house she called out *Imelda-ohhhhh!* so that Imelda would stop what she was doing and come outside. Imelda had been waiting on Tessa, perhaps even without realising it. In Watersgate things became ritual easy, like the rhythm of the croaking lizard found each morning at 10.32 on the croton plant, sunning itself; by 11 moving on to the wall; by 11.44 upside down on the roof. Such was the established order of his day. And while Imelda had plenty of things to do, she was only doing them half-heartedly, her ears in truth waiting for the old woman to call *Imelda-ohhhhh!* at which she would take out a long glass of water, *Here you go, Auntie Tessa.* The washerwoman would rest her bundle, take the water gratefully, gulp down a first bit, then use her thumb to rub the middle of her chest vigorously until a great belch escaped and she would apologise quietly, *de gas, de gas.*

The strange topic of conversation that morning was the state of Tessa's panties – or rather their lack of state – for not one, not two, but three pairs had been stolen from her recently. And though in Watersgate there were those who believed (and Tessa was one of them) that a missing item could be summoned back by repeating its name insistently, it just would not do for a woman of Tessa's age to be going around the streets whispering, *Blue panty! Green panty! Polka-dot panty!*

'Childe, is you one I telling,' the older woman said, 'for it would shame me to repeat this to most people.'

'B-But is a shame, yes!' cried Imelda. Most days she had a very slight stutter. 'What use could anybody possibly have for your p-panties?'

'T'iefing old woman drawers! That is what this world come to. Imagine, this is what I have to live to see! Suppose my Harry was here now, eh? What would he say? And him is a deacon!'

'I remember, yes.'

'I should sue somebody for this!'

Tessa's eyes were raised, and Imelda understood the exclamation was more of a question.

'No, I d-don't think you can sue anyone for your panties. You will just have to call it a loss.'

Tessa made a sound of disapproval in her throat. She had briefly been excited by the vision of a grand court case. It was her custom to watch the Perry Mason show on Saturday evenings, and so she had imagined a quick-mouthed lawyer from Kingston putting all of Watersgate on the stand, catching one of them out on a lie, then browbeating the culprit until she bawled and confessed. Apparently this was no longer possible. Tessa looked at Imelda hopefully again.

'You think this have something to do with The Problem With Mr Solomon?'

Imelda sighed. More and more of the villagers had begun to speak like this. In truth, no one knew if Mr Solomon had a problem. They didn't even know Mr Solomon – and this, indeed, was their own problem. That a man should be practically living in the midst of them, and that they should know nothing about him, filled them with concern and suspicion. Now, whenever something went wrong, you could count on someone to say, 'I wonder if this have something to do with The Problem With Mr Solomon?' Imelda doubted it and said as much to Tessa who frowned and shook her head.

'The place is becoming just as bad as the city. Slowly but surely.'

It was an overstatement. The theft of a few pairs of panties could not be compared to the political violence that was sweeping over Kingston, leaving more young men dead in concrete alleys than had died in the cane fields of former years. Yet, Imelda thought, the washerwoman had said it right: *slowly but surely*. The stolen panties were a sign of things to come, of things worsening. Long after Tessa had taken up her wash load and continued towards her own house, Imelda was still by the gate. She was a resourceful woman by nature. If something had to be done she would do it.

The next morning the sun rose bright over the village – though in 1983, with paved roads just beyond the bridge and JPS poles spaced evenly up and down the street, their untidy wires legally and sometimes illegally snaking into each house, it didn't feel quite right to call Watersgate a 'village'. It was true – they didn't yet have running water in the houses, but there were two

4

standpipes, and when this last obstacle to modernisation was fixed five years later, the people would indeed stop calling it a 'village' and promote it in their talk to a 'district'.

Watersgate wasn't so much a sleepy community as one that was just waking up. With better roads, Alexander Town Square was no more than ten minutes away and the city of Kingston under an hour. A few men and women now began to commute to Kingston for work and brought back not only the new slang and a slightly more aggressive demeanour, but also cheeseburgers and slices of pepperoni pizza for the children, thereby introducing the village to – no one would say a better, but – another kind of life.

Imelda woke up that morning with the satisfaction of one who had gone to bed with a question and had risen sure of the answer. She tidied herself, put on her trainers and went outside into the lime-grass scent of the morning.

Watersgate was loosely a one-road town. There was indeed only one road, but there were houses built behind houses, and houses set against the side of the hill, and you could only reach these by little dirt paths that broke off from the main road which started (or ended) at Imelda's house on the bank of the river. From there the road rose steeply but evenly for almost half a mile, one side set against the hill, the other looking over towards the river. Along its sides were mainly houses, but also two shops, a basic school and a church. At the top of the road was an iron bridge which went over the river and when cars crossed, it sounded like a great zipper being pulled up. Beyond the bridge, the 'good road' started and the village officially ended.

Two houses in Watersgate were different from the others. The first was a small hut set high up on the hill. To get to it, you had to climb a rough path which smelled strongly of kerosene, as if you might throw a lit match onto it and it would blaze up magnificently, a road of sudden fire. The hut was painted red, green and gold and made of bamboo and it belonged to the village's Rastaman, Joseph. He sold kerosene which the villagers

5

often spilled on their walk back down, as if to anoint the ground, giving it its permanent smell.

The second house was not officially in Watersgate. It stood just across the bridge where the good road began – a two-storey concrete house, painted honey-white. The owner, Mr Solomon, was a tall, slim gentleman who was always seen wearing finely tailored suits. He built the house, moved in, but spoke to no one. He left early in the morning in a blue BMW and returned late at night. Watersgate people were not used to such a phenomenon – a neighbour who was not their intimate.

Imelda's objective that morning, however, was neither of these houses, but a quite ordinary one near the top of the road. The woman who lived here was Miss Millie, a thin woman whose smallness of frame was inversely proportional to the loudness of her mouth. Miss Millie had unusually large ears and crossed eyes which were strangely furtive, as if she were always trying to look at three different things at once. Her face was a landscape of constant activity – she looked, she listened, but most of all, she gossiped. Like all persons talented in such a maligned habit, however, Miss Millie did not believe herself to be a gossipmonger. She was the most devout of churchgoers, but her loud, impassioned prayers were the best source of information on latest scandals in Watersgate, and even some of the surrounding communities. It was Miss Millie, for instance, who found out that the man who lived in the concrete house was named Mr Solomon, and that he worked in Kingston as something called 'an actuary'. Indeed it was Miss Millie who had prayed one Sunday about 'The Problem With Mr Solomon,' after which the whole village had taken up the phrase.

Imelda had woken with an idea and she knew if it was to spread through all the village, Miss Millie was the person to share it with.

'M-Millie-ohhhhh!'

Miss Millie poked her head out from around the back. 'Imelda? Oh, is you.' She emerged fully, a pot of peas in her hand. 'Come mi dear, let we sit and talk. You can help me shell these peas.'

The two women sat on Millie's small veranda, a soft wind rattling the sheet of zinc roof above them, their fingers absently delivering peas from their pods into the pot. Miss Millie sighed.

'What a thing though, eeeh, with that girl Sandra getting' pregnant. Oh Lord. Her mother send her to school in Kingston so she could improve herself and look what she gone do!'

Imelda nodded. 'What a thing.'

'Well, I hate to be the one that say it, you know, Imelda, but, like mother, like daughter. Miss Pearl was'n much older than little Sandra when she first get belly.'

'I remember.'

'The good book say it. The sins of the parents is visited upon the child. Imelda, let me tell you as God is my witness, is more than one time I sit out at front and see Pearl coming from underneath that banyan tree out there, every time a different man behind her.'

Miss Millie pointed with her chin to the famous banyan that grew outside her gate. 'You know they call it the *Sex Tree*? Imagine! The good green tree that Father God make, people take it and use it for sin. Pearl couldn't expect no better from her daughter. But Imelda mi dear, let me tell you something, you can't escape from God, you know. You just can't escape from God.'

Millie took a breath, changed gear, then started again. 'And you know who I hear was in Alexander Town Square just the other day? You remember that awful girl, Cutie Taylor, who go to Kingston and come back with her bad ways. Of course you must remember. You and she was friend and combolo growing up. Well, you wasn't here a few years back when she come mash up the people dem funeral with a gun! Eh! Poor Pastor Braithwaite did catch himself an awful 'fraid. I hear him did even pee-pee up himself . . .'

'M-Miss Millie,' said Imelda butting in, 'isn't it just a raas shame how this p-place is getting more and more like the city?'

The gossipmonger flinched. She didn't like Imelda's habit of cursing, and she didn't like to be interrupted. But being comfortable in any talk of apocalypse and calamity, the flinch transformed itself into a vigorous nod.

'Yes, Imelda. I was saying the same thing just the other day to Brother Norman. The young people today just getting badder and badder!'

'B-Before you know it, crime going to be just as bad in these p-parts as it is in the city.'

'Don't even talk it!' Miss Millie shivered. 'But you right. You is so right.'

'And the constable, him only c-coming here once or twice a week and is straight to the rum bar. I admit, a nice gentleman that Young Constable Brown, b-but him is of no real use to us in these times.'

'Not an earthly use.'

Imelda made a moment of silence stretch between them. They continued to shell peas. Miss Millie pouted her lips and shook her head from side to side.

'But you know ...' Imelda said at last, 'when I was l-leaving England, they had something they called *Neighbourhood Watch*. Don't you think we c-could do with something like that here?'

'But of course!'

It was accepted on the island that whatever came from abroad was bound to be superior, so Miss Millie agreed emphatically that a Neighbourhood Watch would be a good thing, although she quickly realised she had no idea what it was. She leaned over, biting her lips in concentration.

'Explain to me again how it work. It was long time ago I hear about it and you know the old brain ain't so good these days.'

'To b-be frank with you, Miss Millie, for us, it would just be a way of holding on to some old-time values ...'

'Amen!'

'We would organise it that everybody look out for everybody. Even when people gone into town or such. We would k-keep a good eye on the lookout, and d-don't allow this damn thing to happen where we don't even know who is living b-beside us ...

8

like The Problem With Mr Solomon. That is what it's like in the city.'

Miss Millie was won over; being a nosy woman by nature, the opportunity to legitimise such practices was welcome.

'It really wouldn't be anything drastic for us,' continued Imelda, 'Just a way to ensure ...' she had to swallow before adding a bit of scripture, 'a way to ensure that we remain our b-brother's keepers, so to speak.'

'You take the words right out mi mouth!' declared Miss Millie. 'Our brother's keepers. Is exactly what this community need. A Neighbourhood Watch. Yes, yes, yes!'

The two women continued to shell peas. Eventually Imelda looked up at the sky and said her goodbyes.

'Miss Millie, I think I b-better go and put some things on the line now that the sun is out fully.'

So she went back down the road and had not even rounded the corner before Miss Millie was leaning over the hedge to her neighbours' house, repeating the words that Imelda herself had stolen from Tessa.

'Lord, Lucinda. It sad how this place getting as bad as the city, eeeh? And when Lucinda confessed that indeed it was sad, Miss Millie barrelled on, 'I been thinking. What we need is a Neighbourhood Watch.'

The story jumped from woman to woman, from fence to fence, tumbling all the way down the village, from the bridge to the river, so that an hour later, as Imelda hung clothes out on her line, her neighbour leaned over and said, 'Miss Imelda, you been hearing talk of this Neighbourhood Watch? I hear it is the newest thing from foreign!'

Imelda said yes, she did know something about it, but they, as neighbours, would have to meet and form a charter; they would also have to go to the man who made signs and ask him to weld a big yellow one which would be planted at the bridge, and it would be like the angel with the sword who stood guard at Eden, confounding evil people and forcing them to turn around and walk briskly away. This new information made its way back up from the river to the bridge, and then back down again, and for the whole week the Neighbourhood Watch was discussed in this way. It was decided that everyone would meet on Sunday to make things official.

It being a Saturday and all, Joan Braithwaite knew to keep out of the way of her husband, the pastor, and to guard his privacy vigilantly, shooing away anyone who might call. For it was on this day, she would explain, that her husband would wait to hear from the Lord, waiting for a vision to come straight down from the throne of God, which the good pastor would then share with his people in church the next morning.

Pastor Braithwaite, on the other hand, had been behind the pulpit too many years to believe everything he said had been straight down from God. Yes, even the business of preaching, it seemed to him now, had its Tamarind Season – a time to struggle and invent and grab at anything that would help compose a lively sermon for the expectant congregation. Nineteen eighty-three was still a couple of years shy of the great explosion of dancehall in which artistes like Shabba Ranks would sing how he *loved punany bad* and Lady Saw would tell about a hood lodged so deeply and tightly in her hole that it could not be taken out – a culture so degenerate and colourful it would provide plenty of venom for sermons. But on that Saturday, Douglas Braithwaite was still in the midst of a Tamarind Season. He had no inspiration, no sermon left in him. His ears were therefore particularly keen to the news that had been spreading around the village: *Neighbourhood Watch! Neighbourhood Watch! What we need is a Neighbourhood Watch!*

The pastor was certain that this talk could only have been started by Imelda Agnes Richardson – the heathen – a woman he secretly despised. She had returned to Watersgate almost four years ago with her head shaved low like a man's, and by the way people told the story, you would believe she had stepped straight from the plane and into the police station where she broke open the jail bars with her two bare hands and took that no-good boy

Zero out of his cell. He had heard the whispers that followed the incident – *no, not even Pastor B. ever have de power or de guts to do something like that. She's a good woman, that Imelda.* All these years he had resented her. All these years he had thought of how to put her in her place.

The sun seemed to set early that evening. Clouds gathered over the hills like it was set to rain in the mountains above and the next morning was dark and miserable. People went out of their houses, an umbrella in hand just in case, and marched solemnly to church.

Though the church was registered in some official book as the denominationally confusing name, Ark of the Valley Apostolic Baptist, the original painter of the sign which stood in front of it, having a reasonably good grasp of phonetics but not of spelling, had simply spelled it the way most people said it. So it became Hark of the Valley Apastalic Baptis, a mistake which the village teacher, Sarah Richardson, used to point out with pedagogical disgust to her pupils each year. The church was a beautiful, small wooden structure with a high steeple. Inside were crude benches which prevented the children from falling asleep, and looking on these humble pieces of furniture you could still make out the shapes of the trees from which they had been cut. It was one of those churches that got going like a slow engine. It started out softly with just a hum, but by the middle of the second song everyone would erupt, spontaneously and yet in beautiful harmony, in a refrain common to all churches in these parts, '*Laaawwwd you're wurddy, wurrdy, wurrddy! Give Him praises He is wurrdy, wurddy! Hallelujah He is wurddy.*' By the sermon, the congregation would break out into ecstasy, with fervent shouts of '*Oh yes!*', '*Preach it!*', '*Hallelujah*' and then other untranslatable words; all in all a few hours spent one day each week to give the people enough faith and stamina and courage to make it through the other six.

When Pastor Braithwaite climbed up to the pulpit that morning, the first bit of thunder rolled across the valley, making the congregation shiver; it seemed now that whatever he was

11

about to say would have the weight of heaven behind it.

'Oh my people.' He pursed his lips and shook his head from side to side. 'Oh my people!' A little louder this time, and the church responded, 'Yes, Pastor, yes.'

'OH MY PEOPLE! Lift up yourn eyes. Look to the heavens. Who has created all these things?'

'Jehovah ! Jehovah has!'

'Do you not know? Have you not seen? Have you not heard? The Loooord our God is God and God alone!'

'Hallelujah!'

Pastor Braithwaite paused and licked his lips. 'In the Book of Matthew, chapters 10 and verses 29, it says are two sparrows not sold for a mere farthing? And yet not one of them shall fall on the ground without your father.'

'Yes, Pastor!'

In a magnificent quaking voice he continued, 'But the very hairs on your head . . .'

'. . . is numbered!' the church cried, completing the verse. 'FEAR YE NOT! YE ARE OF MORE VALUE THAN MANY SPARROWS!'

'Oh yes! Preach it.'

'The songwriter says, his eye is on the sparrow, but he watches over me!'

'Mmm!'

'Our God is watching over us! My people . . . my people . . . Nobody cannot watch you like Jesus.'

'Oh, no.'

'Yu mother cannot watch you like Jesus. Yu father cannot watch you like Jesus.

'No way, Pastor! No way!'

'Yu boyfriend or yu husband or yu wife cannot watch you like Jesus.'

'Say it, Pastor!'

'AND NO NEIGHBOURHOOD WATCH GOING TO WATCH YOU LIKE JESUS!'

For the first time, the pastor was greeted with silence. The silence of fear, of a people suddenly finding out they had eaten a forbidden fruit, worshipped a golden calf; that they were displeasing the very God they lived their lives to please.

'Oh yes,' Braithwaite continued, 'I been hearing the talk. And the Lord wants to ask you today, who do you put your trust in?'

'In God!' This from Miss Millie, quick as always to recover.

'I say, WHO do you put your trust in?'

'In Jesus!', from the whole church now.

The pastor smiled. 'Amen, brethren. For some trust in horses, and some trust in chariots, but . . .'

'. . . we shall remember the name of the Lord our God!' The church said this at different speeds, so that it sounded like a mighty echo resounding and resounding. They went straight into singing that very song, and they worshipped and they spoke in tongues, and each man and woman felt blessed, as if they had been made right before the Lord once more, had turned away from their wicked ways, back into the sweet enfolding of their Saviour's arms.

Imelda would know none of this until later that evening, for she was one of the few people in the village who hardly ever went to church. Indeed, after the service, Miss Millie had felt compelled to set the record straight; that the idea of the Neighbourhood Watch had always been Imelda's to start with, and she, Miss Millie, had told her, 'You can't escape from God!' 'Straight to her face, I tell her. Right there on my patio. I look at her and I say, "Imelda, you can't escape from God." But you all know how she is – her mouth is very foul, and her heart is very hard. Mmm. I pray for that child every night.'

That evening, Imelda waited in vain by the one-room building which was in turn a basic school during the week and a meeting hall on weekends. But there was to be no Neighbourhood Watch meeting. No one turned up, and this caused Imelda to reflect once again on the strange silences and upturned noses that had greeted her all day. She knew for certain now that something was up.

She walked back to her house and was about to climb the three steps to her own patio when the neighbour's little boy called out from the yard in which he had been playing.

'Miss Imelda, is true that you going to hell?'

'Say what?' Imelda turned to him.

'Mama say if people like you don't give them life to God, you going straight to hell.'

'Is that so?'

'Yes, Miss Imelda,' the boy said proudly.

'And what else M-Mama say today?'

The story came out then, and Imelda got a good idea of what had occurred in church that morning. In fact the boy was still chatting away when Imelda suddenly turned her back on him and marched into her house, slamming the door, but not before the words *Fuck fuck fuck!* had resounded like thunder throughout the whole village.

Imelda shed a few tears, but only a few. She was a resourceful woman who could not linger long in the land of griping. She knew this was how life was in Watersgate. In the morning she would visit Pastor Braithwaite and appease his pride. She would explain to him that she was not trying to replace God. For who is like unto the Lord, she would say. This Neighbourhood Watch was just a way of building community spirit, promoting community action – which is something she was sure God would want to see, for didn't he send out his disciples two by two and not by themselves? This was what she planned to say and more. That was her strategy. But Imelda would soon learn that things can change overnight.

Some will say that a river that changes course is a river remembering itself. Rivers having, as most of them do, histories longer than the civilisations that spring up around them are likely, now and then, to recall a different time when they chose to run in a different way.

Geologists and meteorologists would give a more sober explanation as to why Imelda's house ended up in the middle of the river on that dark morning of 29 September 1983. It had been raining heavily in the mountains above, cloudburst after cloudburst. The weatherman had given flash flood warnings if anyone had cared to listen. There was just too much water coming down the hill. The river swelled. The banks flooded. Then the whole thing turned. Smooth as a train changing tracks, it had diverted to a course it had run a long-ago time.

Perhaps it was the sound of the river coming into her house that seeped into Imelda's sleep, for that early morning she dreamed that she was going to the fridge to pour herself a glass of water, but the water in the bottles was dirty. She went to the sink to collect more water, but the water from the tap was also dirty. It gushed out, splashing her and soiling her white night-gown. She woke with a start but could not have imagined the destruction foretold in the dream of dirty water would turn out to be so literal. The river had reached the level of her bed, but she could see nothing – only hear the current all around her. When Imelda swung her feet off the mattress and they sank into the cold bite of water, she was certain for a moment that she was still dreaming.

She got up and sloshed through the water, managed to find the front door and opened it. The water gushed out of the house, taking with it three pairs of shoes, a lamp stand, dishes and cups, a garbage bin, a chamber pot and whatever else had been lying on the floor. Outside and all around was river. Imelda waded back to her room, knelt in the water and pulled a suitcase from under her bed. She packed what she could find quickly, including the red cardigan, and discovered how easy it was to leave almost everything behind. She understood how people could walk across whole continents with barely a change of clothes in their bags.

Back on the patio, Imelda knew it would be dangerous to step into the dark water, and it wouldn't be wise to go back into the house. She would not call out to any neighbour because she knew they would laugh at her – they would say she deserved this because she had tried to replace God. She looked up to the hill above her, to the spot where the red, green and gold bamboo hut was located. She could not see much in the dark but she knew it was there. *If only I had a drum, I could beat it and he would come down to rescue me. He wouldn't care what anyone said. He never did.* But she had no drum, and besides, there was something she felt towards the Rastaman that would have prevented her from beating a drum, even if she had one. And it was this thing too that made her leave Watersgate – just as much as the bad-mindedness of the villagers, just as much as the disappointment in the failed Neighbourhood Watch, just as much as the disaster of the river swallowing her house, it was this other thing. Love.

She was always running away from men who loved her. She didn't think of it this way. But if she had had a drum, and if she had beat it, and if Joseph, the Rastaman, had come down the hill to rescue her, then they would have had to face each other in a new way, in this world suddenly changed around them, and they would have had to answer a question it seemed they had been avoiding for more than three years, about their love, and the shape of it, and its future. She knew that she loved him; she wasn't sure any more that he loved her, and if she had called him that morning, this question would have been answered. But not even Imelda was strong enough to face the possibility of being crushed twice in one morning, so she stood on the patio waiting for the day to brighten, and as she waited she tried hard not to cry again.

When the first traces of the sun rising came from behind the mountain, she stood up tall in the greyness and marched down her patio steps into the river. She tried to float the suitcase in front of her as she crossed. At its deepest point the water reached up to her ribs.

Imelda was so focused on crossing the river without slipping or drowning or losing hold of her suitcase that she did not see three strange objects suddenly surface a short distance above her. She did not see them float down towards and then past her, ominous as Spanish ships. One of them was blue, the other green and the last one pink with black polka-dots.

16

Tessa's panties had not been stolen. Walking up from the river one day, the old woman had tilted a little too much to the left and the three undergarments had simply fallen from her load into a shallow puddle of water. They lay there baking in the ground just outside Imelda's house, and for each person who passed they were pressed more deeply into the earth, camouflaging them. There they remained until the river changed course, dissolving the mud which had encased them, and bringing them back up to the surface.

This was the second time Imelda had left Watersgate. But this time, she thought, she was never coming back. Imelda crossed. She reached the road, and from there she walked out of the village, muddy footstep after muddy footstep.

'Why-o, why-o, why-o,' the people would sing, that's how she come over.'

The Silly Thing Imelda
Believed as a Child

October 1960

One midday when Imelda was barely four years old her father came outside to find her looking up, her small eyes glued to the neat line of smoke a plane was leaving behind it, like tracks.

'Looking on the aeroplane?'

Imelda nodded, careful not to take her eyes away. Desmond heaved the child up into his arms and she squealed. In the swooping-up motion she felt she was brought closer to the sky.

'Papa? There is p-people inside the plane?'

'Yes, Imelda. Plenty people.'

'Where they g-going to, Papa?'

'England.'

It was the answer he always gave, as if, from that distance, he could recognise the specific aircraft, its number and its destination. And Imelda, with the precise logic common to children, put two and two together: if people needed to take a plane to England, then England must be in the sky. She held on to this idea for most of her childhood, so convinced by the simple obviousness of it that she never needed to share it with anyone. And although she never thought of it in exactly these words there was also the notion that if England was in the sky, then it was a kind of heaven; Jamaica, a kind of hell. As if the two places weren't even on the same earth.

His Little Lamb

February 1956

If anyone asked *When was Imelda Richardson born?* the old people probably wouldn't be able to give you the year. 1956. Such details are trivial and quickly lost. But they would be able to tell you when it was. When it was exactly. They would just have to tell you in another way.

It was after a stinking, hot summer, during the time when everyone was holding on to the words of a prophecy. Most people of this world make it through hard times in silence – by waiting them out. Hiding. But Watersgate people were different. They were the kind who made it through hard times loudly. By chanting, repeating verses. Reminding each other across the fence of some promise or other they believed God had made. In truth, they were reminding God. So in the summer of 1956 this is what they were doing: holding on to a set of words that gave them hope.

The pastor at the time, an old man by the name of Noel Baskin, who everyone simply called Old Parson, had given them a prophecy: *Yea, I am the Lord who hears his children crying. I am the Lord who does new things. Look on the barren land and see how I shall give it fruit. Look to the dry river. Watch it rise again.*

That summer, the waters of the Rio Bueno had sunk low, then lower, till finally they went underground. All that was left of the river were small stagnant puddles of water where mosquitoes bred, then rose up in clouds large as a biblical plague. It was the summer of fevers – dengue fever and yellow fever – almost every child running a temperature into the hundreds. Miss Rebecca, who was sister to Tessa, and who lived in a village not ten minutes away, had two just-born babies – twin girls – who died. On the Sunday of the burial, all the women banded around Miss Rebecca, held her, and cried together.

Mothers who had never bought ice before, the ones who preserved their meats by salting them and placing them in cool boxes below their wooden houses, started to flag down the ice cart every dawn. All day they chipped away at the blocks of ice, putting pieces in the children's bath pans, and at night in plastic bags placed inside pillows.

'Sleep cool. Sleep cool,' they whispered, 'and make morning find you alive.' They cursed the hot sun and the swarms of mosquitoes, and they prayed.

It was the summer of maladies, and a time when God seemed to be doing a lot of seeing and a lot of knowing. If you asked Tessa Walcott, for instance, how she was doing, she would sigh heavily, and shake her head from side to side.

'The Lord sees, and the Lord knows.'

It was the summer after the birth of Tessa's first child who, despite being the firstborn, was called The Fifth. It was the summer she became fat, and it was also one of the summers that her husband, Harold, had disappeared. This was not unusual for Harold. Although he was established in Watersgate, he had a reputation for being a man with salt grains on the bottom of his feet. A journey man. A wanderer. Some held it as fact – could not be convinced otherwise – that Harold was nothing but a sugarman. Sweet-talker. Woman's man. Tall guy like him – yellow skin and green eyes – could make you believe everything he said in the moment he was saying it. People said he had another village somewhere on the other side of the island, with a second family, wife and children. And this village was just as much home for him as Watersgate was. Whenever he was present in one, he was disappeared from the other. Owned equally by both places, but at the same time expected to leave both from from time to time. And the rumour, malicious though it was, acquitted him of all sin. Said it was the fate of all pretty niggers like him. The wretchedness of vanity – to wander and wander, and never find home.

The thing was, Tessa knew when Harold was about to ship off. Always, the week before leaving, he would start to visit the local rum bar regularly. He would sit on the barstool drinking JB way into the night, and every evening Tessa would have to make her way over to fetch him. He would hold on to her guiding hands and stumble towards home. Tessa loved Harold always, but the truth was she especially loved him in that week when he was getting ready to leave. When Harold drank there was a sadness that rose up in him. A sadness that was probably always there, but remained hidden. The kind of sadness that makes a woman feel strong and helpful – made her feel that she could reach in and touch what was hurting and make it better. In that week, Harold would also seem to love her more. He was grateful when she appeared at the rum shop each night. Would look up cheer-fully, a smile so genuine she could never be angry at him. It was, in fact, the smile she had come looking for. As if he had always been waiting for her – even as if to ask, 'How come you leave me here so long?'

But that long summer Tessa knew he was about to leave. One night, before going into their house, she looked into his eyes.

'Harry. You can't leave this time. Please. You can't leave.'

'Why I would ever leave you, eh?' he said gallantly, because there was a kind of sadness in her voice – the kind of sadness that makes a man feel strong and helpful.

'Harry, I serious man. The Fifth just born. Times is hard. I can't do without you just now.'

'And I serious too.' Suddenly sober, holding her hands firmly. 'I not going nowhere.'

He was serious. In that moment, in his own mind, he was serious. But it didn't matter. Things happened with a religious certainty in Watersgate – as if the people had no say in their own actions. The next day he was gone. That morning, a neighbour leaned her head over the fence and asked Tessa where Harold was, as she needed a man to help her move a cabinet from one room into the next. Tessa responded with a dignified sadness, shaking her head from side to side.

'The Lord sees, and the Lord knows.'

Poor Tessa Walcott in the summer of 1956. A wretched summer. Her sister's children dead, her man gone, her body suddenly fat, and the river low, low, low, like her spirit. So low, in fact, she fretted about losing her regular work, washing for the magistrate in Alexander Town Square. With the river gone down to nothing she could no longer bring his clothes back to the village to wash them. A new arrangement would have to be made, and if there was one thing Tessa understood about rich people, it was that they didn't like new arrangements. She did not look forward to having to stand in front of Magistrate Rattray and explain to him about the river; that she might need to come in now and do the washing by the two tubs he had installed outside his house. But Tessa need not have worried. Unknown to her, she had a friend in the magistrate.

Magistrate James Rattray had inherited the strangest of habits from his mother. An expatriate Englishwoman who was perpetually bored in Jamaica, Margaret Rattray used to leave money lying about her house. It appeared to be a careless habit but, in truth, she did it knowingly. Maliciously. She was laying bait for the hired help, tempting them every day to steal from her. Small amounts of money. Nothing anyone would miss. She was delighted when it was stolen. To the few she told about her secret pleasure, she offered various explanations: the poor dears, they really didn't get enough pay to survive, what with the number of children they usually have; she was being generous, topping up their salary. Or, it was a social experiment, she was testing the Peasant Character, seeing if they really were all crooks and thieves, which is what people had told her in England. *Don't move to the colonies, Marge! It's a right riot there. Nothing but crooks and thieves.* Or, finally, she was bored, and what was the harm in having a little fun?

When Margaret decided to fire a member of her household staff, for whatever arbitrary reason, she would hold up an exercise book in which she kept meticulous records. To the stunned employee she would read out every petty theft they had ever perpetrated – the day, the time, the amount of money stolen. Then she would give a long, tearful speech about trust. Dignity. Honour. About how the employee had failed her in every way and how deeply hurt she was. How she had lost faith in Jamaica because of them.

'Leave! Leave! Just get out of my sight. I don't want to see even your shadow around here again!'

When he was seventeen, James, smiling, asked his mother, 'Why do you always play that game?'

'Don't start to question me!' she snapped.

Even then she could sense the rebellion that was being born in her son.

When he was twenty-one, a young law student, he didn't even bother to smile.

'What you do is just plain wrong, Mother. It's wrong. And immoral. And', he added just to hurt her, 'it is unchristian.'

She didn't respond.

Then when James was twenty-six, in what became known in family history simply as the Big Fight, a quarrel that was about everything and nothing, as all big quarrels are – the big fight which was so loud that in its aftermath there was a three-year silence between mother and son; the big fight that moved from upstairs to downstairs, from room to room, from topic to topic – in that colossal confrontation, the part of it that took place in the kitchen, James brought everything round to Margaret's strange habit. He yelled something about her being sinister and evil and diabolical. And she screamed back that he was an ungrateful arsehole who hadn't been spanked nearly enough in his childhood. That was the last they ever spoke of it.

So imagine, when, shame of all shames, James Rattray, Magistrate, in charge of his own house, found that apart from his mother's nose, and his mother's thinness, and his mother's very slight lisp, he had also inherited the habit he so despised in her. He told no one, but he did it compulsively. Guiltily. Left money lying about the house for the staff, or in his pockets for Tessa. He too kept a meticulous exercise book of amounts stolen. When and by whom. And this is why Tessa fascinated him. Her name had never been entered into his book. She had never yielded to temptation. Not once. Not ever. And somehow he felt redeemed by her honesty. Forgiven. That this awful habit had led him to discover there was still good in the world. There were still people who did right. Tessa could have asked anything of him, for she was his little lamb, the one who took away the sins of the world.

It was in that same summer of 1956 that Teacher Sarah Richardson stopped seeing her period. She was forty-nine years old and accepted the missed periods with a grave finality — *Well, that is it. No children for me*. She felt she had come to terms with this fact years before and indeed had always been the first one to make fun of herself. When she rode Dorothy into Alexander Town Square, for instance, and the vendors asked about her family, she would pat the mule's back.

'My darlings, my dears, my loves' — she addressed all people like this, easily becoming the most loved schoolteacher in the parish — 'me and Dorothy here are just the same. No children for us.'

The ladies selling would laugh.

'Oh, but you very well know is Mr Richardson we asking 'bout! We know you don't have neither chick nor child.'

Sarah and Desmond had instead played surrogate parents to many of the children who passed through Sarah's classroom and there were times, it seemed to them, that their very barrenness had blessed them with more children than they could ever hope to have or love. But on that morning, when Sarah realised she had not seen her period, a wave of depression hit her, she started to cry, and days later the sadness still had not gone away. Every event seemed to be an occasion to weep, and then she, who had hardly ever been ill in her whole life, started to feel sick. In the mornings she would wake up, hold her stomach, stumble to the outhouse and vomit. She began to eat carrots fresh from the earth, dirty and brown, never bothering to wash them; indeed, it was the sweet taste of soil she was savouring on these occasions. Desmond, who had witnessed all of these things, came to her one evening.

'Sarah, talk to me. Is something the matter with you?'

Sarah looked down at her toes. How could she explain this, and to him of all people? All these years she had accepted that a man who could not have children by his wife would go outside to have them. But Desmond had never played up to the stereo-type, and this faithfulness left her feeling equally grateful and guilty. It was in his eyes that she would occasionally feel most like a disappointment, so to explain to him now her body's last and final rejection was difficult. She thought about the last two months – the missed periods, the sudden need to cry, to vomit, her appetite for dirt, and all at once the truth caved in. Stunned, her body flopped down onto the seat and she reached for her husband's callused fingers.

'My darling, my dear, my love,' she almost whispered, 'we are going to have a baby!'

James Rattray told his wife of the new arrangement with Tessa as they got ready for bed one night. They were both reading books before turning out the lights. This wasn't a habit James enjoyed, but Anna had very firm notions of what 'proper' people did, and one of those things was reading a chapter or so in bed before going to sleep. In the early years of their marriage, James tried to rebel by turning off his own bedside lamp and pulling up the covers, but every page Anna turned would then seem terribly loud, and he was always conscious of the light on her side of the room. He was a man who could only sleep in darkness, every light out and the curtains pulled shut. Now, grudgingly and non-committally, he would read one of her romance novels, but in order to spite her he took pleasure in regularly looking up from his own reading and disturbing hers with some arbitrary comment. That night, he cleared his throat.

'Oh yes . . . the washer woman, Tessa, she'll be coming in to do the washing from now on. I told her that it was perfectly all right, of course.'

Anna ignored him. She was used to his mean disruptions and if she could, would let his comments pass without response. But soon it sank in that he had made a decision concerning the management of *her* household! Have mercy! Men could be so unbearably aggravating! She closed her book and put it down firmly. James smiled at his success.

'But James,' she sputtered, 'why on earth would you do that? What was wrong with the old arrangement?'

'Oh,' he pretended to be engaged with his own book again, 'something about the river. You know, with the summer being so hot, all the water has gone down.'

'Now that's just ridiculous. And you, of course, believed her, James? Rivers don't just run out of water like that. It's not a bloody tank.'

'I think it's perfectly logical. I'm sure we can get somebody who understands geography to explain it to us better.'

'Geography is not the point, James! I just don't like the situation. She's going to be traipsing into our house. Our house! And who is going to keep an eye on her, eh? I already have to watch the other staff. I can't do it. I can't take on one more. It's just too much!'

'It's only two days per week, dear.'

'Two too many! Those people will rob you blind if you're not careful.'

'Tessa won't steal anything from us.'

'You know, James, for a magistrate, you are a poor judge of people. But in this, I know better than you. So take it from me . . .'

James Rattray was a white Jamaican; Anna was brown. But

she was that kind of brown whose family had been brown for ever – parents, grandparents, probably great-grandparents and so on. She had little claim to anything black except when it came to matters like the present conversation and, feeling the need to establish her authority, and wanting to show that she understood more of the manner and disposition of poor people, she happily alluded to the fact that her skin was darker than his without the slightest awareness that she was implicating her own self.

Haughtily, she repeated, 'Take it from me, James, they will rob you blind.'

'Tessa won't.'

Anna closed her eyes, shook her head and turned off her lamp in a fury. 'Well? Are you coming to bed or what?' her voice snapped from underneath the covers.

'In a while, dear. I just want to finish this chapter. It's wonderfully engrossing.'

If you asked Tessa she would tell you things couldn't get no worse than they got in the summer of 1956. That was a stinking summer. Now, on top of everything that had happened, she found herself bent over two concrete sinks in the magistrate's backyard. Her list of grievances was long: first of all, she didn't like the smell of the water that came out of those taps. It burned her nose. She was used to water that had the smell of leaves and roots. Second, she had to be using more blue soap than she was accustomed to. There were of course no river rocks in the backyard, no place to give the clothes a good beating that would loosen the dirt so instead she had to soap and soap, then scrub and scrub in such a small place she felt she had never worked so hard before. Third, she had to be standing up all day. Standing and bending, and in no time her back was aching something terrible. Fourth, she was alone. Washing by the river had never actually felt like work. There was always Jennifer and Sandra and Joline and Melva, and washing was simply what their hands did while they talked and while they watched the children playing, scolding them from time to time with their love.

'Devon! Why dis child can't hear, eh? Don't you hear I tell you don't go too far out!'

'Tessa, I hope your little boy, The Fifth, don't grow to be like this one here.'

'Listen to you mother, bwoy! You want River Mumma to hold you and drown you? Eh?'

'Aah Lord, that one, him take after him father. Stubborn! Notice the other one just sit down quiet over there by the bank? That's how he stay. He like his own company. But that one, Devon, Oh Father help me. He going to get himself . . . Oh look at that now . . .'

'Don't work up youself so, Joline. Him safe, man. Him safe.'

But there was none of this talk at the magistrate's house and the hours passed slowly. Her back hurt. Her feet hurt. And as if physical pain weren't enough, today temptation was hurting her worse than anything. Temptation had become a tight knot in the centre of her stomach, growing and tensing. These damn careless rich people who never seemed to know the value of money, always leaving it about! Satan will trap you like that.

'Lord,' Tessa whispered, 'give me strength.'

The money she spotted was in the bushes near the back door. She had to pass it every time she stepped into the house to take out another bundle of clothes. Two five-pound notes. Crisp. The things Tessa could do with that money, especially now that her husband had gone off. The people here obviously didn't want the money. Besides, it wouldn't be stealing if she took it; it was more the luck of finding! It probably didn't even belong to anyone inside the house. Probably some visitor had dropped it. It was a different matter with the money the magistrate left in his pockets, because then she knew for certain who it belonged to. But those crisp notes lying on the floor . . . they didn't really belong to anyone. She should just pocket the money and thank the Lord for his provision.

But for the whole day she resisted temptation. Bundle after bundle she passed the money, and bundle after bundle she talked to herself, part of her saying no, part of her saying yes. Finally the day wound down to its end. Tessa took out the last load. She stopped at the door. Yes. She would pocket the money and thank the Lord for his provision. Why not? She bent down, picked up the two notes and stuffed them deep into her pocket.

Sarah recovered just as Desmond collapsed. He fell down into the chair thinking about the words his wife had just said. *We are going to have a baby*. A baby? She must mean she was going to adopt – but how could she make that decision without him? No. Sarah was not that kind of woman. So she must mean she was pregnant. But how . . . after all this time and at this age? He looked up to ask her kindly, kindly to explain yourself more fully. ''Cause is like my ears not working too proper tonight. Say each word slow and careful.' He looked up to make this request, but it was only in time to see Sarah running out of the house.

'I soon come back!' she shouted, as if she knew where she was going, 'I soon come back.'

Tears were flooding Sarah's eyes. She hadn't even put on shoes, but her feet were moving and she couldn't stop them. She ran down the patio and out into the road, hoping to bounce into someone. Anyone at all.

It happened that Tessa was on the road. She had just stopped by a neighbour to pick up her baby, The Fifth.

'My darling, my dear, my love!' Sarah shouted and reached over to hug the woman.

'Don't crush the baby!'

Sarah laughed. She continued to embrace Tessa, The Fifth held high above them as if in blessing.

'Is what happen, Teacher?'

'Oh Lord. Tessa. Oh Lord. Good news.'

'Talk straight. Look on you . . .' Tessa laughed. 'I never see you like this before. Is what happen? You win money?'

Sarah parted from her. 'Better than money, my dear. You will not believe this, you won't . . .' she took deep breaths to calm herself, then put her hands on her stomach. 'I am going to have a baby, Tessa. Me and Desmond. We're making a baby!'

'You sure, Teacher?'

'The Lord sees and the Lord knows, Tessa. I'm sure about this one. Yes. I will go to the doctor in the morning. I don't know how I didn't see it before. But my darling, my dear, it's just ... it's just that I wasn't expecting something like this. But I am sure.'

Tessa reached out her hand as if she would be able, just like that, to feel the child inside Sarah's womb. Verify its existence.

'But dat would be a miracle ...'

'Nothing less.'

Tessa's hand rested on Sarah's stomach and she did feel something. Something more dramatic than a baby's kick. The prophecy which they had been repeating all summer leaped into her mind and she gasped. *I am the Lord who does new things. Look on the barren land and see how I shall give it fruit.*

'Teacher! Mi God! Is the prophecy come true.'

Sarah agreed. It must be true. She was going to have a miracle baby. Old Parson had prophesied it. But the fulfilment of the promise filled Tessa with anything but relief as she thought about the second part of that prophecy – the river that would rise again; the God who was still looking after her. She thought how everything was going to be all right after all, and what she suddenly felt was a deep wave of guilt.

'Oh God, Teacher Richardson. I done an awful thing.'

'What?'

'An awful thing. Oh Lord have mercy on me. Teacher Richardson, please take this child from me. I will be back before it get too late.'

Tessa gave The Fifth over to Sarah, lifted up her skirt and ran as fast as she could out of Watersgate. Sarah meanwhile stood in a dual state of puzzlement: the sudden baby in her arms, the sudden baby in her womb.

Tessa could not explain very well what happened after that. When she knocked on the door of the magistrate's house he answered it himself and his face seemed more drawn than she had ever seen it before. She showed him the money, told him how she had found it and put it in her pocket, fully intending to give it back to him. But somehow it had slipped her mind and she had left with it still in her pocket.

Tessa could not understand the magistrate's reaction. How he drew her into his embrace, as if he wanted to cry, and told her he was sorry. He wouldn't do it again. He had done it once too often. And look on that. Look on that, he had said. She had still proved herself. Like gold in the fire. Tessa couldn't understand what he was going on about. Especially when he began to call her his lamb. Tessa, my little lamb. She tried to give him the money, but he said no, how could he ever take it? It was hers, he said. She had earned it. Then he told her to wait, and when he came back he put two more crisp pound notes into her hands. Said she was not to refuse (though Tessa was never the kind to refuse money freely given). She was his lamb.

When was Imelda Richardson born?
    After the summer of 1956.
    How was she born?
    Miraculously. And not the kind of miracle that is really something quite ordinary, like a beautiful sunset. Nor the kind that is only a nice coincidence, like two people who have had been planning to meet bumping into each other on the street. No. It was an honest-to-God miracle. Sarah was fifty. Desmond was fifty-seven. By all accounts they should have been grandparents. Instead, Sarah was putting a newborn to her suddenly-firm-again breasts.

    Imelda was born with her mother's face – the dead stamp of her mama, is the way people would put it – high cheekbones and full lips and slanted eyes that seemed to be a throwback to some forgotten Asian ancestry. And with her father's height – yes, even as a baby some said you could look on the shape of her feet and tell she was going to be a tall woman. She was raised on lots of love. Lots of kisses. And lots and lots of sugar – sweet potato pudding, cornmeal pudding, grater cakes, gizzadas. Indeed she grew to be quite plump.

Imelda was born prophetically. Tambourines had shivered. There was that long, long reverent silence in which women splayed their fingers and lifted them up to heaven. Then the word had come into the silence and Old Parson's kind voice had uttered it: *Yea, I am the God who does new things* . . . And it was this fact that she had been born prophetically, like Jesus, which made her feel, twenty-eight years later as she walked out of Watersgate, that she was about to die. For it is the fate of such people to die young.

The Silly Thing Desmond
Did Not Do for His Child

October 1956

While Sarah sweated and screamed inside a room with Mother Lynette, the village midwife, and two other women attending to her, Desmond was outside pacing, keeping up that ancient tradition of expectant fathers. No one said he wasn't allowed into the room, but he understood it instinctively. He also understood that he was waiting on something. Not just the birth. Something else. But he couldn't put his finger on what it was.

He knew the moment Imelda was born. It was as if all the air in the house had been drawn to the centre, like the house had taken a deep breath, held it, and then let it go. He heard the child cry. The bedroom door was opened and a woman came out and handed him a small plastic bag. This was what he was waiting for. The birth cord. They expected him to bury it in the yard.

Desmond felt self-conscious as he stood outside holding the bag. *This is pure foolishness*, he thought. *Where it come from and what it supposed to mean?* But he knew the answers to both questions: it had come from for ever and he was supposed to tie his offspring to the earth. The world was an unsafe place and sometimes people fell off it. Floated away, just like that. This burying of the birth cord was a way to anchor the child to a specific place and home. But Desmond wasn't sure he wanted to be that kind of father, or his child that kind of child – tied to the

33

same earth that he had been tied to, given a destiny that was never their own decision. He wanted his child to be free. To roam wherever, and find whatever was out there for him or her.

Desmond sat down in the grass, looking out over the river that had finally risen again. He looked back towards the house; Sarah was in there holding their newborn baby. Boy or girl? He didn't even know yet. But, he thought happily, maybe everything would be OK. Just like the river. Everything happens in its season. Maybe it had taken them this long to become parents so that they would have grown and seen enough of life not to make silly decisions. He made up his mind. He was not going to do what they expected him to do. He stood up and threw the plastic bag into the river, watching it bob and sink and float downstream.

No Suitable Pastor

December 1961

Pastor Douglas Braithwaite was not originally from Watersgate. What brought him to the village was a series of incidents that began when Old Parson, Noel Baskin, surveying the congregation of Hark of the Valley Apastalic Baptis, could find no one to replace him. It was 1961. Old Parson would sit at his kitchen table at nights and with a shaking hand, hold his big leather Bible at arm's length, squinting and trying to read the words. It was becoming more and more difficult to read, and where he could once map his failing vision to years, it now seemed he could map it to weeks, even days. By the end of the year he would be blind. But at the age of eighty-six years, what weighed heavy on Old Parson's heart was not his impending blindness, nor was it his senile wife who had, for the past ten years, taken up the habit of going out naked into the yard, displaying her sagging body to all and sundry, and then collapsing. Old Parson, instead, was concerned with the business of succession. He thought himself an Elijah without an Elisha; there was no one to take up the mantle after him, no one to pass the ministry on to. There were three deacons in the church he had built, but none of them would make a suitable pastor.

Deacon Rodney

Deacon Rodney wasn't raised a Sunday worshipper. His family were strict Adventists, but he had insisted on marrying Rose, a young woman from Watersgate who was especially talented with needles and cloth and who impressed him with her long skirts that looked both womanly and modest on her. But although he had stopped going to Saturday church, whenever he and Rose argued he would say something vindictive.

'If I end up in hell is you cause it. I turn my back on my church because of you.'

Some things never left Rodney. He now worshipped on a Sunday but he called it his Sabbath and was adamant that no work should happen in his household on that day. No washing. No sewing. No stove should be lit. No gardening. No reaping. No picking of anything from any tree. This was challenging for Rose who knew, for instance, that Rodney liked a cup of fresh mint tea every morning, but would raise hell if she picked it on a Sunday. So every Saturday night Rose would have to pick what mint needed to be picked and leave it in water overnight. She would have to tidy what needed to be tidied, check her Sunday clothes and his and sew what needed to be sewn. But sometimes something unforeseen would happen – a button would come loose, a hem would fall, something would need attending to, and this would ultimately upset Rodney a great deal. Many a Sunday Rose came to church, brave and proud in her long skirt, and if anyone asked what had happened to her eye she would say she had walked into the mango tree or she had bent down behind the donkey who had kicked her in the face. People weren't idiots though. Everyone knew what was what.

One Sunday morning, Rose ran all the way to church without a skirt on. She had no shoes, and the stockings she wore sported big runs all the way up her thighs as she had run on the long gravel road in them. Blood was running down the side of her face and she held up a little piece of skin between her fingers.

'I want my divorcement!' she whimpered. 'You see how that

36

dog bite off mi ears? I want my divorcement, today, today, today.'

Divorcement. Big People's Affair. The children were sent home at once. Some of them, on their way home, happened to pass Deacon Rodney on his way to church, and later they would contribute to the story saying the deacon was whistling as he walked, as if nothing was the matter. When he arrived, he ignored his bloody-faced wife who was cowering in the corner. In fact, he ignored all the angry eyes fixed on him and eased his towering two-hundred-pound bulk into a bench. He looked up to the empty pulpit and frowned, a self-righteousness in his eyes, asking, *Why de dickens de service don't start yet?* Old Parson walked over and stood before him, not saying a word, and every second that passed was like an hour. When Rodney finally rose to his feet, Old Parson must have grown six inches taller to deliver the blow, for it didn't seem like he was standing on tiptoe or anything, but he balled up his fists and punched Rodney clean in the jaw. The big man crashed into one of the crude benches and a yellowed tooth leaped from out of his mouth and spun like a coin before settling on the dusty floor. Sister Carol, who sang the prettiest descant in the choir, spat a ball of phlegm into his face.

'Fucking dog, you,' she pronounced over his slumped body. 'I hope dat teach you not to bite up woman again.'

Rodney grabbed his tooth, lumbered to his feet and walked out. Walked out on the church. Walked out on Rose. Walked out from Watersgate. He went back to his Adventist family, and so wasn't around to hear Old Parson and Sister Carol apologise from the pulpit the next week. For that matter, neither did he hear the announcement that came right after – that he had been stripped of his position as deacon and for the next six months was to sit on one of the back benches of the church.

Some old women might tell you that bad times are the earth from which miracles grow, and so a most extraordinary thing happened on the day that Rose ran to church demanding a divorcement. Even the children who had been sent home because this was Big People's Affair, even they tell the story as if they were there. After Rodney marched out, people crowded around Rose who had once again dissolved into tears. Miss Millie parted the crowd for her one big scene, and though it wasn't true, there are some who would recall the gentle singing of hymns like a soundtrack in the background. Miss Millie walked over to Rose and prised the small piece of ear from her hand, immediately pressing it against the larger piece it had been torn from. A bar of sunlight streaming into the church hit Miss Millie directly on her hand so it looked to some as if the hand were glowing.

'Oh Fadder Almighty!' Miss Millie squeaked. 'Facider Almighty in whose name all t'ings is possible. In whose name de waters are parted and de sick are healed. In whose name even de great whale does bow down and swallow man and spit him back out when commanded. We are de children of your name and so we calls on you today.'

The people shifted from side to side. They mumbled *Amen, amen.* They muttered *Please, please.* Miss Millie's hand, with the of sunlight on it, trembled. Millie cried out.

'Rose! Rose!'

Rose shivered and dipped.

'Rose!' Miss Millie cried out urgently.

'Yes?'

'Rose. Does you hear what I saying? Does you hear me, Rose?'

'Yes, I hear you.'

The congregation shivered and dipped.

'Say after me, Rose! De Lord is my Saviour and my healer!'

'De Lord is my Saviour and my healer!'

Pandemonium. Miss Millie lifted her hands in hallelujah and spun away dancing. Men and women stomped on the floor and tried to out-shout each other. No one had time to notice the small piece of ear that had fallen back to the floor. As far as they were concerned, Miss Millie had just given hearing back to the deaf. Even Rose would testify about it later, how she had lost her hearing but God had given it back to her that morning.

*

Rose didn't bother with the divorcement. It seemed for the following year that she was divorced anyway. But Rodney did return when the year was over. He had fallen out with his family after he had beaten his small, small sister who luckily had a big, big husband. This big, big husband also had big, big brothers and big, big cousins all of whom had big, big fists. They confronted Rodney who tried to tell them in a big, big voice (although he was shivering) that it was *his* sister and *his* fist and he could beat her all he wanted. It was not the smartest thing he could have said. One of the men whacked Rodney across the face with a bamboo stick and the chase began. They ran him down, they caught him, they beat him. Briefly he escaped briefly. They ran him down, they caught him and they beat him again. Over and over. So Rodney finally ran back to Watersgate, battered, with another tooth missing. He went down on his knees in the wet grass, the door of his own house locked to him. He beseeched Rose with a new lisp.

'I thorry, Rothe. I thorry. I going to do better by you, 'cauthe I done you wrong. Have merthy on yu huthband. Don't make me thtay out here all night. I thtill loves you.'

Only after an hour did Rose accept, and in truth, he never hit her again. Things changed in that household. Rose began to pick stalks of fresh mint on a Sunday morning, she began to sew on a Sunday morning and cook on a Sunday morning. Rodney flinched inside but never said a word at these things. He was afraid of losing more teeth. Eventually, he would even give a moving *tethtimony* in church about how God had *thaved* him all over again. He was reinstated as a deacon, but still, when Old Parson began looking for someone to succeed him he knew that Rodney was not a thuitable candidate.

Deacon Harry

Harry was not pastor material. Harry wasn't even deacon material. The only reason he had any position in church was because

Tessa had come to Old Parson one afternoon, greatly unsettled by something her firstborn, The Fifth, had said.

Harry Walcott came from a long line of British men with the same name. By right, he was Harold James Walcott IV. Harry's grandmother, Lilieth, had happily packed her bags and left the island with a young Scottish soldier whose name was Harold James Walcott II. In her ignorance, Lilieth had thought all of Britain was England, and that all of England was London. She thought that wherever they lived, they would always be able to see Buckingham Palace, and also the River Thames, and there would be not many, but at least a few black people. But London lasted for only a week. She was off to Scotland after that, and she never warmed to the cold village they settled in. She suffered both the loneliness and the noble acceptance of a forest animal forced into a cage, far away from trees and from earth. Escape was not for her, but she was ecstatic when, years later, her nineteen-year old son confessed his apathy towards Scottish girls and declared his intention to go to the island his mother was from and find a wife. Even before he left, Lilieth was already looking forward to his return, when he would bring back things from her lost home. Yes, she wanted a daughter – a black daughter-in-law with whom she could really talk – who would listen to the way she sucked her teeth, look at the way she rolled her eyes, the different ways she pouted her lips, and understand these as words and language, not something to mock gently the way Harold II did, never understanding that he was hurting her. She wanted other things, too. Mangoes, though she knew they would not survive the journey across large water. But she did ask for plantains, hoping against hope, instructing the boy that in the year he was to return he should buy them green, wrap them in newspaper and hide them from the sun.

Harold James Walcott III had been in Jamaica for four months when a chance encounter introduced him to Ruth. He was at the beach and she was with a group of friends. He did not notice her immediately. In Jamaica he was excluded from groups of black people. He found this strange; in Scotland he was one of the only 'darkies' around, yet here in Jamaica he was suddenly seen as white, lumped with the upper classes. Black people looked on him with suspicion, his green eyes and red curly hair. That day on the beach he had not noticed Ruth although she was the prettiest girl in the group. But she was black and that made him not look, which was ironic, because black is exactly what he had come to the island for.

He noticed her finally when a young man draped her over his shoulders and started running towards the water. Ruth began to scream and hit the man's back; the group of friends were laughing and it seemed to Harold III that on the whole beach only he and Ruth realised that she wasn't joking, that her fear was real and swelling into something ugly. Harold intercepted the man, wrestled Ruth from his hold and shoved the young man into the sand.

The man got up angrily, but in the face of what he saw he withered. It was the early twentieth century, and his assailant was fair-skinned and had green eyes and the young man knew that such people were protected by every law. To fight with one of them meant trouble of the worst kind. He stood there seething with his ineffectual anger, feeling all the more foolish and crippled because his girlfriend, Ruth, was holding on tight to this man, crying into his shoulders like she was grateful or something. He marched back to the group of friends, his manhood crumbling to a fine powder. When Ruth finally rejoined him he had no words for her, and days later when he started speaking again it was only to call her a whore, a nasty bitch, a slut. He told everyone who would listen that they had had sex and it had been her suggestion, with no talk of marriage. He told everyone who had the stomach to listen that she had even swallowed his sperm one night, and that is why from then on he had refused to kiss her.

A month later, Harold III met Ruth again. She was in the market selling june-plums and he was looking for plantains, which he had fallen in love with. When he looked up and saw her with five yellow plums, the size of eggs, in her hands, he smiled and asked if she had been back to the beach. This surprised her.

'People like you don't usually remember people like me. You think we all look the same.'

'I could never forget you. I noticed you from long before,' he lied. 'You're very pretty, you know.'

They went out that night, and the next and the next, but after two months their relationship was still just talk and the occasional holding of hands. Ruth didn't understand. She knew that a relationship like theirs was only for one thing – that there was no future in it, except for the child she would hopefully have who would inherit something of his father's complexion which would propel him to a greater place in the world. The day when Harold finally mentioned marriage Ruth felt numb. It wasn't simply that she did not expect it – and she didn't – it was that she did not love him and didn't want to marry him. But it was the beginning of the twentieth century and she was black. Who was she to say 'no' to a fair-skinned man with green eyes and red curly hair who was proposing marriage to someone like her, a tainted woman who had swallowed sperm? Her life passed in a kind of daze after that and she felt it was no longer her own. When Harold III mentioned going back to Scotland, Ruth ran out of the room and vomited. Already she was seasick. Didn't he realise that she had never trusted water? Wasn't that how they had met – he had rescued her from the sea – but now it seemed he was going to throw her right back into it. She didn't know who would save her this time, whom she could scream out to.

When Harold IV was two years old, his parents, Harold and Ruth, prepared to emigrate to Scotland. An impressively large vessel, SS *Queen Mary*, was docked in Kingston Harbour. The Walcott family boarded the ship on a Sunday morning, Ruth holding on to her baby, trembling all the way up the ramp, and Harold III holding a suitcase in one hand and a bunch of plantains wrapped tightly in newspaper in the other. Ruth was committed to not seeing daylight for the next ten days. She was not going to leave the security of their cramped room until the ship had reached its destination and was ready for its passengers to disembark.

SS *Queen Mary* came to a complete halt only two days after it had left port. The vessel coughed and sputtered as it entered the Atlantic and the great white sound of the engine which had previously masked all other sounds, ceased. The world fell silent, even as the ocean, at once, seemed loud. Ruth could hear herself shaking, her baby breathing, and twelve hundred passengers on board opening their doors, asking for explanations. Ruth was certain, even before the porter knocked on the cabin door to say, 'Sir, Madam, please come on deck at once, I'm afraid there's an emergency,' that this was Apocalypse. The world had ended for her. SS *Queen Mary* had developed serious engine problems and was not going to be arriving at any British port. They would have to disembark the next day, right there in the middle of the ocean, on to another vessel sailing back to Jamaica.

There was no consoling Ruth: no husband, no porter, no captain could convince her that she was safe descending that rope ladder down to the raft that would take them over to the next ship. On the day itself, Ruth refused to let go of her child, as if he was her charm, the only thing that would make her safe. She held him between her body and the ladder, his head on her shoulders. Shakily she started her descent. Harold III stayed on deck and looked down, encouraging her.

'Take it easy, my darling. You're going to be all right. One foot at a time, darling.'

She kept her head raised, looking up at her husband. The further down the rope she went, the more he appeared to her like some kind of god, his flaming red hair framed by blue sky and clouds.

'You're going to be all right, my darling.'

His voice as sure as stone. And Ruth believed him; she was going to be all right. She took her eyes from above and looked down. She was much nearer to the raft below than to the deck above, but there was still so much ocean around that she trembled and gasped, and in that movement let go of her baby who fell fifteen feet and splashed into the Atlantic.

This is Harry's first memory: falling into the ocean, being in the middle of the lukewarm water nothing but blue waves in front of him, discovering naturally the oft-repeated assurance: that a body completely relaxed will not drown. His mother never told him this story but he always remembered it. He thought it was something he had imagined, a fantasy, especially since the self he saw in the water did not remain a baby, but grew alongside him. At five, at fifteen, at fifty – his actual self was what he saw falling and landing in the water. On the day it happened, even as the desperate shipmate jumped from the raft and made firm strokes towards him, even as everyone above deck and on the raft screamed, even as his mother on the rope ladder felt her insides collapse, Harry was smiling.

He would never lose this love for the ocean. Growing up in Jamaica with a stepfather who seemed to love nothing more than to call his wife a whore and a nasty bitch and tell the whole neighbourhood that he never kissed her because years before she had swallowed his sperm, Harry found solitude in going out to the beach. It had nothing to do with what people told him – that he had a Scottish father who lived somewhere on the other side of all that water, who had gone back with another black woman when Ruth refused. This wasn't any longing for paternal roots. It was the water that drew him to itself. He would go out with fishermen if they allowed him – out to the Pedro Keys where they hauled in hundreds of snapper and goatfish – out to the California Bank where they caught conch. But he wasn't interested in fishing. His favourite Bible story was the one where the Saviour walked on water; he understood this, how a man could feel more sure-footed on sea than on the earth.

Years later he married Tessa, a woman from Watersgate, but he would still feel the pull of the sea and disappear. He needed those months when he could pretend to be a fisherman and set out on a boat each morning. Once, he took a boat out so far he couldn't find his way back home. He almost died. Harry woke

44

up on the black sands of Haiti. He finally made it back to Jamaica with four refugees, and when he arrived he realised he had been gone for a year. For the rest of his life he would occasionally greet people with 'bon swa' or 'sak pase' and his wife would never understand what these words meant, or where he had learned them.

Tessa naturally fretted over her husband's absences. Once when he returned, The Fifth had looked up dispassionately and said, 'Hi, Uncle Harry.' and Tessa had started to cry, hurt that the boy was growing up fatherless – that he should recognise his father only as some distant relation. She went to Old Parson the same evening and pleaded on behalf of her husband.

'If only him had a little more responsibility, Pastor. If only him had something here which him could take pride in, probably him wouldn't have to leave so much.'

No. Harry was not deacon material – but he was a deacon all the same, for the sake of Tessa, and for the sake of the children who needed a father present.

Deaconess Jennifer

Miss Jennifer never married. Supposedly, the only man she was ever interested in was not interested in her, and the only man who was ever interested in her, she was not interested in. Her subsequent spinsterhood was, however, part of the reason she rose to the post of deacon despite being a woman. She was a proud virgin of fifty-one years and seemed to be above all reproach, she would tell you this herself, that if Jesus were to issue the challenge again, *Whoever is without sin cast the first stone*, she alone could draw a big rock-stone and smash whoevers' face she wanted to smash. She tithed faithfully; she never touched alcohol except for Communion; she did not gossip; she did not fraternise with 'people of the world'; and she certainly did not have sex. The only thing to give her pause some nights was the tribe of goats that was her livelihood. This tribe had started with a mere five which she had purchased twenty years ago – one billy and four does. She had bought the goats because they didn't look like any she had ever seen before, their fluffy grey coats making them seem almost like sheep. She found out later that she was right. The animals were an experiment – part goat, part sheep – and now when she read the Scripture saying God would come to separate the sheep from the goat, she thought about her herd and wondered if, on that Day of Judgement, God would accuse her of having raised abominable creatures. But Deaconess Jennifer never fretted over that for very long.

She had also been given the post of deacon because when the church had been without a building, the congregation used to meet under a tent pitched in her own backyard, and to this day some people in Watersgate and the nearby communities do not call the church by the name, Hark of the Valley Apastalic Baptis, but rather 'Miss Jennifer's church'. So everyone called her Deaconess long before the appointment became official.

The problem with Deaconess Jennifer, and why she couldn't become a pastor, was that she was a cantankerous and miserable woman who was more sour, everyone agreed, than the Sybil oranges used to make drinks. Yet she was the church's Sunday School teacher. One Sunday, Deaconess Jennifer had instructed her class of twelve boys and girls to sing the chorus, 'We Serve A Great Big Wonderful God'. Five-year-old Imelda had never really heard the words correctly and had unwittingly invented her own. The other eleven children sang:

> *We serve a great big wonderful God,*
> *We serve a great big wonderful God,*
> *Always victorious, always watching over us,*
> *A great big wonderful God*

Imelda, on the other hand, belted out:

> *We serve a great one-dollar-full God.*
> *We serve a great one-dollar-full God . . .*

Miss Jennifer gasped at the impertinence. She wondered when the child was going to feel guilty and stop. The utter blasphemy of it – God, who was worth more than silver and gold, devalued in this little girl's song to a simple one-dollar bill. Imelda zealously continued to sing her heresy. Miss Jennifer, trembling now with anger, marched stoutly over to the girl. The chorus faltered and died in the other children's throats. Miss Jennifer didn't say a word. She just made up her face, raised her hand and slapped Imelda so hard the child toppled over. Her frilly white frock rode up and the other children were so frightened they began to laugh uncontrollably.

That morning, Imelda left Sunday School spiritless, her eyes red. Sarah thought the child had come down with something.

'I think I should take her home,' Sarah whispered to Desmond.

Imelda was silent for most of the walk home. Sarah looked down with concern at her daughter and then noticed her dress.

'Imelda, my darling my dear, how did you manage to get your white frock so dirty?'

The little girl started to sniffle, and the sniffle soon avalanched into a full-scale bawl.

'What is the matter? Imelda? What's wrong with you now?'

Imelda bawled even harder.

'Imelda?'

'D-deaconess Jennifer slap me across m-my face and m-make everybody laugh at me.'

Imelda was pulled all the way back to church. The violence of her mother's walk convinced her she was in even more trouble and she cried the whole way, every sob making Sarah angrier. Sarah walked through the church doors, up to the deaconess, the service still going on around them.

'Miss Jennifer!' she shouted. No 'my darling', no 'my love', no 'my dear'. She put aside the schoolmistress properness with which she usually spoke, but not the authority. 'Tell me something ... is because you can't make pickney for youself make you feel you can abuse other people children? Eh? If you want pickney to beat, why you don't get pickney for your own damn self?

Sarah's voice, already loud, was rising with every word. The church was all silence around her.

'Imagine, is that you doing in Sunday School, beating up other people children instead of teaching them about God! A big old horse-steering woman like you ... don't you have no shame? Listen to me woman, is only because we in the middle of church right now why I don't box you to the floor the way you box Imelda this morning. But so help me God, the next time you put a finger on this child, I coming after you. Do you understand me?'

Miss Jennifer's lips fumbled but not a sound came out.

'Hello? I said, do you understand me?' as if she was talking to one of her nine-year-old students. And Miss Jennifer, like the nine-year-old who knows that every answer is the wrong answer, kept silent. Sarah sucked her teeth.

'Imelda, my darling, don't ever let these people take any step with you, do you hear me, child? Don't allow foolish old women like Miss Jennifer here to take liberty with you. Do you under-stand me?'

Imelda understood. She had been redeemed. She nodded smartly and glared at Miss Jennifer.

If Sarah Richardson had ever suspected that Miss Jennifer would take her seriously – take up the challenge, *if you want pickney to beat why you don't get pickney for your own damn self?* she might never have said it, for the boy who would become Miss Jennifer's son was condemned to a childhood full of straps and belts and long pieces of bamboo. All night that Sunday, Miss Jennifer chewed on a piece of ginger though it was not her stomach that was upset; it was her nerves. Over and over again she replayed the confrontation. She, a fifty-one-year-old virgin who was above reproach; she, after whose name the church was commonly called – to be accused like that, and then have that foul-mouthed demon of a child, Imelda Richardson, look on her in such a way,

48

without respect, and in the House of God! Oh, goodness gracious. If it was up to her she would beat the child until she forgot her own name. And all of this brought upon her by Sarah of all people who had been a mule for most her life. For Sarah to bring her womanhood and her womb into question. She had no children because no man had ever known her, and she was proud of the fact! Miss Jennifer fell asleep trembling and chewing on the piece of ginger.

Early the next morning she took an empty suitcase and went to get herself her own pickney to beat. She was not headed for an adoption agency or an orphanage, but across the island to Hanover to pay her older sister a visit. She hardly ever spoke to this sister on account of the fact that she believed her to be a wretched and whoring sinner. Her sister had had seven children by six fathers, and her eldest daughter had recently bettered the record by having eight children by as many men. Deaconess Jennifer would not be surprised if, when she reached Hanover, the niece was pregnant with a ninth. Mother and daughter often wrote to Jennifer asking for assistance, but Jennifer had always insisted she did not have money to give to the likes of them. Still, every Easter and Christmas she had had one of her goats killed and sent to them, until this too had stopped when it was reliably reported to Miss Jennifer that the niece had made a great big pot of mannish water with the last goat head, curried the rest of the meat and invited all kinds of men over. Nine months later to the day she had had her seventh child.

Miss Jennifer arrived in Hanover at midday and almost stayed right out there at the gate of her sister's house. Built from a variety of scrap board, it was not a pretty structure to look at, even with the various colours of planks nailed haphazardly to each other to make the walls. It was a small house, no more than three rooms, and it seemed a miracle that it could contain the great number of children who supposedly lived there. The house did indeed seem to be bursting at its seams; a number of planks were missing, and the three windows around the house had, in all, only five broken louvers between them. Nor was there a

49

front door – only a curtain to separate outside from inside. Miss Jennifer could hear at least two babies crying and a pair of adult voices, oblivious to the wailing, talking about something else.

It seemed that the great progenitiveness that blighted the occupants of the house also cursed the animals in the yard. Two female dogs lounged under a mango tree, their ribs showing, their full sagging breasts larger than the rest of their emaciated bodies. The twelve or so puppies that belonged to them were chasing a great flock of chickens and chicks which were running amok around the yard, shedding great quantities of feathers.

At last Miss Jennifer entered the gate, but did not walk up to the house. She, a proud virgin, would not grace such a place with her presence. She sat on a crate that was propped under the shade of a breadfruit tree and waited patiently for someone to notice her. Soon she heard a voice from inside.

'Mama, somebody sitting out dere.'

'Where? What?'

'Somebody in de yard, Mama. Look.'

'But why them don't come in. But see here!' Miss Jennifer's older sister came outside, her hands akimbo. 'Who is dat? What is it you want?'

'Is me,' was all Miss Jennifer deigned to say in a small bored voice that barely carried over to her sister.

'Jennifer? Jennifer, but see here dear God. Why you outside here kotch off like t'ief?' The sister erupted in bawling laughter. 'Is yu Auntie Jennifer,' she hollered to whoever was inside. 'Den how you do, Jen? Why you don't come inside?'

'Look,' Jennifer said curtly, 'I am here to take one of the children.'

There was silence for only a moment, then a pair of jiggling fat hands was thrown up into the air.

'As there is a God in heaven! I knew you was going to come through for us. I knew you wasn't going to turn you back on family. It is very hard Jennifer, let me tell you with so many of them. My set not even fully grown, and that little girl just breeding left, right and centre. I try to talk to the girl, but she jus' cannot stop herself. She breed again yu know! She don't tell me yet, but I know. A mother always know dese tings. But see here now, you is a saviour to us!'

'Only Jesus saves,' Miss Jennifer said without emotion.

'What age child you want?' the sister asked, as if it was as simple as that – and it was. Like flipping through a catalogue.

'I don't want no baby,' Miss Jennifer replied. 'I want a child who can take care of themself. I pass the age to be changing diaper.'

'Yes. Yes. Of course. Well, t'ree of the little ones soon come home from the school right down the road there. You can take one of dem,' as if it was as simple as that, and it was. 'They mother not here, but it don't matter. God knows she will be as happy as me to see one gone. You is a real saviour to us.'

The three little ones at school who had no idea they were being considered for permanent separation were: Joseph Martin, five years old; his older brother, Kevin Johnson, also five; and their little sister, Natalie Miller, who was four. They attended the Basic School a mere five hundred yards away from the falling house of coloured planks. When the three set out from the school gate at one o'clock, Joseph challenged them.

'On your marks! Get set! Go!'

He gave his siblings a head start but then he was off, catching up easily and then passing them, beating them by *a good donkey length!* And because he was the first child to reach home that afternoon, almost tumbling into his grandmother and great-aunt as they sat beneath the breadfruit tree, he became the chosen one. But the spirit which brought him home ahead of the other two was the very thing that would make him the worst kind of son for Miss Jennifer. His grandmother did not discern this. She sent him inside with the small suitcase Miss Jennifer had brought and instructed him to pack a few things that belonged to him, which in fact was nothing. Clothes and toys were communally owned. Half an hour later, and still confused, he was walking out of the yard with his great-aunt and the still empty suitcase.

'Where we going to, Aunt Jennifer?'

51

'No, no. Not Aunt Jennifer. You will call me Mummy from now on.'

Now she had her own pickney to beat.

All things and all deacons considered, Old Parson was in a tight spot. He could not choose between a former wife-beater and ear-biter, a man who frequently ran out on his wife and children, or a cantankerous old woman who had a soaring reputation for beating her adopted son worse than any other mother in Waters-gate. So it was in this state of there being no suitable deacon, no real successor to take over the pastorate of the church he had started, that fate conspired to arrange a meeting between Old Parson and young Douglas Braithwaite.

We Live and Then We Die

January 1962

At the relatively young age of twenty-six years, Douglas Braithwaite was the proud owner of eight long-sleeved shirts, all black. Three pairs of trousers, all black. Nine pairs of briefs, seven black, two grey. Six pairs of socks, all black. And a shiny pair of gentleman's shoes, black. The shoes sat neatly by themselves on the floor of Braithwaite's closet, and above them his dark clothes were hung, each on its own hanger – from the long-sleeved shirts straight down to each pair of briefs and each pair of socks. The clothes were dutifully washed, starched and ironed, then hung up in the small closet. There was no space left for anything else in that closet, and a quick glance would have one assuming that the pastor was single.

Such an assumption would have been wrong. At twenty-six he had been married for three years, and it was his wife, Joan, who had come up with this arrangement. It was she, not he, who washed and starched and ironed. It was she, not he, who dignified each item of her husband's wardrobe with its own place on its own hanger. It was her own decision to stuff her pretty silk blouses, her linen church outfits and her long skirts all into a chest of drawers to be ironed all over again whenever she decided to wear a particular ensemble. She saw it as an act of wifely submission and one day the Lord would reward her for it. But also, she was proud of her work on Douglas's clothes. She liked opening the closet and seeing that great display of black. She had got into the habit of buying a bit of black dye each month along with the laundry soap. Her method was to wash, then to dye, then to press. Braithwaite sometimes remarked on the way his shirts never faded, no matter how often they were washed. They never grew dull. He congratulated himself on making smart purchases. Buying shirts that lasted longer than most. That always looked new. Joan didn't mind this at all – this praise averted from her. She was a simple woman and she took pleasure in simple things. And she doubted herself. Joan would tell you with her own mouth, she was not particularly smart, not an intellectual. In the church she kept quiet, for she did not think she was someone of spiritual discernment. She felt lucky to be married to a pastor who could explain things to her. Pleasing him brought her pleasure, and to have his clothes hung up in the closet by themselves meant she could open it and smile at the good work she had done.

The predominance of black in the pastor's wardrobe was, of course, due to his occupation. Douglas had been apprenticed to the Reverend Arthur T. Grant, who had a reputation, in the 1960s, of being the best Funeral Parson in Jamaica. Everyone who was anyone wanted Grant to be the one sermonising over their dead bodies; it was as if the forcefulness of his sermon was the last push they needed to get through the gates of heaven. Reverend Grant, however, was not an organised man – he did not have a secretary and never wrote down any of his appointments in a book or calendar. It was not unusual, then, for him to promise to deliver up to three sermons on the same day, at the same time, at three different places on the island. Knowing this, he apprenticed unto himself two young men – Douglas Braithwaite was one – who could, at quick notice, find themselves at some little church tucked away somewhere in Jamaica, giving apologies on his behalf: *Poor Reverend Grant wake up sick this morning, he just couldn't make the journey, but he ask me to come and bring the message.*

54

This is how Douglas Braithwaite ended up delivering a famous sermon in the community of Sugar Park – a sermon which caused grown men of ill repute, hardened criminals, to cry, and the young pastor's reputation to spread.

The funeral that morning was for a boy who had died suddenly. He was only nineteen years old when his heart gave up on him and at the time the kind of machines didn't exist that could have explained to the bereaved community that his heart had always been too small for his body and that his life had always been tentative. Reverend Arthur T. Grant, of course, was not going to Sugar Park to conduct any funeral for a nineteen-year old boy who, by all reports, was growing up to be the kind of dog-hearted criminal Sugar Park was known to produce. So it was Douglas and Joan Braithwaite who arrived that morning: he, decked out in his black long-sleeved shirt, black trousers, black socks and black shoes; she in a slightly crushed linen suit, Bible in one hand, feather duster in the other, dutifully brushing off any speck of dirt brazen enough to settle on her husband's clothes.

'Reverend Grant?' A woman asked at the door, puzzled by his youth.

'No, no. I am Douglas Braithwaite and this is my wife, Joan.'

Joan nodded politely.

'Reverend Grant wake up sick like dog this morning. Poor man. Just couldn't make the journey. But he ask me to come on his behalf and deliver the sermon.'

'Oh, I hope he get better! But at least him still above ground. On days like today you thank the Father for life.'

'Amen, sister.'

'Well, come in, come in.'

The pews were almost full. Old men sweating under their fedora hats, old women already dabbing their eyes, young women in too-tight black dresses. Restless children. But there were no young men. Sugar Park men. No one expected different from them. They had had enough decency to come; enough decency to wear black trousers and clean white shirts, but not enough decency to tuck those shirts into their trousers, or to wear belts, or to enter the church and sit quietly. They loitered outside, chewing gum, already drinking rum. They had even put a piece of plywood on two concrete blocks, and a loud game of dominoes had started. Braithwaite had noticed them all on his way in. Sugar Park men. Wearing their manhood like a threat. He had felt small and almost feminine passing them. He had felt their eyes on him, and understood that among men such as these he had no power. His sermon on the pulpit was for them.

'Something is not right! Something not right here today!'

All week long the old people had been saying exactly this to each other, *It not right for the old to bury the young*, so they responded with fervour.

'No sah! It not right. Not right at all.'

But Braithwaite was talking about something else. He climbed down the pulpit, walked down the aisle and the congregation's eyes followed him. At the door he called out to the yard of young men, the power of God now in his voice.

'Either you all come inside like men, or you leave like little boys. I know plenty of you afraid of God. But is better you don't come at all. Scripture says, "I call upon you young men because you are strong". But none of you here is strong. You don't fool me.'

One of the domino players slammed down a tile so hard it almost shattered the plywood table. He stood up and walked over to Braithwaite. Inside the mourners got up from their seats and peered out to witness first-hand the death of the stupid young pastor, his stabbing, or if he was lucky, just his beating. Braithwaite and the domino player faced each other silently. Finally the young pastor turned around. The crowd in front of him had to part. Braithwaite walked in and the man followed. One by one they entered the church, all the young men, a sloping walk down the aisle and towards the coffin. It broke the women's hearts and they wept all over again.

The new congregants gathered around the coffin. Some of them swallowed many times and trembled to see their friend there, a face that they could remember animated, suddenly waxen and without life. Braithwaite began his sermon right then, with the men standing, looking down on their friend.

'Oh Lord. We have all looked into a coffin today. We have looked into a coffin and have seen our future. We see it clearer than in any crystal ball, clearer than in any palm, clearer than in any card or magic stone. Some of we going to sleep in a bed later on tonight, but all of we going to sleep in a coffin tomorrow.

'Some of us in here is very cunning. Some of us know how to dodge bullet. How to hide from police and soldier. How to escape the law. But hallelujah – when sweet God in Heaven write down the law that say: *We live, den we die* him write it under we own skin. Him write it down on we heart. So we cannot run from it, or hide from it, or dodge it, 'cause no man can run away from himself. Oh my people – we live, den we die. That is the only unescapable law!'

There were no choruses of Amen, and the young men gathered in front of the church looked on their dead friend and felt the sadness of their inevitable future. Some of them started to shake.

'But, ooh Laawwwd Jesus,' the pastor continued, 'You never come to bruk up no law, but to give us a greater one. A better one. And de new law say: if we believe in you, . . . [the church shivered and said their first amen], . . . if we trust in you, . . . [the church said hallelujah], . . . if we follow after you, . . . [someone at the back released the gift of tongues], . . . then our life will follow a new order: we will live, . . . den we will die . . . [a long silence] . . . BUT DEN WE WILL LIVE AGAIN!'

'Sweet Jesus!'

'And we will live again! And We . . . Will . . . Live . . . Again! And there shall be no end to that living because that living is eternal!'

The entire church was on its feet. Two of the men by the coffin stood with fat tears rolling down their faces.

'And if you want to live by that law, den is one simple thing you have to do. You have to leave your wicked ways; you have to understand that you not no badman for God; you must REPENT!'

57

The two men with tears fell down now and started to cry out loud. The other hearts broke as one. Soon more young men were weeping.

'You must repent! You must be born again! If you want eternal life, dis very day, repent!'

Prudence Baskin was not a badman or a badwoman. She was the wife of Old Parson. No doubt she wanted eternal life just as much as the next woman. But at the age of eighty-three she had a more immediate desire. She wanted to die. She had been wanting to die for the past ten years and, in fact, had been practising. She was from a generation that didn't need to look too far back to remember slavery. Her own mother had been property on a plantation. She grew up singing about the sweet by and by and how wonderful it would be when they crossed over to the other side. When she began to decline in old age, losing pieces of her memory, the thing she held on to was this value about the sweetness of death and, on her seventy-third birthday, she told everyone who would listen, 'This is mi last year on earth. Don't mourn for me. I ready to meet the Saviour.'

Then one day she took off all her clothes, from head to toe, so to speak. She started by kicking off her pink slippers. Then she untied her favourite Union Jack scarf from around her head. Then off came the light, billowy dress with its pattern of orange and purple flowers; she eased out of her black slip; her green baggies were last; and everything was thrown into an ugly, mismatched pile. Prudence then went outside in all her aging, drooping glory. She stood in the open yard for only a second before falling to the ground. Her body began a series of convulsions and white froth started to bubble up from her mouth like a never-ending river. A neighbour who had been outside raking the dirt of his yard the way country people do, as if to make the dirt neater, saw all of this. A shout went out and soon a crowd of worried people were streaming into Prudence's yard, trying to revive her with stinking toe, smelling salts, or just by shifting the position of her body. But all of a sudden the old, naked woman became very still and very stiff. People started to bawl right there and then. Poor Prudence! Prudence dead and gone!

Prudence herself was convinced that she was dead. But she was so touched by the outpouring of emotion around her that she opened her eyes and stood up. She thought it was her spirit rising out of her body, but people started to scream for joy, and somebody touched her and said, 'She not dead!' And before she could explain that she actually *was* dead, that it was just her duppy, people had already lifted her up and taken her into the house and sat her down, forcing a cup of tea down her throat which really did burn her tongue and convince her of what they all realised before she did – that she was not dead.

She did the same stunt at least once every two months after that. People grew bored with the performance. They also found it indecent. Why did she always have to be naked? Whenever Prudence dropped down someone would slap her face and say harshly, 'Prudence, you not dead! Git up!'

She was disappointed. It was a wonder the disappointment didn't kill her.

Prudence started to prepare for death in different ways. Some Saturdays she would go all the way to Spanish Town just to see the processions driving towards Dovecot Cemetery. It was really a procession of processions – a hearse followed by ten or so vehicles, then another hearse, then ten more vehicles, then another hearse, and on and on like that for the whole afternoon. Sometimes there was competition between the funeral groups – who could sing the loudest and most mournfully. She would watch it all and plan which songs she wanted sung at her funeral, what kind of coffin she wanted as her final bed, which hearse she wanted to carry her body. The hearse from Campbell's Funeral Home, for instance, had a tendency to break down, and it was painted red which didn't seem like an appropriate colour to her at all, as if it were taking its passengers to hell instead of to heaven.

She also started attending every funeral she could. If she knew someone who knew someone who knew someone who had died, she was sure to attend the funeral. She made more notes. More plans. How long the service should be. What kind of flowers she wanted, if she wanted flowers at all, and how long the casket should be kept open. So Prudence was in Sugar Park the day Douglas Braithwaite delivered the sermon that converted all the young men and made them give their lives to the Lord. She leaned over to the woman beside her while Braithwaite was busy praying, and said, 'That young man is quite a good Funeral Parson, eh! When I die, I want him to conduct my funeral!'

It was the last thing Prudence ever said. When the service was done, she walked out of the church, took one look up at the sun and then collapsed without so much as a 'Mmm!' Just like that. Stone dead. No frothing from the mouth, *and* she was fully clothed. Hat and gloves. So decently decked out, in fact, that they put her in the freezer without taking anything off. On the day of her funeral they simply moved her from the freezer into a coffin, her black dress ice-cold and her hat frozen.

When Prudence collapsed the woman who had been sitting beside her ran to Braithwaite and relayed the old woman's final request. He and Joan agreed; the next Saturday they would make their way across to St Mary to a village called Watersgate where Prudence Baskin was to be buried.

The funeral went well. As per her request, it started promptly at nine a.m. Sister Carol sang two songs: 'We Go to the Garden Alone', which was an appropriate funeral song, and 'Great is Thy Faithfulness' which was Prudence's favourite hymn. Her coffin was a simple one, made from pine wood. And there were no flowers at all in the church – no roses, no lilies, not even an orchid. Prudence had fallen in love with the phrase she heard on radio death announcements – 'No Floral Tributes Please' – and so she had asked that donations be made in aid of the School Building Fund, which in truth hadn't existed prior to her funeral.

Old Parson sat down in the pews, glad that he didn't have to officiate. He read the eulogy – told everyone that Prudence had been a good wife and, with a sheepish grin, that he hadn't been worried at all when her head started to come and go and she had began taking off her clothes in front of the whole village. It reminded him of a time that was too, too long ago, when they were younger and used to take off their clothes for more than just bathing purposes. The men laughed at this and the women blushed easily. Old Parson then sat back down and became sentimental and contemplative. He listened to the younger man who went up to occupy his space on the pulpit.

A single thing separated the two men, the old pastor and the new. That thing was love. For Old Parson was a man who loved his wife, loved his village and loved almost everyone in his church – and this love made him see only good in the young Pastor Braithwaite. The man had verve, he thought to himself. Had a way with words. He was a natural up there.

The religious see almost everything as a sign, a small piece in the great plan of God's supreme architecture. Old Parson smiled inwardly. There was no suitable deacon in his church, but Prudence had found him his Elisha. He would invite this man and his wife over to the house afterwards and he would offer it to them. The house. The Church. Watersgate.

The Silly Games Children
from Watersgate Played

1961–1970

When Imelda was small, the girls would play dress-up.

The boys played marbles. There was nothing more exciting than getting a whole bag of glassy-eyed marbles as a birthday present.

Together, they played ring games. *Bull in the pen! Yu can't come out! Bull in the pen, yu can't come out!*

'What this fence make out of?'

'Straw!'

'So-so straw?'

'That's what we just say!'

The bull would dig his heels into the earth, his head bent low to show off his imaginary horns. He would huff and snort and flare his nose and kick up dirt, and all the children holding him tight in their circle would become tense. Then the bull would charge. *Bull in the pen! Yu can't come out Bull in the pen . . . Catch him! Him get out!*

Some days they played Mama Lashy, and Mama Lashy would pretend to be whichever mother it was they all agreed gave the worst beatings. The children discussed this often, whose mother beat the worst? They agreed that everybody's mother beat equally the worst, but Miss Jennifer beat the worstest. When the shopkeeper found out her son Joseph was stealing sugar out of

62

the bag by the door, Miss Jennifer dragged the boy home from school, untied his pet goat and put the rope around his own waist. She beat him right there in front of the whole neighbourhood, who laughed at first to see the poor child running around the tree and tying himself up even tighter. But after a while it stopped being funny, especially when she just left him there all day. Some of the other mothers went over and told Miss Jennifer that she was taking things too far, that the punishment was larger than the crime. Even Mr Edwards said the boy had had enough which really should have made Miss Jennifer ease up, for Mr Edwards was the shopkeeper and it was his sugar the boy was being punished for. But Miss Jennifer was a hard woman. So whenever the children played Mama Lashy, the child with the belt would almost always invoke her.

'Watch how I go I beat all yu bottom soft soft like Miss Jennifer!' and the other children would scatter.

They also played games that children all over the world played: hide and seek; tag; Simon says. And when parents weren't looking they played, 'You show me yourns, and I will show you mines!' which always led to a lot of giggling. Strange – it was nothing they hadn't seen before; all the children bathed in the river and swam naked together, but that was with their parents watching. Everybody knew nakedness was bad when adults weren't around.

Watersgate was a deeply religious community and from day one the children knew of a game they should never ask about, should never even mention, lest they be cast into the pit of hell. A game only their parents were supposed to play, because that game, more than anything else, was Big People's Affair. But also in those days, it was still a community a couple of years away from having electricity. A bad combination, that: religion on one hand, no electricity on the other. Little in this world will lead to so much sex – the deep guilt and the ample opportunities. When they were old enough that their hormones began to kick in, the children would meet each other in the darkness, especially under the Sex Tree, a large banyan with vines hanging down in a canopy

63

so thick you could go underneath it and be completely hidden. The game they played there was private and sweaty. Sometimes they called it boom-boom. Or bang-bang. Sometimes they didn't call it any name at all; they just winked and rotated their pelvises knowingly.

Imelda played this game too. She lost her virginity when she was fourteen years old and she lost it to Miss Jennifer's sixteen-year-old son, Joseph Martin, the boy who played drums well, who, five years earlier, had been tied to a mango tree and beaten for stealing sugar from Mr Edwards's shop. Joseph was a tall, lean boy and when he and Imelda walked together in the village people called them 'Fatty and Skinny' and said they made a cute couple. Luckily for Imelda, for the two do not often happen together, it was also with Joseph that she discovered the joy of orgasms. It happened almost by accident. They were under the Sex Tree. They had begun to do it frequently. He was inside her and she was tolerating it the way she had learned to – not feeling bored exactly, but with an odd curiosity that was even mildly pleased. They heard a sound that could have been someone else approaching. Joseph made as if to get up and in that fumble ended up sliding into a position he had never slid into before. Imelda felt a sudden jolt of pleasure, wrapped her arms around him and held him there as he struggled to get up. She pulled him in; he struggled up; she pulled him in; he struggled up; then finally she let him go, weak from pleasure and shuddering in delight.

It would amuse her later in life to think that her first partner was Joseph Martin – Miss Jennifer's son who stole sugar and who used to play drums in church, and in truth never stopped playing drums, though he did stop going to church. Joseph Martin became Watersgate's first Rastaman. Bongo Man. Bhinghi Man. Nyah Man. Lion. Warrior. Heart-bless. He built a house out of bamboo painted red, green and gold, and set it on the hill, higher than everybody else's house. You would need to hike to reach up there. He sold kerosene oil to make a living and so, years later, children who simply wanted to play bull-in-the-pen or

Mama Lashy would groan when their mothers called them in and pressed money into their little hands.

'Here, child. Go up to the Rastaman and buy a small bottle of kerosene oil for the lamps.'

The First Leaving

November 1974

1974 was, like every year, a bad year. Which is to say it was average. Which is really to say, in time some might even acknowledge it as a good year. All of five people from Watersgate got married in 1974. And there were two funerals – which were nice funerals, because the people who died were old and more than ready to meet the Saviour. And the five weddings plus the two funerals added up to seven big pots of mannish water, ten goats killed, several bunches of green banana boiled in salt water, soft, soft, so you could mash them with just a little butter. Not to mention the whole heap of currying that went on – curry mutton, curry chicken, even curry fish – and the many nights of rum-drinking and celebrating, all crammed into the same year.

But it was in 1974 that the news had stumbled back to the village – oh Lord have Mercy on our Souls! – that little Jonathon had been lured away by a golden comb. The boy's sister had run home crying for everyone to hear and, carrying his shoes limply in her hands, had collapsed into her mother's arms, Miss Dorcas, and blabbered something about River Mumma. River Mumma had taken her poor brother – Miss Dorcas's son. Just like the legend. Tempted him with the golden comb. Now he was drownded. And when Miss Dorcas heard this, she too collapsed, without having anyone to catch her. Flat out on her doorstep.

The other children who had been playing by the river soon arrived – they had not run as fast as the little girl who was energised by a grief she should not have known at that young age – and they backed up her story. Yes, Miss Dorcas. Yes, is true. Her little boy was drownded. No. They didn't see exactly how or when. They was just playing a game of hide and seek by the river and everybody know Jonathon was a boy who loved to play it dangerous – loved to go into the river and hide. Hold his breath under water whenever someone come near, for who would look for him in the waters? Don't it? Don't they had all seen him do that before? Yes. Yes, they had. And don't they all tell him, him play too dangerous. Dat him luck was going to run out – don't they had told him? Yes, the children all agreed with each other. They had told him. Well, sure as fate, this time the worst had happened. They had found his shoes by the river, but nothing else. All the children had called and called. They had gone into the water. His sister had called and called, for over an hour. The sun was about to set, and all of them had looked up just in time to see the light glinting off of a rock. And didn't all of them see it? Yes – all the children nodded that they had – glinting on the stone, something that looked like a golden comb, a sure sign of the River Mumma who tempts children her way, then drowns them.

By now everyone had gathered, but although they all had much to say, no one immediately knew what to do. It was with the relief of sheep – people who lack the strength or conviction to make decisions on the most important things – that they heard a sound like a mighty zipper and looked up to see the jeep belonging to Young Constable Brown crossing the bridge above them.

Young Constable Brown was neither young nor was he, in fact, a constable. In his less-than-impressive career in the force he had managed to be promoted once, but only once, and technically, he was a notch above 'constable'. The name Young Constable Brown had stuck, however, and though it did not acknowledge the solitary promotion of his whole career, he thought that at least it credited him with a kind of youthfulness and vigour.

The performance of his constabulary duties in Eastern St Mary brought him to Watersgate once or twice a week, driving up in his government-plated jeep. To the people of the village, the constable was a well-respected man, the most official person they encountered on a regular basis. Their first link with Government and the wider, complicated world. When Young Constable Brown sat in the bar, sipping charlies and water (usually on the house), zealously telling stories he had only just read in the *Enquirer* or the *Star*, the rum-heads drank it all up. This is why many of the silly things he believed, the whole of Watersgate ended up believing as well. For instance, they believed that the prime Minister had installed in his house a two-million US dollar bathroom; fountain in the middle, golden taps, jacuzzi the size of an Olympic swimming pool. They believed the whole process of elections was nothing but a sham because in truth every politician had an obeahman working for him or her, and so all the election results proved was whose obeah was the strongest and most potent. They believed that the CIA had killed Bob Marley because there was a coded message embedded in those reggae songs that would liberate black people all over the world, and the CIA couldn't cope with the thought of an uprising or the incongruity of a black president in the White House. And so it was to this officer of the law that the people flocked on the day news spread that little Jonathon had drownded.

The constable tried to be very official, asking the children to 'repeat and corroborate' their stories so he could write an official report, but when Miss Dorcas started weeping bitterly, and he said no, no, no, it was more important, much more important, of utmost importance to find the body first. Soon everybody was walking down to the Rio Bueno with candles and lamps. They had to hold Miss Dorcas up and carry her the whole way. The children were silent and serious as they made up the rear of the procession. At the river, the men rolled up their trousers to the knee and women tied their skirts up high.

'Fan out, fan out,' instructed Young Constable Brown.

They all walked into the water, slowly down into and around it, feeling the bottom with their feet, searching for something softer and larger than simple river stones.

All this time little Jonathon was watching from the top of a mango tree, fearing what was surely going to happen to him, for he realised he had taken the joke too far this time. He was in trouble and he knew it. If Miss Dorcas beat him all the way into next year, he would count himself lucky. The mango tree he was in was in fact the same tree under which they had laid Miss Dorcas to cool down. Jonathon tried to get her attention softly, throwing down leaves at her. Little twigs. Hoping she would look up and discover him herself. But Miss Dorcas only shook off the disturbances, and then sighed loudly.

'Oonoo find him yet? Oh Lord!' calling out to the people in the river, who called back to say no, they hadn't. They feared he had probably floated too far downstream by now. Probably all the way out to sea.

Jonathon knew he would just have to call out to his mother. He tried to do so softly.

'Mama.'

But he said it at one of those strange moments where everything is suddenly and completely silent. Like the world had paused and the earth had ceased its turning, so that his sound alone could exist. The soft 'Mama' wasn't soft at all. It seemed to fill the whole river. Women screamed. The children waiting on the bank spun around agitatedly, for they had already seen River Mumma today, and now it seemed as if they were going to see a duppy, and they couldn't handle so much of the supernatural in one day. Miss Dorcas alone looked up into the tree and saw her son, and there was so much anger in her eyes that little Jonathon climbed down faster than if he had dropped. Without a word to him or to anyone, she dragged him all the way home. When they reached the house she hugged him hard.

'I not going to beat you. I won't make you father beat you. No. I think you know what trouble you cause already. You scare you

69

sister so much, you will have to make it up to her. But I not going to beat you.'

She put him to bed, and there he cried harder than if she had indeed beat him.

And that night, everyone spontaneously gathered outside – Miss Josephine, Maas Jeffery, Miss Millie, Teacher Richardson and Mr Desmond, Pastor B. and Joan – everybody was there, and Miss Dorcas made a big pot of hot chocolate to share. And they drank it and ate water crackers long into the night, telling stories and singing songs. Wasn't that a good time? Wasn't that the kind of thing that makes a year good?

And 1974 was the year when Mother Lynette got a telegram from her son Brendan, the one who won all the scholarships, who had brains more than sea had water, who everyone agreed 'him bright-can't-done!' He was now a big doctor of something and teaching at a university in Canada. Mother Lynette told everyone the story, how she got a letter from him saying the University was so impressed with his work that they had promoted him. Given him a chair. And she had written back to him saying, 'Tell them to keep the furniture. Tell them you want money.'

'Ole fool like me,' Mother Lynette laughed, 'who never know what University chair was.'

Everyone who listened laughed with her, though they knew they might have made the same mistake. But they felt proud with her too. And wasn't that a good year? 1974, when Brendan got chair, and they could laugh and feel foolish and proud at the same time.

Yes. In retrospect, there were good things that happened. But years, like wine, need time to improve. Living through a year is a different thing from reflecting on it. And living through 1974, no one would tell you about the five weddings or the two nice funerals or Miss Dorcas's little boy who never drownded or Mother Lynette's bright son. They would tell you instead that it was a bad year. Like every year. Mostly they would tell you about the hurricane, which hit hard. A few of the houses had been getting used to the constant buzzing brightness called electricity, but the hurricane came and plunged them all back into the great equaliser called darkness.

Living at the very end of the village, the Richardsons had had no electricity to begin with, so Desmond's concerns in the weeks after the hurricane were about other things. The roads, never good from day one, were now completely impassable and the question of how to get crops into town was a daunting one. Still, the farmers would have found a way around this were it not for the second problem: there were no crops.

All the fields were devastated. Coffee plants had been uprooted. Banana trees torn up. Coconut trees had fallen by the thousands. The land was so waterlogged by the time the rains left that the only sugarcane that had managed to survive was worthless, only as sweet as the fresh water surrounding it. Prices tripled and then tripled again, and for three weeks straight the young Pastor Braithwaite spoke from Psalm 60: *Thou hast made the earth to tremble; thou hast broken it. Thou hast shewed thy people hard things: thou hast made us to drink the wine of astonishment.*

One evening, a couple of weeks after the hurricane, Sarah was sitting in the living room, the doors and windows flung open as she used the last of the day's light to catch up on her reading. Desmond came in, sat down in the chair opposite her and cleared his throat. But after a long moment he had not said anything. Sarah peered at him above her glasses, shook her head, then went back to her book.

Desmond got up, paced outside, then returned to the seat and cleared his throat again. Sarah put down her book with much exaggeration.

'Des, if you have something to say, it is best you just say it.'

'Yes my dear,' he started, grateful that she knew him so well. 'It's just that ... is just ... Well, we is not young any more.'

'You don't need to tell me that, thank you very much, Mr Desmond. I have my own eyes and I look in the mirror every morning ...'

'And what a lovely sight it is to see, eh?'

Complimenting her was second nature to him. She grunted, pleased, but unwilling to give him the satisfaction.

'But is something else I trying to say . . .' He paused.

'Then say what you mean to say, nuh! As you put it, we don't have all the time in the world. Mind you or me dead before you get off whatever it is on your chest.'

'Chu man, Sarah. You so provoking at times . . . but, I just thinking. You know, when our own parents send us into the world, is like they give us something. You know. The island needed building up. And is like we do a bad job, Sarah. We don't have nothing to leave the next set of young people. The country just mash up so bad . . .'

'I know,' Sarah said softly, taking off her glasses.

'I is seventy-five years old now, and I wonder what kind of world I leaving behind for Imelda.' He looked up at his wife. 'Sarah, we have enough money saved. I been thinking . . . We should send Imelda away. Send her to England, where it have opportunity for young people . . .'

'Oh no, Desmond. Oh Lord, no. Not this again.'

An old-fashioned Jamaican man, Desmond kept his face still and waited for his own emotions to subside.

'Is probably the best thing we can do for her.'

'But send her away to do what, Desmond? You can't just send a child cross the ocean like that.'

'How you mean? Look how many people do just that,' he protested. 'But she could go to school. We will make arrangements.'

'Too late for that, Mr Desmond. Too late.'

'We can make arrangements,' Desmond insisted. 'She can stay with someone for a while. Work for a year. Settle into the place and then apply for school next year. She is a bright girl. And in England people can be anything they want to be: lawyer, doctor or Indian chief.'

'No, Desmond. No [N-n-no] [N-n-no!] no!'

And this outburst of 'no's came in melody and harmony: the melody of 'No, no no!' from Sarah and the harmony of 'N-n-no,

N-n-no!' from Imelda. For she had entered the room from the back. To walk in suddenly and hear her parents plotting to take the world away from her made her dizzy. She ended up on her knees, and it was from here that she made her very first and loud reproach to her ageing father – 'N-n-no!' – an outburst that soon dissolved into tears. Imelda then recovered her strength and ran out of the room, Sarah stumbling behind her.

Desmond waited for his voice to compose itself. He continued to speak to the empty chair as if Sarah were still sitting there.

'And most importantly, my dear, I don't want the child to see us die.'

This latest concern was a new one for him, but the desire to have his daughter leave was old. What started out on the day of her birth as magnanimity on his part, the throwing away of her birth cord, this generous gesture, the allowance that she should be allowed to go wherever she chose, had soon become a mission for him. Throughout her childhood he was always scheming and suggesting which boarding school in Montego Bay she should go to or in St Elizabeth, or saying she should be sent to live with a relative in Kingston because any good parent who wanted their child to become something in life knew that child had to grow up in the city.

But what about the child's language, Sarah had asked. You know Imelda doesn't have the cleanest mouth. People won't understand her. They would expel her immediately. And what of Cutie Taylor? What good did Kingston do for that one? You forget already? Cutie and Imelda are the same age and they sent Cutie to Kingston but not a soul can argue Kingston did her any good. Do you remember how every holiday when Cutie came back it was another scandal? Thirteen years old and she was winking at every boy who knew how to use his willie. Fourteen years old, and she said she was done with boys. She wanted only Big Man now. And so said, so done. Have you forgotten, Desmond? You and I saw it with our own two eyes – Cutie walking into Maas Jethro's house at night! Old Maas Jethro – a man who could have been her grandfather, and with his poor old wife in America on a six-month visa cleaning house for rich people and sending the money back home to him! And do you remember how, when that summer was over, Cutie went back to Kingston but she was in the family way? Is that what you want for our daughter? The argument Sarah had used to put a decisive end to all Desmond's scheming was when she told him, quite sternly, *All this talk of sending the girl away will make her think we don't love her.*

But that was four years ago. That was when Imelda was fourteen, not eighteen. A young teenager instead of a young woman. That was before the hurricane. The suggestion now was for her to go to England, not Kingston. And though his daughter and wife had run off, leaving him alone in the living room, he knew the point had registered because this time he was right.

In her room, Imelda complained. 'Mama, tell him for me. Tell him I not going to no raas c-cold country!'

Sarah placed her hands on Imelda's thick, wild hair.

'Oh, my darling, my love. You're almost eighteen. You are your own woman now. You don't have to go anywhere you don't want to.'

'Good,' cause I not going. I staying here with you.' This made them both cry, for each knew the other was lying. They didn't know the language or trust the love which could say two things and feel two things. They didn't want to hurt each other. So the daughter could not say, 'Yes, I would love to leave', and the mother could not say, 'I would love for you to go'. Instead, one said she wasn't going anywhere, and the other said she wasn't going to let her go. But this was just their way of saying they loved each other. Between them, they already knew the future. It would be silly to turn down this opportunity. In those days almost everybody was waiting for a ticket out. Great Britain had taken so much from her colonies, the colonies were now taking back. Caribbean people landed by the thousands on English shores, many without a place to stay or a plan of what they might do. They arrived with the simple conviction, that England had something to give them, something they were entitled to, and they weren't going to leave until they got it.

It was a hurricane that blew Imelda towards England, but was that such a bad thing? People on an island will tell you that the trees grow most brightly in the aftermath of a storm. That great and powerful act of nature is nothing more than God pruning his Eden – tearing off dead branches from the tallest breadfruit and eucalyptus trees that no man would bother to do himself. So that year, when opportunity blossomed bright for Imelda, wasn't that a good year?

The Silly Things People Told
Imelda about England

November 1974

In the 1950s, Jamaicans started to migrate by the hundreds and then by the thousands. All of them, walking towards the boat or the plane, would turn to their loved ones and say, 'Look for us with two eyes. We coming back for sure. This is home,' but for years no one came back and some didn't even bother to write. By 1974, the trickle back had finally started and even swelled. Many people were returning, some of them with money to build houses for their retirement, some of them with shattered minds needing to heal, but each with a story of what it was like living in Mrs Queen's country. Once people heard the news that Imelda was to leave and seek her own fortune there, they quickly told her who she was to go and see – *they will sit you down and tell you exactly what is what. They will give the full rundown about what you need to know to survive.*

Mr Kiddu, a man from Watersgate who in truth had only been to England for two months to visit a daughter who lived in the Derbyshire countryside, spoke very flatteringly of the place. He informed Imelda, quite seriously, that cows up there were decent and mannersable. Much more than the old teggareg cows we has down here. For if you leave a pen open in England, he said, the animals stay right where they was. Imagine that! Civilised cows. Brought up proper. Not like the bad-breed local herd who, everybody know, leave the gate open and soon as no one looking they lift up their tails and trot off fast, fast, gone to do whatever gallivanting and shenanigans it is indecent cows get up to. And then you have to spend all evening rounding them up!

Mr Kiddu also confirmed that it was true, English cows could divine the weather. If they were sitting down it meant it was going to rain, and if they were standing up it meant the day was going to be bright and sunny. This, of course, never worked in Jamaica because some cows always stood up while others always lay down, and the all it meant was that some was lazy and some was up to mischief. No, no, he told her. You can't put too much stock in Jamaican cows, for they have no respect for the Government or the Queen.

Marie Patterson who lived near Alexander Town Square told Imelda that she would walk untold distances. Miss Patterson had arrived in England with three tattered cardboard boxes, yards upon yards of brown tape holding them together. She had arrived with three boxes, but only two hands. The money in her pockets was too precious to spend on taxis, and her sister was working a double shift that day and could not come to meet her. Marie Patterson said the buses were so tall they didn't even have a rack on the roof, much less a young man up there who could help lifting heavy loads. Instead, she herself had to load the three big boxes on to the front of the bus, and nobody offered to lend her a hand. The bus driver and all the passengers even looked disgruntled, as if she was wasting their time. She told Imelda how the final journey from the bus station to the house was only one mile but she ended up walking five. She would take up one box and carry it for twenty yards or so, put it down and then go back for another one and bring it forward, and then go back for the last. This is how she made her way, slowly, slowly, to the house, and she realised this was the lot for black people in England. To walk until them foot drop off.

Albertina George told Imelda she couldn't too too remember much about England. She remember the boat ride across. She remember the largeness of the ocean – how it frightened her to

77

have so much water and no land. She remember thinking that the ocean was bigger than a day, and bigger than a week. Beyond every horizon was only more water. When she finally arrive, the whole place was just mist, and it was like she step inside the mist, and the mist step inside of her, and her brain became soft, just like that. She know that she learned to ask the question, 'Any spare change, sir?' She learned how to find the warm parts of buildings – the sections near pavements where a vent would exhale gusts of hot air. And she remember that some people were nice to her, but others would spit on her. And she remember a nice, white hospital she would go to at times that had plenty people from Jamaica and St Kitts and St Vincent and all over the West Indies. And she remember the man from Trinidad who did tell her, 'They say we mad, eh? Well, we really mad to leave home and come here!' And Albertina remember the day she hear a voice cutting through the mist saying, 'Mama, Mama? Is you that? You know how long we been looking for you? Mama, is this what you really come to?' Then suddenly she was on a plane and, looking down through the window, she realised the ocean had shrunk. It was only hours big now. She arrived back in Jamaica and it was as if the mist left her mind at the same time, for everything became clear again. They told her she had lived in England for twenty years. They told her she had grown old in England. But she couldn't too too remember.

So Imelda put it all together one night in a dream: she imagined England was a long, long road covered in mist. And on the side of the road were cows wearing tiaras who bowed down graciously whenever the Queen passed by.

Imelda's Sermon

Arrogance is the inevitable condition of every city. The feeling settles not only on the people, but also on the buildings, on the cars, and even on the rusting rubbish bins filled to overflowing that line the streets. Also, in the lights. In the ubiquity of the streetlamps, in the flashiness of the theatre lights, in the glare of 2,000-watt stadium bulbs, in the red and blue excitement of sirens. The villages and towns that lie on the outskirts of the city, or even further afield, seem like unexciting little pockets of darkness – backward places whose shadowy people are always running to the city for their own little piece of brightness to take back with them. But after the hurricane, Jamaica's capital city was humbled. It had nothing to distinguish it from the rural sections of the island because in the storm, light-poles were felled as easily and as plentifully as trees. Kingston, no stranger to power outages, experienced one that lasted two months. On the night that Imelda left for England, airport staff led the passengers out onto the tarmac using flashlights.

In the plane, Imelda sat beside an old man who tried to talk to her. He admitted that this was his first time flying, and produced from out of the briefcase he clutched in front of him pictures of a son, the son's wife and their two children, who all lived in London and were doing well and had sent for him. Imelda wasn't sure when she had turned away from this conversation, but she found herself looking out of the window onto the dark tarmac and then up at the viewing deck with its crowd of silhouettes – people either waiting to see their family off, or hoping, even in this darkness, to catch a first glimpse of relatives alighting from a recently landed plane. One of those silhouettes belonged to her mother and another to her father. She turned back to her neighbour and found him packing up the pictures that had failed to impress her. She wanted to apologise but didn't know how, so she turned back to the window, ashamed to look at him.

Safety instructions were given. The old man beside her had his eyes closed and seemed to be praying. Imelda felt her ears close as the plane lifted off. She looked out of the circular window; the dark island growing smaller and smaller. There was a rumble from below. Then a flash of light. Thousands and thousands of lights came on at once. After two months, power had finally been restored and the city blazed up like Christmas. It was as if the plane had pulled a veil off the city, and Imelda imagined the darkness was there behind the plane, being drawn by a long rope, going with her all the way to England.

What was missing in the hurried postal communications between Sarah Richardson and her second cousin, Maisy, now living in Peckham Rye, all the envelopes that passed between them marked URGENT as if this would make them cross the Atlantic faster, was not Imelda's time of arrival: nine-thirty in the morning. Nor was it a plan of what was going to happen immediately after – they had already decided on that: Maisy would take Imelda home and she would stay there for at least a month. Maisy had even gone as far as preparing her speech for Imelda. She would tell the girl as she set her up in the living room, pointing out the couch that would be her bed, that *no, no! This wasn't convenient for [h]er at all, at all.* (She didn't pronounce most of her h's.) *This is, after all, our living room, and right beside the kitchen. So don't worry if John (my [h]usband, you'll meet [h]im later) [h]as to walk through [h]ere in the morning to get [h]is coffee. Because John needs [h]is cup of coffee in the morning, because [h]e goes to work so bloody early. Because life [h]ere isn't so easy like it is in Jamaica. We [h]ave to work [h]ard [h]ere. So bloody [h]ard. You'll [h]ave to learn that soon, you [h]ere? But this is your room for now. No, not convenient for us because we can't bloody well entertain with someone sleeping in the living room. But that's all right. It should be all right. And [h]ow is your mum?* All these details were worked out. What was missing was something far more simple, and far more crucial – for when Sarah wrote that Imelda's plane would land at nine-thirty, and Maisy wrote to say that wouldn't be so convenient because she would [h]ave to take time off work but it was all right, it was fine, and she would be there to meet Imelda at the airport, it did not occur to either woman that there was more than one airport in London. So Imelda arrived at Gatwick, while Maisy waited for hours at Heathrow, the cardboard sign with 'IMELDA RICHARDSON' useless in her hands. So it was that the two were destined never to meet.

When, two weeks later, a frantic Sarah sent a telegram to Maisy asking, 'Is Everything All right?' – meaning, of course *has Imelda landed safely? Did you meet her at the airport? Is she settling in?* – a still angry Maisy interpreted the note as an apology – *so sorry for wasting your time, for making you take time off from the job and go to the airport for no goddamn reason. Can you forgive me?* And because Maisy had decided she would never waste time or money on Sarah again, she returned a simple message: Yes. Which of course meant, No.

Imelda hugged her father's old grey jacket tight around her body; it was the warmest piece of clothing she had. In its breast pocket her mother had stuffed a piece of paper, saying as she did so, 'My cousin Maisy will meet you at the airport. But here are two other phone numbers. I haven't telegrammed them, but they are good people, and will help you out if you're ever in a spot.' So when Imelda found herself in a spot, five hours waiting for Maisy and not a sign, she tried both these numbers. Sadly, neither proved useful. Maybe these two former students of Sarah's had moved

81

on and up with their lives and had neglected to inform their old teacher about their latest ascent. Or, as Imelda would think in later years, maybe she had done something incorrect. Probably she had used the Jamaican coins in her right pocket instead of the British coins in her left; or not inserted her finger in the right hole of the dial and spun it all the way around till it clicked; or maybe she had put the mouthpiece to her ear and the earpiece to her mouth. It was the first time she had used a payphone – too proud to ask for help, and too nervous and self-conscious to do anything correctly.

She walked away from the phone, out of the airport and into the cold afternoon. She watched the taxis, big and black as hearses, coming and going, dropping off and picking up people who seemed at ease with the world. Imelda felt exposed. Small. She started to panic. She reached into the inside pocket of her jacket. There was a fistful of dirt there. The morning before leaving Watersgate she had bent down in the yard and closed her fingers around the soft earth. It was this same earth she was touching now, for comfort, for balance.

'May I help you, ma'am?'

She turned around. The young black man in front of her seemed stupidly dressed in a red hat and blazer. He was smiling, his teeth perfect and white in an angular face. Quickly she tried to compose herself.

'Yes. Yes . . .' she looked around her. 'I was wondering what b-bus you take to . . .?'

Her sentence trailed off. A bus to where? She had already arrived in England, but what kind of destination was that – so big and wide and meaningless? People do not live in whole countries; they lived on streets, in flats, in apartments, in houses, and almost always with specific numbers assigned to them. She wondered how she could not have realised this before – that the world was too big for any one person, that each man divided it into small fractions in order to make sense of the whole. But now Imelda found herself in the broad world, without an anchor.

The porter pressed her. 'What bus do you take to where, ma'am?'

'Excuse m-me!'

The food she had eaten on the plane was rising up in her throat. Imelda grabbed her suitcase and ran for the Ladies'. Squeezed inside a white cubicle, she retched into the porcelain bowl. She did not ever want to leave. The world was too large, and she decided this small space would be enough to contain her. It would be her permanent address: Ladies' Toilet, Cubicle 4, First Floor, Gatwick International Airport, London, United Kingdom. Maisy clearly didn't want her, so maybe this was it.

When, after many minutes, there was a knocking on the white door, it was with a sense of proprietorship that she called out, 'Yes, who's there?' But the sound of her voice, echoing in so small a place, destroyed her illusions immediately. She opened the door.

'You OK?'

'This is the Ladies!' Imelda protested.

It was the man with the red cap and blazer. He smiled defiantly.

'I'm OK.' Imelda relented.

'Do you have somewhere to stay?'

She was surprised by his directness. Was her situation so obvious? She shook her head.

'Look, I can take you into London when my shift is done in half an hour. You could leave your suitcase in storage here at the airport. You wouldn't want to be lugging it around.'

'Storage?'

'Don't worry. I can do that for you. They charge three quid though.'

Imelda reached into her pockets for the money. People had warned her England would be expensive. She followed the man out of the Ladies.

'I'll be back round here in half an hour,' he called. He was walking faster now, and not looking behind him. She watched him walk away with her three quid and her suitcase and only when he was nearly out of sight did it dawn on her, with a kind of sad defeat, that she was probably being robbed.

He didn't return after half an hour, nor after an hour, and when two hours had passed Imelda started to cry. But only for a minute. She was a resourceful young woman by nature, who and would not be beaten down by self-pity. She wiped her eyes and mounted the connected seats of the airport waiting area, standing up tall and looking England square in the eye. All through her life, when people heard Imelda's stutter, they would say of her 'she has a heavy tongue'. She wanted to explain that it wasn't her tongue that was heavy, but that words were too light. When she wasn't careful, words would slide out and fall on her tongue. This is why she took so easily to cursing. Curse words seemed to have more weight to them, and they would never slide. They came out whole, complete and eloquent, and could even steady all the other words surrounding them.

'Bomboclawt,' Imelda said softly to the airport that morning.

'Bomboclawt.' A little louder. And then a little louder, and louder still. A rising crescendo of *bomboclawts*. No security guard dared to stop her; no woman from customer services tugged at her sleeve to offer *a cuppa tea*. She was shouting with such conviction, *bomboclawt*, *raasclawt*, *raashole*, *bumbonought* to a stunned congregation of travellers. There was even a Chinese missionary in the airport that morning who listened to her with a growing sense of comfort. He did not understand Imelda's words, not knowing much of the English language beyond 'Jesus loves you, amen'. He thought, however, that he understood her spirit, and decided that hers was a pure and holy one. Indeed, to him, every *bomboclawt* and *raashole* Imelda shouted sounded like words from an angelic tongue, and so in his heart he responded to each one of them: 'Amen, Jesus. Amen.'

After her sermon, Imelda was silent. She did not speak a solitary word for two whole days.

Inside almost every immigrant there are two impulses – the impulse to shout, and the impulse to be silent. The second is by far the stronger impulse, for at some point almost every day, the immigrant is afraid of speaking. She is afraid that the sound of her voice will be a loud banner confirming to everyone else her deep fear that she does not belong. Ironically, the impulse to shout comes from the same reason, for the immigrant will want to hear in her voice proof that she belongs somewhere else, the melodious evidence of a nation that accepts her.

From Gatwick Airport, Imelda followed the signs that pointed passengers to the TRAINS. This was something she could understand without thinking: England had built the first train network in the world; Jamaica had built the second. So it was something she was familiar with. Trains took you somewhere you needed to be. She boarded and watched the land pass by and then a voice shouted 'Last stop, everyone disembark,' and with the small portion of her mind that she was using to move and to breathe and to survive, she understood that it was time to get off. She came out into the great cathedral of Victoria station. There were more trains that she never saw, and there were black taxis and red double-decker buses that she never saw. She just kept moving – walked down the road and past Buckingham Palace, but she never saw that either. She thought it was safer to keep looking at her feet, to make sure she still had them. So, on her first day in London, what Imelda saw was this: the hem of her green skirt, her feet in black stockings, her black shoes with one-inch heels going clip-clop, clip-clop. She saw various squares of pavement and many patches of green grass and cobblestones. She saw one dead pigeon and a thousand live ones defiantly weaving in and out of many feet.

She saw feet in slippers and platform shoes and bell-bottomed trousers. She saw bird shit and dog shit, black banana peals and empty fizzy drink tins. Her eyes followed her feet to Piccadilly Circus and then to Trafalgar Square, and when Imelda was tired, she took off her jacket, wrapped it around the one bag she had and laid down in the grass in front of the National Gallery and went to sleep.

The next morning Imelda lifted up her eyes and really began to see England for the first time. It surprised her the great number of toilets there were in the country. Shop window after shop window, billboard after billboard, every new construction going up, all of them advertised in bold letters the fact that they had a TOILET. In actual fact, the signs were advertising space to rent, but Imelda's mind, not familiar with the phrase 'To Let', had magically filled in the missing 'I'. With this great over-abundance of toilets, the thought had come to her, *I know it all along. This country full of shit.*

But even as she walked around and saw London, only the smallest part of her mind was engaged with what she was seeing. It was as if she had decided to cocoon the rest of it – put it safely in storage. London and then all of England passed through her like an amnesia. She remembered only what she needed to remember, and only at the moment she needed to remember it. Day after day she walked the streets; she paid a few pennies to wash in the train station bathrooms; she bought fresh fruits at pavement stalls. And night after night she slept in parks – but the next day she would not remember which streets she had walked on, what she had eaten, or which park she had slept in. Take, for instance, this fact: it was only on the day that she came to a building that said 'Social Agency for Homeless Families' did she remember a night spent sleeping on Clapham Common. The missionaries had come with their candles, and they sang 'Rock of Ages' while handing out food and blankets to the homeless. The woman who had held Imelda's hand and prayed for her that night had mentioned this same building she was standing in front of.

'You really must register at the Social Agency for Homeless Families. They will sort you out.'

A Word That Sounded like Home

December 1974

Jamaicans landing in Britain found the names of places fascinating. In London there was Kingston and Barbican and Paddington, and although they knew that England must have been the origin of these names, it still seemed they had been stolen from Jamaica. They knew the English had tried so desperately to remind themselves of home that even today in Jamaica the red otahiti fruit, which isn't an apple at all, is called one. So the migrants wondered – if colonisation had happened the other way around, would the English apple have been called an otahiti? Would berries have been called guineps?

Other place names stood out: places like Pity Me and Ramsbottom, which would remind them of place names in Jamaica that had whole stories behind them. Wait-a-bit. Save Mi Rent. Nine Miles – which always begged the question, 'Nine miles from what?' There was a place in England called Calamity Hill, which disturbed them. It was as if the people living there must be waiting each day for the ground to vanish and the walls to fall in. There was another place nearby called 'Bury', and some wondered if the residents had made up their minds to die. They would think of all the wakes and nine-nights in Jamaica, the old people drinking rum into the early hours of the morning, men beating drums like it wasn't even them playing, and the women singing in rounds that went on forever, *Yerri me, mi nana, yerri me. Bongoman a dig hole to bury me!*

Imelda did not stay in London for long. The woman behind the glass counter at the Social Agency for Homeless Families had asked her through a microphone, her voice disembodied and eerie, if Imelda had any ties to the city. The woman told Imelda she would be guaranteed a job in Manchester if she was willing to go, and she could even stay rent free for a month at the Mary Grant Hostel for Women. So Imelda took the bus to Manchester, another place name Jamaicans would be familiar with.

On the island, Manchester was a red-dirt parish. In England it was a redbrick city. Redbrick buildings and redbrick roads. All the redbrick houses were held tightly together as if they were trying to keep warm. Above the city there was a kind of fog that wasn't really fog at all, but the exhaust from millions of chimneys, too tired to rise any further, so that it hovered over the city like a grim angel. In 1974, Manchester was a city that was slowly rotting. Almost a hundred years had passed since the end of industry and cotton, but the shock had not worn off. Hundreds of empty factories and warehouses just stood there, their broken windows open like surprised mouths. The Victorian architecture was reduced to being a canvas for the work of street artists, boys who painted elaborate graffiti onto the walls. And while progress had stopped, inflation hadn't. A steady stream of immigrants kept pouring in, rushing into this centre of poverty as if to claim a piece of rot for their own. They rented dark rooms all around the city – in Moss Side and in the Northern Quarter – hoping against all hope that one day they might be able to move to a place like Didsbury or Oldham and own a home with a front room that didn't need curtains – was just there on open display for everyone to see they had finally arrived.

Imelda found the women's hostel and settled into a yellow room that was almost her exact impression of a jail cell. The nine other cots showed evidence of the other women who slept there, women Imelda would never really meet because even at nights, each woman stayed in her own private world. No one seemed to make friends with anyone.

Imelda got a job at a supermarket. She presented the official slip of paper with her A-level grades on it to the store manager who didn't bother to look.

'Do you think you can manage the tills?' was all he asked.

'I think s-so.'

'Good then.'

Months later she would present the same A-level slip to the admissions officer at Winchester University. He did not look at it either – not until he asked, with boredom, what she wanted to study, and Imelda, remembering how her father had said – *In England you can become anything you want: lawyer, doctor or Indian chief* – elected for the first thing on that list and said, *I w-want to study law*. It was then that the man scrutinised her grades, and finally nodded.

'Yes, I think you should be able to get a place.'

Imelda worked her shifts and then in the cold evenings she would walk up and down Portland Street, or along Oxford Road, turning off the side streets into Hulme and Old Trafford, or heading back to the city centre and across to the Northern Quarter. But Hulme was the place where she most wanted to find herself a room. Just the sound of it – Hulme – a word that sounded like Home.

For colour's sake alone, Purletta Johnson belonged to the Jamaican bourgeoisie. She was fair-skinned, had light grey eyes, and worse, she spoke the kind of upper-St Andrew English culled from the BBC news which radios in middle- and upper-class Jamaican houses were always tuned to. In America at the time they would have described her as 'yellow'. In Jamaica, she had been 'red'. In a future England they would call her mixed-race, but at the time Purletta arrived in the country there was no such denominator, so she was simply coloured.

Only briefly did this new assignment of class and race disturb her. Others in her position did everything to pass for white; they straightened their hair even more and then lightened it; they bleached their faces. These young women would have counselled Purletta to do the same, arguing that she had a distinct advantage with her grey eyes. She had arrived in England in the late 1960s, burdened by her mother's idea that she should live there long enough to transform the UK-Right of Abode stamped into her Jamaican Passport (a gift from her father who was a citizen), into a full UK passport. No doubt Purletta's mother also wanted her daughter to come back a cultivated English woman. But Purletta did the opposite. In the land of the BBC she suddenly abandoned her BBC accent. Away from Jamaica, she learned to talk Jamaican. She braided her hair close to her scalp and thereafter gave in to every possible stereotype, whether negative or positive. She became loud and colourful. Learned how to laugh from her gut, clapping her hands, leaning over and placing the palms of her hands on her thighs, shouting *woooooooooiiii*. She became fat and started to walk a kind of walk that was all hips. She got a gold tooth. Then she transformed herself into the kind of person who, as they said in Jamaica, *any pan knock she was there!*, so she started to go to every reggae show and would boogie all night until she was sticky with sweat. Purletta began to grow ganja on her balcony. She smoked, especially on evenings when she was getting ready to go out, and this would make her even louder, even more outrageous. A bona fide hooligan.

The neighbours did not like Purletta. The woman living across from her considered at great length which authority or council she could call to get her neighbour evicted. Possibly even deported. Mrs Mildred Farquason had spent her working life as a member of the auxiliary staff of British Rail, humbly cleaning train stations around Manchester. Now that she was retired and living off government funds, she felt indebted to the system – to a country that made you work when you should work, but allowed you to rest when it was time to rest. She thought that a life of such privilege was uniquely British. As an old woman, she had, of course, developed firm notions of what was appropriate and what was not. But what was appropriate was invariably

British, and there was nothing appropriate about her neighbour.

One evening while Purletta got ready for a concert, smoking her ganja, blaring music and occasionally shouting 'Jah Rastafari!', Mrs Farquason, fed up to the brim, walked across and banged on the door.

'Oy! Oy in there! Miss Johnson! Miss Johnson!'

Purletta opened the door, smiling, her eyes red from the ganja.

'Howdy, Missis. How yu do?'

'Not well, Miss Johnson. I'm over there, tryna have a little rest and here you is making a right racket. I can't even sort out mi own thoughts! I don't care what it's like in your country, Miss, but it's not how we do things here. It's a residential place, this is.'

Purletta was Jamaican, and for her 'residential' meant upper-middle-class. Hulme was barely a step above the ghetto. She looked up and down the street, as if seeing it for the first time, and laughed loudly.

'*Residential?* This piece of shit?'

Mrs Farquason staggered back. She became indignant.

'Miss Johnson, I was tryna be reasonable, but I see a person can't with your sort. Well then, I wasn't born yesterday. I know what you've got growing inside your house. Blooming pothead is what you are! I'm tempted to call the coppers on you. Yeah. How's that?'

'The coppers?'

'The police, Miss Johnson!'

'Police?' Purletta giggled. 'You think *me* 'fraid of police? But is what wrong with this wrinkle-up old woman who come to disturb mi peace, eeh? Think say big woman like me 'fraid of police?'

Purletta slammed the door on Mrs Farquason, and then, to make her point abundantly clear, she proceeded to call the police on herself.

From across the road the old woman watched in alarm as sirens approached. Purletta ushered two uniformed men into her living room. She sat the officers down and poured two mugs of ganja tea for them. The tea had been brewed with peppermint, cinnamon leaves and then sweetened with condensed milk and the two young policemen sipped it all the way to the dregs, commending Purletta for the soothing exotic blend of 'island tea'. They inspected her house, saw the marijuana plant on the balcony but dismissed it as something else. She wouldn't have called them and left something like that out in the open. They left as confused as they had come, a little more mellow, however, and happier, and that evening three teenaged boys who would normally have been locked up for public mischief (they had been caught spray-painting graffiti on the side of a building) got off with a light reprimand, and even a 'Cheers, mate'.

Mrs Farquason thought it best from then on to look for somewhere else to retire.

Imelda decided to knock because the sign in the window said 'Room for Rent' and not 'To Let'. Here was someone who spoke her language. The woman who answered the door was wearing nothing but a bra and a pair of blue shorts. Her ample stomach hung in folds over the waistband of her shorts and she had a broom in her hand.

'Is what you want?'

'P-Please, is the owner of the house here?'

'But Saviour divine! Then what you think *me* is? De maid?'

Every word became light on Imelda's tongue and she stammered more than usual a sentence that made no sense. But the woman in front of her was looking down on her own self and was surprised. It was true – she did remind herself of a Jamaican helper, and for someone who had tried for so many years to be humble, Jamaican and black, this proved to be the ultimate compliment. Imelda tried to apologise but Purletta had exploded into laughter.

'Nuh worry yuself mi love. Nuh worry. Come inside. Come sit down. Wait, is nothing you trying to sell me?'

'No, m-ma'am. I just saw the sign. Is the r-room I come to ask about.'

Purletta stepped back and looked at her appraisingly.

'Yes,' she said finally. 'The answer is yes. Is yours. Now come inside.'

'The rent, ma'am. I don't know how much . . .'

'Have mercy . . . if English people hear you calling me ma'am they will think you is mi daughter. The name's Purletta. I look old enough to be somebody's mother? You even have a job yet? My dear, it look like you barely just come off the plane.'

'Yes, ma'am, I mean, Miss Purletta, ma'am. I got a job. I work the t-till at the supermarket.'

'Good for you! Industrious. Well, we will work out the rent. I not trying to make money here. It's just good to have somebody else in the house. Where are you tings?'

Imelda observed herself briefly in the face of this woman whose personality was larger than anything she had seen before. She heard herself answering quickly.

'I don't have m-many things, but I staying at the hostel on Slopen Road, m-ma'am. I mean, P-Purletta. The Mary Grant Hostel, that's where I staying.'

Purletta insisted on moving Imelda out of the hostel at once.

'They steal milk out of coffee at dat place. Come, come. Let me just put on a shirt and lock this door.'

Imelda allowed herself to be led, secretly glad there was someone to anchor her to the world again. For the whole walk she listened to a never-ending stream of advice. What kind of people to avoid in England. Who was going to try to bring her down. Where to bank. Where to find bargains. What English food would give her gas and rot her teeth. Where to find saltfish and ackee and plantains. Where to find good warm clothes, like the red cardigan she would wear often in England, but not in Jamaica. 'And mi dear – just between me and you, you have to do something 'bout that head of hair. It don't look good.'

Imelda reached up and touched the three big plaits she wore as if she were still a schoolgirl.

'Don't worry, I can braid it up nice and neat for you.'

'No,' Imelda said, finding her voice finally. 'I'm going to c-cut it off.'

'Child, you will look like a man.'

'Maybe.'

The Silly Thing England Assumed about Her Colonial Subjects

Like most mothers, England hoped she had been a good one –
and even if she didn't give out much money to her children, she
expected at least that they had learned the important things: how
to behave properly and in a civilised manner; how to eat with
their mouths closed; how to say please and thank you and cheers,
mate! So when the likes of Purletta Johnson arrived, England was
taken aback. England was put out. England frowned. England
said, 'That's why none of you will ever get anywhere', not understanding that it was this very brashness and coarseness that
would help the immigrant Purlettas of England not only to
survive but also to fit in. England would bend to them, and not
them to England.

Take, for instance, the whole matter of housing and tenancy.
In the 1970s it seemed that all the laws privileged the tenant, and
so the owners of a house who had rented it out to bad-minded
people who had no intention of ever leaving could find themselves with their hands tied. Even if they wanted to reoccupy
their own house, they couldn't. Many were the stories of house
owners forced to sleep in parks at night, or sleep in their friend's
garage, like the fellow who was reported to have died because he
had been cold and had turned on the ignition of the car, trying
to get a little heat, but was overcome by the fumes. Houses just

stood where they were, earning their owners nothing but debt, because every week they would have to fix the fence or the roof or have electrical work done, and the rent they had set ten years ago was still the same because some clause in the law prevented the owners from raising it.

At the same time the surge of West Indian immigrants had come of age; they had worked in England long enough to think about buying their own houses. The English landlords who found themselves with their hands tied thought they'd pull a fast one and offload their occupied houses on these immigrants – for black people had broader backs and could more easily take on the burden of debt.

But the West Indians had the last laugh. They knew instinctively and immediately that the bad-minded people they had inherited as lawful occupants of their houses had no intention of leaving simply because they were English and because their former landlords were English; because they had all been brought up properly and knew how to eat with their mouths closed and how to say please and thank you and cheers, mate. Purletta would have none of this. She was the recipient of one of these houses, and when she was through terrorising the tenants – legally, of course – setting up and sleeping under a tent in the back yard (the council office said this was completely within her rights as owner of the land); peering into the house through the kitchen window as the family prepared meals (the council office said she wasn't trespassing); banging pans against the door at night (the council office said technically she could not disturb her own peace), the tenants packed up and left in tears. The wife who had been on the dole, claiming that her nerves were making her unwell, had an honest claim for once. They left Purletta with her own empty house that she could do with as she wanted.

The Marching Band

One morning in January, when the weather started to get cold in truth, Imelda woke up, stirred from her sleep by the long *paaaaawww* of a French horn. She didn't immediately start to shiver as she usually would, for the sound had become part of her dream and transported her back to the heat of the island.

In high school, Imelda had been a member of a marching band. That in itself had been a small miracle. She had tried out and failed. The bandmaster, a retired soldier by the name of Major Riley, had fitted a red drum around her neck like an apron. On it he beat a simple rhythm. Imelda had to ask him to beat it again, she listened intently, she focused hard, tried to reproduce the sound, but couldn't. The kind of coordination that is able to beat a steady rhythm with one hand and more complicated syncopation with the other was simply one that she didn't possess. Major Riley shook his head.

'No, no, young lady. This won't work at all.'

'It won't,' Imelda apologised. She took off the drum.

It was this that surprised and moved the major – this sensibleness in a child who refused to whine or beg – this adult acceptance of the world and its limitations. He suddenly wanted to offer her possibilities.

'But . . .' he began, 'you can do something else for us. You can be our majorette.'

'A wh-what?'

The major knelt down to Imelda's height.

'A majorette. It's the most important job really. You would march in front of the band at all times. You would be the one to lead everyone into battle. You would make everyone feel proud of themselves and confident. Do you think you could do that?'

Imelda's eyes shone so brightly the major knew he had done the right thing. That same evening Imelda went to Rose, the seamstress in Watersgate. Rose's husband had bitten off a small piece of her ear and somehow she had become deaf from the incident. But Miss Millie had healed her, or so the story went. Still, as far as Imelda was concerned, Rose was hard of hearing to this day. Although she was a talented seamstress, she had an old-fashioned sense of style, and was not particularly innovative and almost always refused to hear what it was people wanted sewn. So sitting down in front of her in the back room of Rose's house, Imelda carefully explained the kind of outfit she wanted, drawing diagrams and making several notes. It was supposed to be a bright yellow pair of trousers with a stripe of blue running down the side of each leg. Rose interrupted to ask if she was sure, as a girl, that she wanted to be wearing trousers. Imelda insisted and moved on. Rose was to use the same blue material that had been used to make the stripes to make a shirt – long and double-breasted.

'Like a jacket?' Rose asked, perplexed.

'Yes. Like a j-jacket,' Imelda told her, 'and with b-big yellow buttons, and yellow epaulettes.'

Imelda was a hit – a one-woman cheerleading team. She walked in front of the marching band twirling her drumsticks, throwing them up and catching them. It was more than just theatrics; there was a confidence to her walk, a sureness in her smile. She was asked to lead the school's cricket team to Pigeon Pea Oval and the teachers agreed it was that march that inspired the team and gave it enough gusto to wallop St Mary's High School, the parish champions and favourites.

So that morning in November when Imelda woke to the sound of a French horn, she began to dream a dream that was really a memory: she was in her blue and yellow regalia marching up Hope Road, the horns, the bugles, the trumpets and the drums making a magnificent sound. There were so many people by the side of the road waving flags and wishing they could be where she was, in the middle of the road twirling a baton and walking towards Her Royal Highness, the Princess Anne, who was visiting Jamaica. Imelda woke up then. She rubbed her eyes and it took more than a moment for her to realise that she was not marching towards any princess, and that the Kingston sun was not beating down on her head.

The French horn sounded again, followed by clarinets.

'Miss P-Purletta? Miss Purletta, you hear that?'

From her room, a sleepy Purletta muttered something about her name being simply Purletta.

'What that you s-say there, Miss Purletta?'

'Nothing.'

Imelda pulled on her father's old grey jacket and ran outside. Her excitement surprised even her, but there was nothing festive about this marching band. No blue and yellow pom-poms. No children in fancy dress. Just hundreds of sombre men and women with red poppies blooming on their chests. The tune of the horns was sad. A funeral march, maybe. An old man in khaki fatigues led the band. He wielded a gold baton and every now and then shouted an instruction in the thick, gruff Northern accent Imelda still had not grown used to. He was followed by eight young men in tartan kilts, their bagpipes slung over their shoulders, the exposed parts of their legs white from the cold. A brass section followed, twenty men strong, owners of the horns and bugles that had pulled Imelda out of her sleep. Then the ratti-ti-tat of drummers, and then fifty or so young cadets in green, marching smartly. Three old women followed and in their wrinkled hands, they carried wreaths of chrysanthemums and daisies.

99

None of this dampened Imelda's spirits. The need had arisen in her to walk; there was something in the sound of horns, she felt, something in the abeng, conch shells, bullhorns – something that called the dispossessed of the world to rise up and march. Imelda followed the band out of Hulme, down into Morris Valley, Fathington, Kerring, and then Portside, where the dead lived. Portside was a green cemetery, and if a tall man stood in the centre he could look as far as he dared in whichever direction, and would still see neither fence nor road, just gravestones losing themselves into the distance.

At this point the old women stopped and laid down their flowers.

The band left the cemetery and continued, marching back up through Fallowfield and Rusholme; past the stretch of Indian restaurants known as the curry mile; past the universities and colleges; up Oxford Road, a tall blue-domed clock watching them with the word 'palace' flashing red on each of its four sides; and on towards the city centre. Imelda walked and she walked, and if the band had marched into the night, she might have followed them into the night, but just outside the city centre she passed a makeshift stall with a rack that held the item she knew at once she had been marching towards all day. A red cardigan.

England had struck her as a grey country – not because of the weather, but because of the colours people chose to wear. She had arrived in September; oranges and reds and greens had been packed away in boxes, donated to charity shops, sealed up for the season, and greys and blacks had flourished instead. The red cardigan drew Imelda's eye because it bloomed like a hibiscus in the middle of the cold. She walked over to it, trance-like, lifted it off its hanger and held it out in front her. It was too small. She knew just by looking at it.

But what Imelda knew was wrong. Something strange had happened to her in England. The solid slab of stomach which had been a faithful companion for most of her life had just upped and left. A tropical creature by nature, the stomach could not survive the long cold months ahead and had evaporated so quickly Imelda had not immediately realised her mid-section was now slim. Imelda didn't realise that she was changing – that already she was no longer the chubby child from Watersgate who grew up on gizzadas.

The shopkeeper observed her interest in the cardigan.

'That'll look great on you, love.'

Imelda smiled at his kindness. The shopkeeper insisted.

'Would you like to try it on, love? Ain't no harm in that.'

'It won't fit.'

'Oh but of course it will, love! A small thing like you.'

Imelda laughed.

'Go on then. Give it a try.'

Imelda shrugged. Why not? She took off her father's jacket and slipped her hands into the sleeves of the cardigan, surprised that they went through so easily. Imelda breathed out and spun around.

'Aye, that does look lovely on you.'

She walked over to the mirror and looked at herself, surprised with what she saw. Her short hair made her face beautiful, and the red cardigan suited her body. She turned to the shopkeeper suddenly. Holding the material of the cardigan between her fingers, she baffled him with the question: 'Will the winter get c-colder than this?' as if temperature was something that could be measured in wool.

That evening Imelda walked home with two new purchases – the red cardigan, and also a rosemary bush which she would place on her windowsill and would always consider to be partly Jamaican. Of course she had bought it in Manchester, but she placed into its pot of earth the fistful of dirt she had taken with her from Watersgate.

The Silly Thing Purletta
Believed as a Child

1950s

She believed that language was in the teeth – that when people spoke, the words that were formed came not from the tongue, but from the thirty-two or so molars and incisors in that person's mouth. Purletta came to this conclusion when her mother, an uptown Jamaican socialite, made the casual remark that the woman who washed and cleaned for them, Cynthia, spoke Broken English.

Purletta never knew before that English could be as fragile as the crystal vases her mother didn't allow her to touch, or the glasses she wasn't allowed to drink from because people said she was too butter-fingered. Still, no one could convince her that Cynthia's language was broken. You could sit down and listen to Miss Cynthia forever. Every expression was a story. When Purletta said she wanted to become 'the biggest singer in the whole wide world', Cynthia smiled and said something cryptic.

'De higher monkey climb, de more her batty expose.'

Cynthia told her other strange things.

'When tiger ole, dog bark at him.'

Or, 'If yu have yu hand in lion mout', wait suh till him yawn.'

She used words like 'hautoclapse', meaning calamity, or 'screbbe-screbbe', meaning not well put together, the kind of words you would not find in any dictionary. Sometimes she made words more full by adding an 'h'.

'Hi his hup to mi neck hin work!'

So as far as Purletta was concerned, Cynthia's English was more complete and whole than anything else spoken in the house.

Then one day it finally occurred to Purletta that Cynthia, old woman that she was, happened to have a mouth full of broken teeth, so they must be the source of her wonderful, broken language. The day Purletta ran into a guava tree and lost her own two front teeth, she went to bed more excited than ever. Her mother, tucking her into bed, noticed how brightly her daughter's eyes shone, how much energy there was still bottled up in that little body, even after a whole long day of playing.

'Goodness me, child. What has you so excited today?'

Purletta only smiled and shook her head mischievously. 'It'th a thecret.'

She knew instinctively to keep this from her mother. But now she had a mouth that resembled Cynthia's, so maybe, come morning, she would wake up with the gift she had always wanted. Maybe, finally she'd be able to speak Broken English.

Three Enemies of Pastor Braithwaite

1. Ras Joseph

1961–1982

Some people used to laugh and say Joseph Martin beat drums as well as he did because his mother, Miss Jennifer, used to beat him as much as she did. It was true – Miss Jennifer was a terror. And maybe, in truth, that was part of his talent – for sometimes the boy could become so solitary, so withdrawn, and would sit down all evening rubbing his thumb across the drum, his thumb across the drum, his thumb across the drum, until it blistered, and the drum would make a sound like a soft wail, almost like a violin, and Joseph could pull from it a kind of music most people couldn't.

But another person would tell you Joseph was a master drummer because nobody knew his instrument better than he did. Every drum he played, he made himself.

Miss Jennifer had told one person the story of how she had brought the boy back with her from Hanover. He was the child of a niece who had not learned the skill of locking her legs and so had too many mouths to feed. Being the good Christian, Miss Jennifer went there to help the situation, to ease the burden: to take one of the children and raise it as her own. But when she was walking out the gate with Joseph, his grandmother was suddenly sad to see him go and had run after them with tears in her eyes. She said to her sister Jennifer, 'This one, he like animals. He like animals a lot.'

When Miss Jennifer reached Watersgate she went to her farm and brought back one of her young sheep-goats. She told the boy he would have the responsibility of raising it, but it wasn't a pet, and he should not grow attached to it. When the goat was fully grown and fattened, and it was time to kill it, the little boy Joseph insisted on doing it himself. Over the years many persons would see him lead a goat out into the field and speak to it gently. When he took up the knife, the goat would only look up with a sad wisdom and nod. It never protested, never bleated as the red life poured from its slashed neck.

Joseph kept the skin for himself. He washed the blood off it himself. He cured it himself. He dried it in the sun; he stretched it; he made a drum out of it himself. People said he played drums so well because, in a way, he had grown them – and it was like he was trying to bring his goat back to life, to make it open its mouth and make a sound again.

The first time Joseph played in church he was only thirteen years old, and it was nothing short of Pentecost. The service did not end till after dark. Tessa danced, and the way her body moved on those thin ankles you just wouldn't believe. People spoke in tongues they had never spoken in before. Brother Ezekiel, who had lived in Panama for years, could attest that Teacher Sarah Richardson, who was not the kind of woman who usually got caught up in the spirit, spoke in a beautiful tongue which he admitted was not Spanish, exactly – not to his memory – but sounded to him like Italian.

Whenever Joseph played he could draw down Holy Spirit from heaven. People invited him to play at dead yards. In the deep night he would go into deep bushes where white hens were slaughtered and blood was thrown to the air. He played Kumina and drew down Kumina spirit. He learned how to play Poco-mania, draw down Poco spirit. He learned how to play Myal and draw down Myal spirit. Learned how to play Gereh, how to play

Dinki Mini, how to play Revival and how to draw down any spirit he wanted to draw down. When he played, people became possessed, and there was even one time when he became possessed. He felt his eyes rolling back and there was the strangest sensation of being outside and inside of himself at the same time. He felt the rough sensation of his spirit lifting out of his body, like a tearing, and his heart was racing. He knew his spirit was ready to travel and it would leave behind only the faintest trace of itself; his body would become a zombie, a vessel ready to be possessed by any of the gods. The experience terrified him and he lifted his hands off the drum, thinking that if he stopped playing the rhythm, the thing happening to him would stop. But when he took his hands off that night, the drum did not stop playing. The rhythm did not quit. His spirit travelled. His zombified body was possessed, and that night he spun and danced and jumped with everyone else while the drum without a drummer kept playing.

But not everyone will dance Kumina or Poco or Revival. Some people are afraid of such spirits, and will stay back in the darkness praying to their good Lord and Saviour Jesus Christ. These people watched with concern Deaconess Jennifer's boy who seemed to be leading the heathens into devil worship. Word got back to Pastor Braithwaite who plotted.

When Sunday came around, the pastor instructed the singers to sing. He waited for Joseph to start a rhythm and when the first clap of the drum sounded, Braithwaite stumbled dramatically as if he was about to collapse. The singers stuttered. The drum stopped. Braithwaite coughed. Holding his hand up in the air as if to regain his balance, he announced that something was not right. He felt something wrong wrong wrong in his spirit. Something wasn't pure about the worship. Pastor Braithwaite closed his eyes and lifted his hands to heaven. Suddenly, he flung his eyes open as if revelation had come to him in a burst.

'You cyan't serve God and Mammon!'

'No, pastor.'

'You cyan't serve God and the devil.'

'No way!'

'You cyan't be filled with the Holy Spirit and have all manner of evil spirit inside you.'

'Mm.'

'Something not right 'bout the worship today.'

He stepped away from the pulpit. He walked down the steps and over to the drum.

'I tell you, Church, truly, this drum been used to lead the Army of Satan! We cyan't use it to make music unto the Lord.'

Braithwaite grabbed the drum, went to the front door and flung it out of the church. Everyone heard as it hit the ground and the barrel cracked.

'THE DEVIL NOT WELCOME HERE! And no demon welcome here neither.' Braithwaite scrutinised the seventeen-year-old Joseph. He put his hands on the boy's forehead and shouted, 'Come out!'

He had fully expected the boy to do what was required – to fall on the floor, twitch and speak in a deep, guttural voice all kinds of blasphemies. Pastor B. would cast out the demons, send them to dry and barren places, and the whole church would rejoice. But Joseph didn't fall. He quietly got up and walked out of the church as if the words had been directed to him personally. He would never return.

Joseph Martin would tell you that was not a good year. His drum had been damaged and he had been read out of church. That evening Imelda visited him. She would not have called him her boyfriend exactly, but for the past year they had been sneaking out at nine in the evening, meeting in the dark under the Sex Tree to play their secret game.

'It wasn't right what P-pastor did today,' she consoled him.

'Well, everything happen in its season. I realise something today. I not supposed to stay here in Watersgate. I know now, I going to Kingston.'

'Joseph? You mad? N-nobody have anything good to say bout the city. Things real violent down there, you know.'

'It don't matter. I will risk it. Nothing more is here for me.'

Imelda was silent.

'And one day you will leave too.'

'I won't,' Imelda protested.

'Nothing is here for you either.' He said it as if she hadn't spoken.

'Everything is here. M-Mama and Papa is here. My friends is here. And even if I leave, I would c-come back. You can't stay away from the place where them b-bury your navel string.'

'Mine not here. So I can always leave.'

'It's j-just an expression. What I m-mean is that here is home, and you can't turn your back on that just so. You think you c-could go to Kingston and never come back?'

'Sometimes is like I hate everything about this place.'

Imelda swallowed. She understood this to mean that a part of him hated her.

'Imelda, I hate that woman who is not even my mother. I know is a sin to say things like that, but is true. I want to leave this place and forget it.'

Don't forget me! is what she really wanted to say, to beg; instead she said stoutly, 'You can't forget a p-place when is part of you.'

'You can!'

Joseph knew this because he had almost forgotten Hanover. He had been back to visit but by then his real mother seemed to him more like an aunt. His siblings were like distant cousins, and they kept secrets from him, whispering to each other whenever he left the room. His grandmother, whom he had loved so much, was now a strange old woman. He realised guiltily that he no longer cared to know any of them. He wished he cared. Sometimes he wished he could beat a rhythm and become possessed by his past. He wanted his eyes to roll back in his skull and his spirit to travel to the time when he was a little boy. He wanted to remember the school he went to, not far from the house – the four big trees along the path that all year round shed white and yellow flowers on the ground. Running home, he would crush these blossoms under his feet, unconscious then that the sweet smell he forever associated with Hanover was the fragrance released when he trampled them. But all of this was almost forgotten now. He understood then that a place could be forgotten. He turned to Imelda, softening.

'Imelda, you ever think bout the rest of the world? I think bout it all the time and it must be real, real different from Watersgate. Better and worse at the same time. Don't you think? I want to find this out for myself now. I want to do more than just think bout it.'

Imelda put her hand in his.

'There is one person in Watersgate who will miss you, I p-promise.'

Joseph felt everything inside suddenly rise to his eyes. He did not squeeze Imelda's hand, or look over at her, or speak, because he knew he would cry.

Joseph lived in Kingston for six years, and for those six years he never found a steady job. There were hundreds like him – young men from rural villages who came to the city and ended up sucking salt, ended up learning that their muscles were not strong enough to beat the system. He lived in a shanty town near the polluted harbour, in a house with three other men. Two of them began to wear blue shirts and wave blue flags, the colour of the political party they were henchmen for. They tried to get Joseph to join them, saying blue was going to take over the country and blue was sure money. Blue was concerned about poor people and blue was the ticket forward. But when one of them was stabbed in the arm by a boy who supported the colour red, Joseph understood that 'blue and red' was dangerous business.

The fourth man in the house was Diggy, about whom everyone repeated the sayings *Silent river run deep*, as if somehow in his semi-reclusive habits he still managed to earn people's fear and respect. Young and unlucky and poor like the rest of them, he had never been heard to complain, had never been found on the street corner slapping down domino tiles with all the anger that had built up in his body over the last frustrating week. People said Diggy was obviously all right – he wasn't looking for a way forward and was content with his poverty. After all, he used to go to Hudson Valley in New York once a year to pick apples and never took the opportunity to lose himself in the Bronx or in Brooklyn or across the border into Toronto. Everyone knew that Diggy had stopped looking for work seriously when he stopped cutting his hair. His Afro began to clump into the clear beginnings of Rastafari. He began to pass the evenings in spliffs, filling the house with the sweet incense. On these occasions he was more talkative than usual and would tell Joseph things.

'The problem with this country is it don't make for black people. Our heart belong to Africa. It beat to Africa.'

Joseph thought he understood. He had already sent people to Africa with his drum, and it was true; it did seem like a better place. He also understood the business of beats.

Another night the ganja had made Diggy sentimental, and he began to recount, not in a boastful way, but with the worshipfulness of nostalgia, every woman he had ever slept with, the ones he had almost slept with, and the only one he had loved – Cutie Taylor. Cutie was barely five foot three but it was like Cutie could take on the world. He found that out when, one Saturday, he took her to a village called Watersgate and she'd mashed up an entire funeral. She had gone out of respect. It was the funeral of her first baby's father, Maas Jethro, and she thought it only right and proper to take her eldest child. But when Cutie stepped into the church Maas Jethro's widow came up to her.

'We nuh want yu here, Cutie! Guh back to Kingston!'

Oh, God have mercy on us all. Cutie saw that as an opportunity to tell the grieving old woman about her pussy, the tremendous size of it, the uncalculable age of it, its peculiar state of dried-up-ness, what and what should be put in it, and how it should be discarded thereafter like a lump of shit. Well, who never faint came to the widow's immediate defense and Cutie took them all on. She told one man that he was as bald and ugly as a johncrow. She told another that his face was as wrinkled up as the widow's pussy. She told another that he looked like something that needed to be scraped out of a chimmy-pot. And no one could count how many people she told to fuck themselves.

Then it dawned on Cutie this just wasn't proper. This was a man's funeral. This was her first child's father. She took a deep breath and walked away from all the shouting. Just like that. People were still quarrelling before they realised Cutie had left the scene.

Now, as Cutie walked away, she realised that all this talk about old, dried-up pussies, johncrows and self-fucking had made her throat completely dry. She decided she would go to the car, take out her handbag and purse and buy a drink from the shop across the road. People muttered as they watched her go into the car. But when she came back out with her handbag, a strange old woman with large ears and furtive eyes screamed.

'Oh Lord, she have a gun! She have a gun!'

As old people say, every jack man and woman, every dog and cat and fowl and roach scattered. The pallbearers dropped the coffin, and the pastor completely pee-peed up himself, shouting as he ran away, 'The blood of Jesus is against you, Miss Cutie!'

Diggy said besides himself, there were only three people left at the church – Cutie, her daughter and the dead body. And even though the story of the gun wasn't true, it could have been, because that was Cutie for you. And that's what Diggy had loved about her. They had been living together for a year, he and Cutie and her three children, when he proposed to her.

'Cutie, why we nuh get married?'

She looked on him and smiled in her knowing way that made him feel, always, like a boy who didn't know much about the world. But she would never patronise him.

'You not strong enough.'

Simply that. He had been weighed in the balance and found wanting. He understood what she meant. It wasn't that he wasn't strong enough for her, he wasn't strong enough even for him. She had seen in him the kind of man who is always searching for himself. Strange. Other people read his silence, his intense introversion as strength. *Silent river run deep*. But only Cutie understood it for what it was, and that made him love her all the more, for it was as if she alone on this earth really knew him.

And did Joseph, hearing this story, stop Diggy at any point to tell him that he did in fact know Cutie Taylor? Did he bother to tell Diggy that he himself was from Watersgate?

No. But his mind did go back to the village, and he too began to fall in love. This was, of course, impossible because it was Imelda he was falling in love with – but it couldn't really have been her, only a sentimental re-creation. In the vast loneliness of Kingston he suddenly reached for and held on to the memory of the young woman who had held his own hand and promised she would miss him. He began to believe in her missing him – to be strengthened by it, and also to be pulled back by it. With his mind now always going back to Watersgate, it was easy for his body to go back there as well. But he did not know who Imelda had become, and she in turn did not know who he had become. It was infatuation, nostalgia, a dream – but then again, it was love. Because while we all reach our destinations by different means and different fictions, having reached it, the simple fact is we have. And so it must be said: on the day that Joseph finally did see Imelda again and the earth changed around and inside him, what he felt was unequivocally and indisputably love.

Joseph never found a job in Kingston, but he did find Rastafari. He learned how to beat a new heartbeat rhythm and how to call down Bhinghi spirit. When he returned to Watersgate Braithwaite saw him, his unkempt beard and dreadlocks.

'The devil really have you now! You are Lucifer's child!'

Joseph just looked on him calmly. 'I and I know you for who you is now. You is the downpresser man. You is Babylon. You come fi tell the people how fi hate each other, but I and I don't follow that script no more. I and I deal with love. So don't come talk to me again, Mr Downpresser man. 'Cause you is not my friend. You is my enemy.'

2 Eulan Solomon

Circa 1950 – September 1983

Eulan Solomon was gay. It must be written that plainly because he thought of it that plainly. Without guilt or conflict or any great overwhelming sense of terror. Growing up in the 1950s, he did not yet know he was supposed to feel oppressed. Eulan accepted life was as life was, and it was this oh-so-quiet way in which he moved through the world that made Miss Thompson tell the rest of the teachers in the staffroom of St Peter's Primary that the little boy Eulan – him have no soul. No heart. No nothing.

He grew up in Golden Springs in a house far from other houses and, like his mother and father, he was an only child. When he was nine the small household of three became even smaller; Mrs Solomon suddenly became ill one Tuesday, and by Saturday she had died from a cancer she never knew she had. Eulan was absent from school for a week. There were no aunts or uncles or neighbours to help. Funeral arrangements had to be made, meals had to be cooked, apologies had to be sent out, and then there was the whole business of grieving. No word reached Eulan's school to explain his absence. When he returned, Miss Thompson, a grade-school teacher stout in body but meagre in intelligence, who aspirated every word that began with 'w', greeted him wickedly.

'Hwell, hwell, hwell. Whom do hwe have here? You've decided to join us again, Mr Solomon? How good of you.'

'Good morning, Miss,' Eulan continued towards his seat.

'Oh my! Only that, Mr Solomon? No explanation of hwhere you've been? Hwhat you've been up to? I'm sure everyone in the class hwould love to know about your vacation. How hwas the beach?'

The class paused. Miss Thompson smiled wickedly. Eulan answered flatly.

'Mummy died. I went to the funeral.'

No soul. No heart. No nothing. That's what she said

indignantly in the staffroom, but back in the class she had stammered.

'Oh! Y-y-you p-p-oor dear! Hwhat a tragedy!'

She apologised profusely. Stroked his head. Bought him lunch.

The death of Mrs Solomon brought a final and irrevocable silence upon the house. It wasn't just the fact that she was being mourned, but that Eulan and his father were naturally quiet people. Without her morning songs and her lovable, clumsy ways, there was little to be heard. Though they lived in the same house, Eulan and his father hardly disturbed each other and it was as if they occupied two different worlds. Eulan grew up with the freedom that other men only gain by running away or migrating: the freedom that his life was his own. He had no family legacy to live up to; no community to let down. He became an actuary not because it was a prestigious profession he had been pressured into, but simply because it was what he gravitated towards. Naturally. He slept with men for the same reason.

But his teacher was right: he had no soul, no heart, no nothing. For it wasn't just that he was quiet. Quietness in him became a kind of arrogance. He developed a bad case of cynicism and an unrelenting sarcasm that kept people away. He liked few people, did not care for community and so when the time came, he chose to build his house far away from Kingston. He bought a plot of land in St Mary with a few orange trees and tall bhama grass. The day he attached his looping signature to the end of a document and the land officially became his, he drove there and parting the itchy grass, walked until he was standing right in the middle of that acre. Then he lay down on the ground disappearing from the sight of five children from Watersgate who had been spying on him and who spread a rumour that a man from the city was doing strange things in the bhama grass. On the ground Eulan listened to the quietness that was not really quietness: the roar of the river, the wind rubbing tree branches together, the shout of birds. He lay there with cow tics marching over his now-dirty linen suit and thought of the house he would build. He was going to build for himself that world which had always been his alone. He was going to build seclusion. Quietness. That was the problem with Mr Solomon.

Two years later the house was finished and the furniture moved in. On the first Sunday he slept there, Pastor Braithwaite's voice booming from the church's microphone woke Mr Solomon. He found out that Sunday, that despite his intentions, he did not live alone in Watersgate. Eulan stormed onto the balcony and shouted.

'You down there! You down there!'

But no one could hear him. The church was so close he could hear them, but too far away for them to hear him. He would need his own microphone, and the thought of this angered him all the more. The church, from where he stood, looked primitive – a one-room building with rough walls – yet inside they had installed a PA system with loudspeakers and microphones. He could not understand this. Someone from the church might have explained to him that it was an investment in the silencing of stones, for God had said in his word, 'Lo and behold, if *you* do not praise me the rocks will cry out *glory and honour*.' And who could handle that kind of apocalypse? – all the stones marching out of the river with their mouths open? The church was therefore playing its part, filling the valley with praise.

Eulan developed a ritual. Whenever Pastor Braithwaite got to the mike, he dressed quickly, jumped into his car and drove over to the nearby community of Highgate where an old acquaintance of his lived.

Without his uniform on, specifically the khaki bush jacket with its breast pocket decorated with all colours of badges, Travis Carmichael did not seem like a police officer. He was of a gentle and kindly disposition, and his bald plate and easy smile made him look like everyone's favourite grandfather. He had risen to the rank of Superintendent of Police in charge of the parish of St Mary because he was well educated, and people were generally impressed with the sharpness of his perceptions and his eloquence. Still, St Mary was a quiet parish without much crime.

He had been given responsibility for the parish because he was perceived as too soft and gentle a man to do the tougher kind of police work needed in the city. Still, it was a little odd that he had been superintendent for over fifteen years and had not been considered for further promotion. Travis Carmichael was actually quite content with his current posting and did not, himself, want to be transferred up or sideways or otherwise, but there was the hush-hush talk in higher circles that for a man at the age of sixty never to have had a wife or girl or even the slightest hint of a lady friend, a man so quiet and soft at that, it must mean, or it could lead some to think, that he was 'that way inclined'. Now and then rumours would surface to give credence to this talk, but Carmichael commanded enough respect in the force that such rumours were never investigated. Still, it had been decided by someone that it was best to keep him where he was – Superintendent of Police, in charge of a quiet parish.

The superintendent was a collector of many things – stamps, antique furniture, jazz records. But it was a very private collection that he was most proud of. Through the years he had found many men who were like him – professional, quiet, and, indeed, 'that way inclined'. Their names and addresses were kept in a brown, leather-bound address book. Eulan Solomon's name had been in this book for years, but it was only recently that they had begun to establish any kind of friendship. Carmichael had thought Eulan a bit uppity and generally unfriendly, but after moving to Watersgate Eulan had surprised him one Sunday by showing up at his door. He came almost every Sunday after that and Carmichael began to look forward to these visits, understanding that the unfriendliness in the young man was only a strange immaturity – a part of him that had never grown up.

On the Sundays that Eulan did not show, the intensity of the superintendent's disappointment was a surprise even to himself. He would replay their last interaction, wondering if he had done or said something wrong. To his great pleasure though, the next Sunday he would hear the familiar purr of a BMW pulling into his driveway.

So because Eulan Solomon had found an enemy in Pastor Braithwaite, Superintendent Travis Carmichael had found a friend in Eulan Solomon.

3 Miss Millie

Circa 1980

Small fire burn down big forest. Who know the story – how Fire make fool of the spider? Anansi say he want to invite Fire to dinner, but Fire keep on putting off Anansi. Fire say he too tired. Fire say he don't have the energy. Anansi don't understand why Fire don't want to come to his house for dinner; he know that Fire is a man with a big belly who can eat from early o'clock in the morning straight through to late o'clock at night and don't feel full. Anansi ask Fire, why you don't want to come to my house? Fire say is 'cause he have no feet. He can't walk, but if Anansi would just lay down some dry bush from his house all the way to Fire's door, he would be able to travel like that. Anansi wife warn him and tell him not to do it, but Anansi don't listen to his wife. So he lay down dry bush, all the way from his house to Fire's house. Fire burn up all the bush along the way and when he reach to Anansi's house he make a big jump and burn up everything.

Listen, I 'fraid o' fire bad bad. When I was a little girl we live in a house with only two room. It was too many of us to have no Mommy and Papa in one room and the children in another room. How we work it out was that Mommy and the girls sleep in the back room, and Papa and the boys sleep in the front room. That way if anybody come in the house they have to face the men first. But you know, true Mommy is the mommy, the boys always coming in for them love up and kiss up and everything like that. Well, one night when we all was sleeping, the littlest boy come into the room and I hear him crying, 'Mommy, Mommy, Mommy.' And when my mother wake up, he saying, 'Sorry, Mommy.' Mommy ask him, 'Sorry for what, child?' But he not saying anything more. By this time all the girls wake up and is then we start to smell smoke and hear the men in the next room coughing in their sleep. We had was to go and wake them all up, because fire was all around them. We couldn't even get out the door because the way was blocked. Everybody crowd into the girls' room and my father and all the boys push hard against the board window and break it open, and that's how we all jump out of the house. My poor mother. All she could think 'bout as we watch the whole house go up in smoke was the blanket that for eight months she was crocheting for her sick auntie. Was the prettiest blanket I had ever seen and she was almost done with it. To see eight months of work gone like that, the gift she was going to pass on to Aunt Mae before Aunt Mae pass on to the other world, that hurt my mother even more than seeing the house destroyed.

In the morning we go through the shell of the house. Is like we was fire dancers, because we don't have no shoes and the coals beneath our feet was still warm. I swear to you, let God strike me dead if is lie I telling: two things we find in that house that didn't burn. The first was a picture my mother had on the wall with the Blessed Saviour and his Twelve Disciples eating the Last Supper. The picture wasn't on the wall no more. That wall did collapse. Instead, it did wrap up in Mommy's blanket, which didn't burn at all. Glory to God! I tell you, that blanket did not burn because it was pure. Is because my mother make it out of complete love, and such things cannot and will not burn in fire.

Understand what I am saying, there is a way to be safe in the furnace. There is a way to breathe in the midst of smoke. When the Babylonian King set up a statue, ninety feet tall and ninety feet wide, made of pure gold, him call all the big-shot people: the ministers, the judges, the officials to see this statue, and when them see it they issue a decree that everyone would bow down to it when them hear music, lest they be thrown into the fire. But there was three young men who ignore this decree – Hananiah, Mishael and Azariah, who you probably know better by their other names – Shadrach, Meshach and Abednego. They decide they not going to bow down to no statue. Even when they drag them in front of the King they tell him, 'No, Your Highness. We not bowing. And if is dead we have to dead, is dead we going to dead. But we believe our God is powerful enough to save.' You hear me? Their God was powerful enough to save. This is how you can survive fire – you have to serve the right God. Listen, they say the fire was so hot that the guards them who take the three young men to be burned fell dead. Heat stroke! Yes, my dears – they fling the three Jews into the furnace, but them guard never come back alive. Those three boys should have died too, but when the King him look into the fire, he don't see three men; he see four. He rub his eyes again and again to make sure. And I tell you, it was the Lord Jesus himself who did walk around in that fire with those boys. And he same one who protect those young men, is him same one who protected my mother's blanket.

Small fire burn big forest. Is no lie. But I pray to God that I survive every fire that he send during my life. I want to face them like gold, and come out pure. I living my life in such a way that I will be spared from the final fire, because I fret over that one bad bad. God gave Noah the rainbow sign, no more water but the fire next time. But same time, I praying that I will have the right fire. The fire of Pentecost. I want that fire on my tongue. I want the kind of fire burning in me, that it catch up in my neighbours' hearts, and they run off shouting glory, glory, glory.

What kind of fire do you have?

This is the first sermon that had come to Miss Millie in its completion. If she had asked Pastor Braithwaite once, she had asked him a thousand times, if she could not please, just one Sunday, take his place in the pulpit. God said so many things to her when she was praying, so just one Sunday, just once, she wanted the opportunity to share it.

But Pastor Braithwaite never took her on. Sometimes he ignored her. Sometimes he told her next week, Miss Millie, next week. But next week never came. He asked her, 'Shall the sheep lead the sheep? No. That is the job of the shepherd. You tell me what God been telling you, and I will use spiritual discernment and decide whether I should share it with the flock. It's not everything we hear that we should speak.'

Miss Millie never complained. But in her heart of hearts she was upset. Slowly, Pastor Braithwaite was making an enemy out of her.

The Silly Thing Pastor Braithwaite Believed as a Child

1940s

He had grown up in Portland and lived on a cliff. It was one of those points where the island curved. If you stood in front of the house you could gaze out to sea, and if you stood at the back of the house you could gaze on another, or so it seemed. Two different pieces of the Caribbean right there. Few people grow up with so much ocean around them and so much sky above them. The magnificent ocean everywhere.

But what used to scare young Braithwaite was not the sea around him, or the sky above him. It was, instead, the train below him. While he became used to the hungry churning of salt water and the sky's terrible wind and the crows who yelled as they flew by his house, he never got used to the sound of trains. The track was much further down the cliff. It too followed the curve of the island. And sometimes at night, when the train came chugging around the corner, it would toot its loud horn.

If he was sleeping, Braithwaite would bolt out of bed and run to the window. He looked up to the sky and prayed that it would stay closed. And he looked out to sea and though all of it was black, he wished that it too would remain closed. For the train horn, he always thought, was the final trumpet. Was the sound of God coming. And that would mean the heavens would part and Jesus would come riding down on a white horse, and the seas would open and issue out the dead. He had heard all of this in church. But Braithwaite had the sense of a whole important life to live and wasn't ready for no final trumpet.

'Stay closed! Stay closed!' he would pray. 'I too young. I not ready.'

The Man Who Loved Dictionaries

March 1976

It was widely claimed that Imelda was the first black student to register at the University of Winchester for a degree in law. The editor of the local newspaper, always starved for news, heard this from his nephew who had presented him with a bottle of coconut rum on his birthday.

'Aye lad,' beamed the uncle upon receiving the gift, 'I reckon this'll be done in one week tops. It's mi favourite. I'm still planning mi trip to the Caribbean. I'll be so smashed within a day, I reckon I'll miss the plane back to this country, which would be bloody fine with me.'

'There's a lass in our class from Jamaica,' the nephew said then, jokingly, 'I'll see if she can't arrange to get a regular supply of this stuff shipped to you. Enough to see you through till your liver rots.'

'Fantastic!' Then after a moment he became serious, 'From Jamaica, eh? Quite an international programme, ennit? Can't be many like her around, can there?'

'They say she's the first black student at Winchester to study law.'

In fact, Imelda wasn't the first; she was only the first in six years. But no one on the faculty had been teaching for more than five, and records weren't kept in those days of which student was white or which was black or which was Pakistani. In 1968, for instance, the University had awarded a law degree to Marcia Ross – a black British woman who would never practise law but instead open three beauty salons, her staff consisting mainly of women she had met in the Caribbean, convincing each of them to migrate illegally to Britain where she would have employment ready for them and where she would school them in the virtues of feminism, the repulsiveness of men, eventually inviting them up to her room where she knew, if all went wrong, at least no one was going to accuse her publicly of sexual harassment. In 1960 the Cameroon ambassador's son had graduated from the same law programme, and as far back as the 1930s there were two brown West Indian men who had studied law at Winchester, hating England and all that it stood for. They returned to their islands to lead the fight for independence.

So although Imelda was at least the fourth black person there, no one cared to research these facts, particularly not the newspaperman. For weeks he tried to arrange an interview with Imelda. He sent a message via his nephew and one through the school but she did not get in touch with him. He called her and she told him she was not interested – the idea of reading a story about herself, having a picture taken that would be displayed to anyone who paid a couple pence, frightened her. But the editor persisted, and when Purletta found out she scolded Imelda.

'You is one selfish cunt if you turn down that offer. Black people in this country catching hell from the moment we reach here. They blame us for every raas thing. Is we bring disease. Is we putting strain on the system. Is we boxing bread out of English people mouth. Now the one time we could read something good 'bout weself, you denying us the opportunity. Because what? You feel too cute?'

The newspaperman arrived at the University with his cameras, telling Imelda just to lead him around the campus and they'd have a casual chat. It was 21 March 1976 and though spring had officially begun the day before, the days were still cold and the trees still bare. A casual chat? Newspapermen must be schooled in such lies, Imelda thought to herself, whatever it took to get their interviewees to relax, to get their guard down so the journalist could find a loose thread, then pull it, unravelling some colossal scandal. Imelda did not intend to relax, lest she reveal how, when she came to England, she had thought the place was full of toilets. Or, she might have told him, as they walked across the park, how the constant green kept surprising her. She thought that the grass would have gone brown in winter, or would have disappeared completely. But the green never faded, as if it were mocking the cold, and if it was for the grass alone, on a day when the sun was shining, you might look outside and think it was summer and begin to plan a picnic. On these days, Imelda felt the green grass and all the white people would laugh at her for her ignorance.

If Imelda had let her guard down, as she and the newspaperman crossed the small bridge that spanned the River Meddock, she might have told him how the fact there was a river had excited her. Her first day on campus she had walked around, desperately looking for it, had crossed the bridge three times looking down at the brown water below before realising that this *was* the river. It didn't look anything more than a glorified gutter to her. The banks were made of concrete; the water was dirty; there were no stones at the bottom. She thought of the river back in Watersgate. Early in the year she had left, the news had spread that little Jonathon was drownded. She remembered going with everyone into the river and Young Constable Brown telling them to 'fan out! Fan out!' Imelda had looked back once to see how Miss Dorcas was doing. She was groaning under a mango tree and leaves were falling onto her face like giant green tears. Imelda had glanced up into the tree and seen little Jonathon breaking twigs and leaves and throwing them down on his mother. *Dat little raashole!* She had almost laughed out loud, so relieved was she to see he was alive. She pretended to continue the search, though, until the moment when the little boy's voice had filled the river causing the women to scream and a few of the children to run all the way back up to their houses.

Thinking about Watersgate and the river, Imelda might also have told the interviewer how, in the summer when she was eight years old, she used to wait anxiously for her godmother, Tessa Walcott, to walk by the house and shout, 'Imelda-oooohhh!' She would say goodbye to her parents and run and follow the woman to the washing section of the river where the water gurgled over rocks into two still green pools. Tessa had six sons but no daughter, and people in the village insisted that she and Imelda resembled each other if only for the fact that they were both fat. Yes, Imelda would have to say to the newspaperman if she had told him all of this, I used to be fat. By the river Tessa taught Imelda the only thing she could teach — how to wash clothes: how to beat a dirty collar against a rock in a way that would lift the dirt but not damage the shirt. She showed Imelda the blue rocks that you could put a stained shirt under, submerging it in the river for an hour or two, sometimes overnight, until the stain lifted. Imelda thought Tessa was a kind of John the Baptist, taking these mountains of dirty clothes and dipping them like sinners under the water, then bringing them up again, restored and clean. Imelda would look to the heavens, waiting for a dove to descend onto Tessa's shoulders and a voice to resound, 'This is my daughter in whom I am well pleased.'

But Imelda said none of this; indeed, she said nothing that would show her to be a real person. She refused to relax, and the interview was stilted. So were the photos taken. As they walked around the campus, the newspaperman asked Imelda now and then to stop while he took pictures. He liked none of them. Her poses were too posed, her smiles too fake.

'Love,' he asked as they walked across the grass and inspiration suddenly hit him, 'could you just look up to the sky and point?'

Imelda could see no harm in this. She obliged, looked up and pointed to the clouds and the newspaperman flashed his camera. The next Sunday it was this picture that appeared in the papers — a young black woman, curious expression on her face, pointing to something above her. The caption read, 'Imelda Sees Her First Robin'.

'Robin! Who never see raas robin b-before!' Imelda shouted, and if Purletta hadn't laughed so hard Imelda might have stayed upset, but eventually she too saw the humour in it. The picture also made her remember one of those first nights she had spent in Manchester. She and Purletta had been outside one evening, and looking up at the sky Imelda had shouted in excitement, 'L-look, Purletta! Look!'

'What is it?' Purletta looked up frantically but saw nothing remarkable in the sky.

Imelda laughed self-consciously. 'Nothing, nothing. Sorry. It was j-just a shooting star.'

She would never admit that it was the moon that had caught her attention. She had not expected to see it in England. It was silly of her, she knew, to think that the moon belonged to the Caribbean. But all the same, the sight of it had filled her with excitement and she had stood there staring for a long while as if her eyes alone were keeping it in the sky. The moon, at that moment, was a sign. For the first time she understood, perhaps, that while she was no longer in Jamaica, she was still on the same earth.

Imelda saved the article with the picture of her pointing at an imaginary robin. She would have kept it for ever, except that ten years later, back in Jamaica, it was stored in the bottom drawer of her dressing table. And then came the horrible morning of 29 September 1983, when the river turned and flooded the house. Imelda did not manage to save anything from the bottom drawer. Neither the article, nor the large batches of letters and Christmas cards she had received from a young man named Ozzie Francis.

She didn't mind losing these letters – some of them love letters. Even when they were together, she realised that she did not love him and he did not love her. The letters – wordy and circuitous, without a drop of anything that could legitimately be called love or passion – were, in retrospect, proof of his insincerity. This, at least, is what she told herself. The only thing Ozzie really loved was dictionaries.

*

As a boy going to school in Antigua, Ozzie Francis learned an easy way to impress teachers. He would swot two of the bigger words from the dictionary each morning and then try to use them in conversation during the day. 'Miss,' he might complain to the teacher as he approached her desk, 'the homework last night was very EX-ZAS-KER-BATING' or 'Miss, this boy beside me is trying to COUNTER-FEET my work!' His primary-school teachers encouraged him by calling him either Young Shakespeare or Young Rhodes Scholar. He beamed with pride whenever he heard such things and he believed in the truth of them, though Ozzie was neither bright nor talented.

When he was younger, he hardly ever pronounced the words correctly or used them accurately but even when he was older he was never interested in the music of words but rather the hoarding of them. His logic was simple: everything he would ever really know in this world was contained in a word, and all the words in the world were contained in some dictionary or other. The more words you possessed the smarter you were; the more dictionaries you owned, the more knowledge you had.

The only statistic that was true, however, was that the more words Ozzie acquired, the less friends he seemed to have. He didn't mind. He felt glad to be excluded, thinking this was proof that he was above them. After all, he could speak so much better. He believed that in their eyes he must have seemed foreign anyway – a young Shakespeare. His true home was not Antigua, it was England, home of the Oxford Dictionary. He had always felt it, and when he reached that country, friendships would happen naturally. Love would happen naturally. Every good thing that was supposed to happen in his life would happen naturally, because he would be with his fellow countrymen who spoke well, spoke with ease the big words you found in a proper dictionary. So he read every night, working his way from A to Z, preparing himself.

Ozzie had been working for two years in a government office when his supervisor finally presented him with the chance of going to England for six months to do a course in public administration.

'You is the kind of man who could reach well far in the civil service,' the supervisor said, probably recognising in Ozzie a pretentiousness and the kind of focused and intractable anal-retentiveness that is often mistaken for intelligence. Ozzie jumped at the opportunity. Yes, yes, he agreed. He concurred. He acquiesced. He would go away to learn skills to equip him to do a better job back home in Antigua. Because of course, certainly, indubitably, he would return, repatriate. But Ozzie knew from the get-go he was never coming back. Not ever. No. Negative.

Friends didn't happen naturally in England. Ozzie thought at first that it was just a matter of them needing to hear him speak. Once he did that he would be identified immediately. He would be accepted into the fold as a long lost son. So he became talkative. Garrulous. Loquacious. The bus driver would be simply giving him back change: 'Oh, sincere appreciation, sir! It's just absolutely wonderful . . .'

'Could ya move down in tha bus, sir!'

In the supermarket, the cashiers would cut him off as well: 'Thar's other people behind you, sir!'

In class, he always put up his hand to answer questions, and his response would be a long-winded discourse about what was 'the bottom line, the crux, paramount to the case', what was 'absolutely and intrinsically germane to this particular situation', how any other approach 'utterly flabbergasted' him. One day when he put up his hand the lecturer snapped.

'Mr Francis, might you be able to make your point in under ten minutes, perhaps?'

The class exploded in laughter.

Then Ozzie thought that if he could just learn the unique words of this new place – its slang – then things would be all right. He had turned up his nose at the Antiguan dialect, of course, but this was England. Surely there was nothing wrong with English slang? He was living in Manchester and in the Northern mouth words like 'pocket' became 'pooket', 'fuck' became 'fook' and everyone was endearingly called 'loove'. Words like 'law' and 'saw' had a soft 'r' at the end. Double Ts were always silent: bo(tt)le, ca(tt)le, li(tt)le. Ozzie thought if he could just bend and roll and twist and flatten his tongue in these new ways it would help. But nothing he did made a difference, and all at once the loneliness set in. He finished his course, got a job in the city, rented his own flat with a green welcome mat placed outside the door. But nothing made England a friendlier place.

So Ozzie did the only thing he had always known how to do: he read dictionaries. But now he was visiting second-hand book stores and buying different kinds. *The Dictionary of Mental Illnesses. The Dictionary of English Flowers. The Dictionary of Comic Book Terms. The Dictionary of Space and the Galaxies. A Stamp Collector's Dictionary. The Collin's Spanish–English Pocket Dictionary. The A to Z of European Place Names. The Official Scrabble Player's Dictionary. A Baker's Dictionary.*

Occasionally, when he was tired of finding out that a) Acute Distonia was a side effect of certain drug therapies that caused the neck and eye muscles to contract and sometimes left the patient unable to think, or b) BA-DOOOOM! was the sound of an explosion in Captain Eddie comics or c) Cranberry Custards should be placed on the window sill to cool, he would take a walk up Oxford Road, across Portland Street and into Piccadilly Park. The centre of the city. It was here one Saturday afternoon, with the winter almost finished, that he saw a woman sitting on a bench, the red cardigan she was wearing bright and defiant in this place. She was tall and slender, and . . . not pretty . . . pretty was too soft a word for her. But handsome. Comely. Pulchritudinous. He went over and sat down beside her. 'Loovely day, ennit?'

'Excuse m-me?'

Ozzie frowned. He took a deep breath and tried again.

'De day does pretty for true, eh?'

'Yes,' Imelda agreed. 'Pretty for true.'

She wondered why he had switched accents. She had said excuse me only because it surprised her for a moment that a black man had come up and started a conversation with her. In those days it seemed that all immigrants in Manchester were either West Indian or Irish, and all the West Indian men wanted Irish women, and all the Irish women wanted West Indian men. So began that generation of coffee children, wild-haired children, half Irish/half Jamaican, half Irish/half Trinidadian, half Irish/half Guyanese, half white/half black or half Indian children. England suddenly becoming mixed, and multicultural, and beautiful.

'De name is Ozzie.'

'I'm M-mary.'

'Mary. Loovely name.' He had switched accents again.

They observed the birds flying around, and stared at the bare trees as if by paying close enough attention they might see the first leaf of spring erupting from inside the wood.

'How long you been here for?'

'Just an hour,' Imelda said.

'No. I mean, how long you been in England?'

'Oh. Almost two years n-now.'

'Yeah. Same as myself.' Ozzie smiled. 'But you're from ... Jamaica? You sound Jamaican.'

'Yes ... and you don't s-sound as if you decide where the raas you're from.'

Ozzie laughed nervously. Imelda turned back to the view of the park, realising she hated these kinds of discussions. Tentative and awkward. She watched various people walking through the park. Most were wearing a layer less than the usual winter gear, although a few were still firmly bundled up, while a final set were down to t-shirts and sandals, as if spring had already arrived. An old man stopped by their bench and asked for any spare change. Ozzie was in the middle of saying, 'No. Sorry, mate,' but Imelda reached into her pocket and gave the man a five-pence piece. He winked a thank-you as if they were co-conspirators; and in a way they were. It was a man like this that Imelda had become used to talking with in the park. If the space beside her hadn't been occupied, she suspected this one would have sat down and said

131

something like *Mighty kind of you, loove*. She would have smiled and he would have started talking because he knew instinctively that she would listen with all the respect of a grandchild. He would tell her then about the days of the factories and the mills; the Salvation Army which had closed its doors only two years ago and where poor children could go on Sunday afternoons to have dinner and watch a film then all walk back home together, as many as thirty of them, and up to all manner of mischief; nothing to harm no one, mind you, loove, but mischief all the same; and swimming in the canals even when you were shivering ya noots off, though he hadn't swam in 'em canals since Timmy dived in for his house key and never came up. Imelda learned about coppers who, in those days, was nice blokes, not like these kindergarten fools who'll be harassing you all day saying you can't lie down on the benches, it ain't a place for sleeping, you have to be sat up.

Imelda liked these conversations because all she had to do was listen. She didn't feel the same with the man sitting beside her now – Ozzie. She didn't know what was expected.

'So what do you do up here?'

'S-study.'

'Okaaaaay.'

He had stretched the word out, trying to draw from her an answer that was longer than one word. It didn't work.

'What do you study?'

'Law.' She got, up suddenly. 'L-look, it was nice meeting you. B-but it's getting late. I have to be getting back home.'

She gathered her things and began to walk away. As Ozzie watched Imelda leave, a sadness larger than anything he had ever known began to swallow him.

'It's just that I don't know plenty people!'

Imelda stopped.

'I sorry,' he continued talking to her back. 'I never mean to scare you off, Mary. Is just that I don't know nobody here. Nobody at all.'

If she were to trace it all back, Imelda would tell you that that was the moment. Not the moment she loved him, but the moment she decided she would allow herself to be loved by him – because he had spoken honestly, in his own voice. She turned to him.

'M-my name is actually Imelda.'

Purletta waddled over to the couch that evening, her fat thighs rubbing together. She sat down, carton of orange juice in one hand, bottle of vodka in the other. She opened both and generously poured from the vodka into the juice.

'Aye, mi child,' she said at last, 'that is where all the problems begin. Now listen to me . . . when it come to man, I don't keep them. My mother was like that too. Except she was fool enough to keep on marrying them. But me? No way. Men have them season, Imelda. Every now and then you will need a treatment, of course. We have needs after all. But other than that, I don't mix up with them.'

'All I said is that I m-meet a nice young man in Piccadilly today.'

'And is that 'cause all the twinkle twinkle in your eyes? What you want me to say? "*Oh Imelda, you meet a man; how nice! And did you two talk about the weather? And will you meet up with him again to talk more about the weather?*" I don't have time for bullshit. You tell me you meet a man, and me and you know what that mean. So I telling you straight, that is where all the problems begin.'

Imelda sighed.

'Like I say, them good in them season. But after that, you have to find a way to get rid of them. Me? Usually I call up the fellow and tell him I catch crabs or something like that. Then I don't hear from him again. That is usually the best way – 'cause man prefer to be the one to leave you. If you try to leave them, they will hang on. But I have my solution for that one too. I make sure I don't take on no muscle man. No fat man. My man have to be smaller in body than me, so that when it come to it, I can fling some lick on the fellow. Make him run with him tail between him legs – which not so hard with English men. Sometimes you only have to say bumboclawt, and them run gone. But if is between me and a man to get lock up for domestic violence, it better be me!'

'So what is it you s-saying then? I m-mustn't bother with this guy?'

'No, no, no! I don't give advice. I only say what is on mi mind to say. You ... you must live your own life. If you like the guy, talk to him. If you need a treatment, get a treatment. I just telling you that's where the problems start.' Purletta lifted the box of orange juice in the air. 'Here, here. To man and to problems. Without them, life would be boring.'

Only months after that toast, Imelda would discover that Purletta was not so strong after all. She came in one night with a white fellow she had been dating and the couple laughed all the way up to her bedroom. Imelda was in her own room ironing clothes for the next day. The walls were thin, and Purletta's voice had a way of carrying, even when she was whispering. Imelda heard the first time she said *No!* She heard it the second time, more distinctly, preceded by the word 'Please.' *Please. No. Stop it!* She heard the man's voice, more like a growl, and she heard Purletta whimpering. Imelda never panicked. She never ran screaming for help. She simply turned the iron up to its highest setting and went into the kitchen to fetch something. Purletta was calling out for help when Imelda opened the door to her room, walked over and stamped the sizzling face of the iron firmly into the man's naked back. He jumped up hollering, his penis immediately flaccid, and threw himself wildly. She produced a knife from behind her back and held it to the man's neck.

'Don't fuck with me today,' she said. 'Leave this house and never come b-back.'

Ozzie's first letter to Imelda arrived in the post two weeks after the Sunday they had met. It was the first of 107 things he would write to her – a combination of typed letters, handwritten notes slipped under her door, cards, postcards and spontaneous poems

134

written on napkins of the various restaurants they had visited. She eventually kept the complete anthology in three separate batches, bound by green rubber bands, in her bottom drawer at the house in Watersgate. But on 29 September, 1983, the river came into the house and destroyed all of it, spread the ink into nothing. Imelda tried to tell herself that she didn't mind losing the notes, but this was of course a lie. Sometimes she would read over his letters and it had caused her to remember England – not just the small details, but the large parts as well. It was frightening when she realised how much of it she had forgotten, how much of it she had not engaged with. And so sometimes Ozzie's letters had reminded her of a feeling she had had at a particular moment, and also the world that had surrounded that moment and that feeling. It was if he had been documenting her own experience for her because she had failed to do it herself. So when the letters were ruined, in a way, England was ruined too.

Some Letters Ozzie
Wrote to Imelda

 1

Dear Mary/ Imelda/ nice lady from the park,
When I walked you home I made a note of your address. It
must seem strange, me writing to you, when there is no
ocean or mountain or great quantity of miles between us.
Forgive, pardon, excuse me. It is only that sometimes I
trust my voice on paper more than I trust it on my lips –
trust it to say most precisely exactly what it is I want to
say.

   For today, I simply want to say salutations and hello. It
was very nice to meet you.
   Yours,
   Ozzie

 4

Imelda,
Something that might tickle you: today I argued with a man
who wished me 'a pleasant, good afternoon'. I informed
him politely that this was a tautology, but he seemed not to
understand me. So I explained to him that it was
repetitious, redundant and pleonastic to say 'pleasant' and

136

'good'. After all, is there any such thing as a pleasant, bad afternoon? Well, he proceeded to call me an 'uppity nigger' and walked off.

I do not believe this gentleman to be English. Welsh perhaps, or a Russian immigrant. But the English know how to use the English language. It is strange, isn't it, to meet so many barbarians in this country. Yours, Ozzie.

11

Dear Imelda,

Maybe you've had the experience of speaking to someone but only after the conversation has ended does something finally occur to you, and you think, If only I had thought of this during the conversation, it would have been a consummate, unimpeachable and serendipitous point to make.

About our little disagreement . . . while you graciously allowed me to choose another performance (which in the long run you must agree was incalculably more enjoyable), I still feel you do not fully appreciate the point I was trying to make.

The point that finally occurred to me was that the term 'West Indian theatre' is an oxymoron. Nothing but a bunch of people running about, shouting, gyrating and trying to have sex with each other. Consider the great playwrights – Shakespeare or Oscar Wilde. They would never stoop to the kind of lewdness our people seem to revel in.

I am not someone to boast, or advertise, but as a man who could just as easily have made a career in the arts, I know that it would only take the smallest fraction of my talent to write a typical West Indian play.

Yours truly,
Ozzie

12

Imelda,
I cannot believe you are still not talking to me. When will this silliness end? Well, I still wish to register two small points: 1) I have indeed been to countless Shakespearean and Wildean plays and so I do know of what I speak. I resent your rather crude statement that I am 'full of bomboclawt shit'. 2) You called me a 'xenophobe'. I happen to have a Dictionary of Phobias, Manias and Philias and, as I suspected, xenophobia is the fear of *foreign people or strangers*. I cannot be a xenophobe towards my own countrymen. There's patroiophobia (the fear of heredity) and anthrophobia (the fear of people) but neither is exactly what you meant. I'm sure the appropriate word exists and when I encounter it I shall pass it on to you. But I would still disagree with the point you desired to make, even if you didn't find the appropriate words with which to make it. I walk with my eyes open, and I will call a spade a spade.
  Ozzie

 14

Dear Imelda,
I am glad we have resumed our friendship, though your comment about me having an 'unearned arrogance' will continue to sting even more than all the expletives you used on me. I will agree with you that on some topics we agree to disagree – but still, you are different from most West Indians, whether you admit it or not. If you do not reject them, they will reject you. I have found this out for myself and I imagine you will soon too.
  But on to more pedestrian, mundane topics. My week has not been good. The woman whom I find myself working directly across from, Mrs Clement, who has indeed been

my partner on several assignments, is an idiot. Incompetent at everything besides sitting on her posterior. It is my conviction (and I know I shan't be proved wrong on this) that she has been telling untruths about her credentials and qualifications and so has landed her present job in a manner that is altogether fraudulent.

I have taken my superiors into my confidence, but until yesterday they did nothing in the way of launching an investigation. On Tuesday, however, as was always bound to happen, Mrs Clement made a blunder more catastrophic than her usual. I am sure it is this which made management announce that all employees were to come in with their certificates, etc. so personnel could review them. Not surprisingly, Mrs Clement has called in ill with a terrible bout of food poisoning. I am certain such scheming shall not spare her the noose this time around, and when it is discovered that I have been right all along, perhaps they shall honour my astuteness and consider me for a promotion. Even into her position.

I do look forward to seeing you this weekend. Maybe we shall have reason to celebrate.

Cheers,

Ozzie

✉ 25

Dear Imelda,

I went to the pool this evening and in the changing room an old man, surprised no doubt to see both men and women in the same room, asked me if all the changing rooms were 'ambidextrous'. I looked at him curiously and so he explained that the word meant something used by both men and women. I dared not correct him for fear he would call me an uppity nigger.

Cheers

Ozzie.

Dear Imelda,

No doubt you were trained by the Gestapo. You want to
know why it is you often turn around to find me staring. I
have been coy, but about 'matters of the heart' (if I may
employ that cliché) I have never enjoyed much confidence.
It is only now, sitting at my bedroom desk and weighing
things more ponderously and deliberately, that I am finally
questioning my shyness, my inhibitions, my timorousness.
What really is the point of it all, when the history of
mankind is, in fact, the history of people falling in love.
From Adam and Eve right down. Indeed I read in my
Dictionary of Greek Mythology that several would rank
Eros as the most powerful and influential in the pantheon –
yes, even above Zeus.

So yes, I shall finally admit it. Why not? I find myself
smitten by you. But 'smitten' is not the right word. They
are, none of them, the right words. I am everything –
enamoured, absorbed, attracted to, beguiled, transported,
bewitched, transfixed, delighted, captivated, charmed,
dazzled, enchanted, engrossed, enraptured, enthralled,
entranced, enticed, tantalised, excited by, fond of,
hypnotised, infatuated and intoxicated, mesmerised,
overpowered, sent, sold on, gone on, hooked on, stuck on,
sweet on, turned on, wild about, you!

My dear Imelda, you are beautiful.

With love,

Ozzie

The Silly Things Harry Walcott
Would Not Do

During the longest stretch that Harry would ever stay at home without leaving Tessa and the children – a total of three years and four months – Tessa woke him one night to tell him, 'You been dreaming of de sea again.'

In his grogginess he admitted the truth. Yes. He had been dreaming of the sea. But then the grogginess lifted and he realised he had never shared this recurring dream with Tessa or anyone. He looked at her with alarm and curiosity.

'How you know?'

'Because whenever you have that dream is like you want to push me off the bed. And I look at yu hands and yu feet, how you spread them out like this, and move them back and forth like this, soft soft, and I realise dat is how people move in deep water. So I see all this time is de sea you been dreaming of.'

'Yes,' he said again, astonished. 'That is true.'

All these years she had observed his troubled sleep, listened to his nonsense mutterings, hoping that one night he would reveal to her the name of whichever woman it was he disappeared off to see. Or else, she hoped he would whisper her own name, so that she could be convinced that she existed in the deepest part of his mind. But all she had ever observed were his hands and his feet spread like that, moving back and forth like that, soft soft, as if he were treading water. Then all at once Tessa understood something else.

'So that's where you always going off to. You been going off to sea.'

Guilt rose up like the ocean. Harry could not understand why he had not told her. What must Tessa have thought? He held her plump, soft hands that did not feel like a washerwoman's and kissed them.

'Yes. I been going off to sea. Did I ever tell you, Tessa, 'bout falling into the ocean?'

'No,' Tessa said. 'You never told me about falling in love with the ocean.'

So that night he told her – about every boat and every ship he had been on. He held her in his arms and together they rocked across the dark sea to Haiti. Together they threw nets and caught conch and shrimp and fish. Then it was morning, the time when boats must go back to shore, and they had not slept nor were they tired, and Tessa found that she could not look into Harry's green eyes.

'You must go back.' she told him. 'I understand now. Is something you have to do.'

Harry could not look into Tessa's eyes either, but he understood something else, as a man will after being married for five or ten or twenty years; that night, he had fallen in love with his wife again. He squeezed Tessa's hands and she squeezed his.

With his wife's permission Harry went to work on several ships and sailed to more countries than a diplomat might visit in his whole career. In the Caribbean he went to Curacao, Panama, Mexico, Trinidad, Barbados and the Bahamas. He stopped at almost every major port along the East Coast of the United States – New York, New Jersey, Philadelphia, Baltimore, New Orleans and Miami. He sailed further north to Canada. He sailed to England, Scotland, across to Europe, once to Africa, once to Shanghai and twice to New Zealand.

And what was the silly thing he did, or rather, did not do? He never disembarked. Even when they dropped anchor in Scotland and the crew rushed back to tell him there was a man in the pub who had olive skin just like his, green eyes just like his, a thick curly red afro just like his, and was named Harold James Walcott IV just like him – he knew they were telling the truth, and that this must be his half-brother. His replacement. That this was an opportunity to meet the other side of his family – his father, if he was still alive, and his stepmother; to see the life that would have been his if his mother had not been so afraid of the water he loved.

But he was not interested. Nor was he interested in the things other sailors lived for – the sounds foreign women made, what they might scream during that most intimate act, in French, in Italian, in Swahili, in Cantonese. He did not take the opportunity, as many did, to run away – to lose himself in another country, to find himself in another language. He never took the opportunity, as every other sailor did, at least to walk on all that foreign soil, to experience the culture, albeit fleetingly. It was all the same to him. All of it – the same earth.

Instead, he was interested in shades of blue. There were thousands of shades and he could tell them all apart; he was also interested in the deep black of night that an ocean could suck into itself; in the rock and pull and swell of the vast kingdom below him. He was interested in those days when the ship docked and he could stand on top of the deck and dive – twenty, thirty feet – into the water, without a splash.

Harry disembarked only in Jamaica and headed straight for Watersgate, depositing onto the marriage bed his full salary.

'This is for you and the children,' he would tell Tessa. Then he would stay for a month, maybe two, and he and Tessa would make love every night and every morning, their hands and legs spread like this, going back and forth like this.

Some More Letters from Ozzie

 63

Imelda,
I ain't give a flying fuck if that big beast of a landlord of
yours don't like me. The feeling here, I assure you, is
returned, it is mutual, it is requited! She was repugnant,
distasteful and quite frankly, vulgar. How it is you
continue to live with her defies the very pillars of logic. I
renew my commendation that you try to find more suitable
accommodation, with people of more refinement and
civility.
   Ozzie

 64

Dear Imelda,
I apologise for my previous disgruntlement, but you must
confess it was warranted. I am still livid about how that
whole evening went. I went to visit your landlord and
friend. I assume she wanted to meet me, your boyfriend.
It is my understanding that such occasions call for
politeness on all sides. I did not go to be laughed at and
certainly not by an ignoramus. But that is how it is with

West Indian people. As soon as they see someone of any true breeding, they become intimidated.

You told me once that her grandfather was some kind of deputy-governor in Jamaica. Clearly that was a lie, or her family line has hit rock-bottom with her. I mean, where is the proof of any breeding in her? All she speaks is Broken English. Even accusing me with it, saying that I was 'speaky-spokey', 'hoity-toity', stoosh'! What kind of words are those?

But I did not appreciate your flippant response that my feathers were too easily ruffled. That I should just relax. You should have been equally if not doubly insulted by that Purletta woman! We are a couple now. If she insults me she insults you!

I am not returning to your house if she is there. Not ever.
Ozzie

✉ 78

My dearest Imelda,
As I write, I am observing your figure, stretched out and sleeping on the bed across from this table. In this first blush, the early light of morning, the vision does make for a wonderful sight, and were I photographer with the appropriate equipment, I would capture it so it could be framed and mounted permanently. I must say, if either of us were believers and practitioners of any religion we would have to abandon it now. Fornication or adultery, or the breaking of whichever commandment it is that was broken, is a splendid and rapturous and wonderful act. We must break it again. And then again. Become repeat offenders, blasphemers struck by a bout of echolalia! What was that strange coinage you used – 'Treatment'? Appropriate, I think. What a treat it was!

Your partner in hell
Ozzie

✉ 85

My dearest Imelda,
As you already know, I have been thinking about our life together. You know it is the predisposition of us males to be forward-thinking and always projecting into the future. I think we should seriously consider moving south, to London. I know the city is big and unfriendly and makes Manchester seem by comparison like the deepest part of the country, and as you complain, no one in London calls you 'loove'. But I will always be there to call you 'loove' my love, or 'soonshine'. Whenever you want. Wherever you want.

And there is something about travelling on the Underground to Trafalgar Square or Covent Garden, when it gets so crowded you're being crushed by the throng, but who knows, the person who is inconveniencing your well-being by stepping on your toes could well be an MP or a council man or a music star. Just being there makes you feel like you're a part of something so much grander – a spoke in a mighty wheel.

So we must think about starting our careers in London. It would only be for the first ten years or so. Then we could do what most people on the up and up do, and buy a bigger house somewhere in the country.

Wouldn't that be a grand life?
Yours lovingly,
Ozzie

✉ 97

Dear Imelda,
I found out from your friend Purletta that she was flying down to Jamaica for the funeral, and asked if she could deliver this letter to you. I hope you do not destroy it before perusing its contents.

First and most importantly, I really do offer my condolences. I was exceedingly sorry to hear about your mother's passing and your father seeming as if he, too, will go at any minute. I admit, in the clearer light of day, that my comment was badly timed, inappropriate and insensitive and though violence is never, ever an appropriate response to anything, I don't even need you to apologise for breaking that vase over my head. Other than a nasty cut, you'll be glad to know it did not cause any great damage.

So I am sorry for saying 'let the dead bury the dead'. Quite frankly, I only said it because I was hurt. I know now it was probably only the grief speaking in you, and that you probably weren't serious about not returning to England. Because really, what is there for you in Jamaica? And what about me? Where does that leave us? And what about graduation? You are the first black person – and a woman at that – to graduate with a degree in law. You deserve to be on stage with the whole lot of them. You are the one always going on and on about community and living for other people – well, there is a community here that needs you to see your success all the way through. And to celebrate with you.

I just cannot abide the thought of someone with your capabilities going back to a little village school in Watergate, or Watersgate, or wherever, to do administrative work that your mother in her eighties could have done with her eyes closed. It's not what you were destined for.

But I do not mean to fight again. This is meant to be an apology – contrite and penitent. I mean to say I'm sorry. I am indeed very sorry. For what has happened to your parents and for how I did not support you when you were most desperate and in need of support.

Yours always and always with love,
Ozzie

103

[Inscription on a Christmas Card]
Yours with much love
Ozzie
1979

 104

[Inscription on a Christmas Card]
Yours with much love
Ozzie
1980

 105

Dear Imelda,

Just the briefest of notes to keep you up to date with my life; it seems at one point you were such a crucial and integral part of it that even now I feel the need to tell you how it is developing. I have begun teaching English at a centre for Adult Education, and am quite enjoying it. The discipline of pedagogy is of course is far more rewarding than my previous profession, which I now have to admit was all rather clerical and tedious. Most of my students are from other European countries who have just migrated to good old Britannia. I can't imagine being so fearless – to move to a whole other place without knowing its language. I myself studied English for years before I came to England because really, our creole is just as foreign as French or Spanish – though without the history or the poetry.

I have met someone. One of my students. Her name is Jessica and she is from Bulgaria. I hope you are so lucky in Watersgate. We had good times, did we not? But I imagine it is indeed time to move on.

Yours,
Ozzie

106

[Inscription on a Christmas Card]
Best of the season,
Ozzie
1981

107

[Inscription on a Christmas Card]
Season's Greetings
Mr and Mrs Ozzie Francis
1982

PS So sorry you could not make it over
for the auspicious occasion of our joining in matrimony.
We do hope all is well with you.

The Silly Thing Imelda
Thought When She Returned

June 1979

To pack up and go back home is not an easy thing. For every item folded neatly and stuffed into the bulging suitcase, the packer will ask him- or herself, what am I really going back to? Most will believe, with all their heart, that there is a place there waiting for them. But this is foolish thinking. For every man exists in the world the way a body exists in water: the moment you leave, the space you occupied will close over. What is left is not even the shape of your body, but the memory of it. There is no such thing as return. We leave one place. We arrive at another. But the person who arrives is never the person who left. We grow. We change. There is no space waiting for us. Only a memory.

Imelda went back to Watersgate to bury her mother. Everyone greeted her warmly. They said they were so glad to see her again. *What a way you grow up! What a way you turn big woman! What a way you lose de weight and look good! What a way you chop off all yu hair? Is so English woman wear them hair? But it look good on you, my dear. We is real glad to see you, Imelda. We is glad you come back.* And Imelda felt, yes, this was where she was supposed to be. This was home. A place had been waiting for her.

But at first no one knew she was planning on staying. They probably were glad to see her in truth, but people cannot remain enthusiastic for ever. They had their lives to live, and the return of any long-lost neighbour is only a minor diversion until that neighbour leaves again. When it became apparent that Imelda was staying, they simply went back to their regular living – and they had learned to live without her.

To pack up and go back home is not an easy thing, for there is no space waiting for us. We must create that space all over again. People grow. They change. Imelda found, for instance, that she was no longer the kind of woman who could go to church every Sunday. She could no longer find entertainment in village gossip. These two facts made it hard for her to integrate, and people eventually sensed in her a kind of aloofness. A superiority about her manner. What was more, the last time she was in Watersgate she had been a child. She had come back a woman. If it weren't for the incident when she had walked into Alexander Town Square and come back with the boy they called Zero it would have been almost impossible for her to fit in. But after the incident people began to come to her for all kinds of advice, and Tessa made it part of her routine to stop at Imelda's house on her way up from the river. Still, people are fickle, and when, only a few years later, Imelda was virtually run out of the village, at least one person sat by their window watching her leave, turned around to their family and said: 'Serve her right. She should have never come back.'

The Six Sons of Tessa
and Harold Walcott

From circa 1952, the birth of The Fifth — July 1979

Tessa and Harold Walcott IV had six sons. To recite their names in order, from the first to the last, you would think one was counting down to a great disaster. It all began with the birth of their first child who Mother Lynette, the village midwife, made the great mistake of calling 'Junior'. After all, he was named after his father and she knew no better. Harry Walcott protested loudly.

'Mother Lynette!' His voice held an equal measure of offence and pride but both feelings were kept separate by the white rum Harry had been drinking all night in celebration. 'I know that you is a simple woman and not versed in such things like names of a more noble sort. But let me tell you, for your own education and betterment, that this boy who is my first son is no Junior! Just like King George the Third was not a Junior, and Pope John the Second was not a Junior. No — he is The Fifth!'

And out of spite the whole village took this up for their education and their betterment, and the boy's name became The Fifth.

The village thought to extend the joke when they nicknamed Tessa's next son, not The Fourth (for that was rightfully the father's name) but more simply, Four. The child after that was Three, then Two, then One and finally, Zero. Thank God Zero was Tessa's last son, for the villager's rudimentary mathematics would have failed them after, and they would not have been able to conceive the name, Negative One – though another person might tell you it was the villagers' inability to conceive of a new name that in turn made Tessa unable to conceive any more children.

The six sons of Tessa and Harold Walcott did not grow up, not one of them, to be extraordinary men. Or perhaps they were extraordinary in their ordinariness. The Fifth had the dubious reputation of being incapable of taking any woman down the aisle, which was not exactly true; he did take at least one woman down the aisle, proving on that occasion that the thing he was actually incapable of doing was saying 'I do'. The church was crowded on that Saturday morning, an abundance of white cloth and pink flowers was draped over the altar and ran as streamers from bench to bench. The bride was smiling from ear to ear, her gloved hands firmly holding the bouquet of flowers that would soon shed their petals when she began to shake softly, then violently, enduring the great shame and tragedy of her never-to-be-husband's silence. The Reverend had put the question to the Fifth.

'Do you, Harold James Walcott V, take this woman to be your lawful wedded wife? . . . Mr Walcott? . . . Mr Walcott, can you hear me? . . . Do you take this woman to be your lawful wedded wife? . . . MR WALCOTT! Do you hear me?'

But not a word. Eventually everyone would walk out and go back to their houses, disappointed, and the only people left in the church would be The Fifth, still standing there like some zombie, and his almost-bride who, in a final act of commitment to him, refused to leave him there by himself, clutching in her hands a bouquet of only stems.

On the occasion before that, The Fifth had not shown up at the church at all. The bride, another unlucky woman, was fashionably late by an hour, but when people saw the old blue Volvo that was carrying her turn into the churchyard, they sent someone out to tell the driver to go back out and circle for a while until the groom showed up. The car circled and circled for almost two hours after which the driver took the weeping bride home, not because he wouldn't have waited any longer, but because the vehicle was almost out of petrol.

The Fifth did the slightly more decent thing on his third marriage attempt by calling off the wedding a good week before it was supposed to happen. Now he was dating a new girlfriend, Sofia, who everyone had forewarned, *Don't look for a wedding ring from dat one. Just enjoy what you have while you can.*

Four, Three, Two and One were almost indistinguishable one from the other – not only because they were born, like clockwork, ten months after the other, so that it seemed to some that Tessa Walcott was pregnant for three and a half years straight. It was not that they looked so alike, forging between the four of them what would commonly become known as the 'Walcott Boy Look': short black men slender enough to appear taller than they actually were, with high cheekbones and pointed noses and always that same full head of curly black hair that had in it a tint of red. But what made the boys truly indistinguishable from one another was that at the ages of fifteen or sixteen they all left the village, as if they had grown up simply to become statistics, part of the great unstoppable wave of migration. Two of them went to Kingston, another to Canada and another to America. People forgot who went where. In each case, their leaving was final, as if they had inherited their father's ability to disappear, but not his inclination to come back.

The last son, Zero, became the disaster his name seemed to foretell. But once again, not an extraordinary disaster – just a mild one, like the mild retardation he suffered. He was extremely slow in the classroom and was virtually incompetent on the sports field. The villagers understood and forgave the boy his imbecility. They would say, *Him is not quite right* or *I tink him kinda touch up hereso*, tapping their index fingers against their own foreheads. But Zero was only a mild nuisance: he would walk up and down the streets and beg you for money ten times a day if he saw you ten times a day; sometimes he would trap you in conversation and tell you stories so fantastic and unbelievable and childlike when all you wanted to do was free yourself and go about the business you were supposed to be off doing; and yes, he had his occasional streaks of mischievousness when he would torment whichever dog he could find, and on a number of occasions Zero would run home bawling, rubbing the place where a fed-up mongrel had finally bitten him.

Then one day, in his own way, it was as if Zero had grown up. This is not to say he suddenly came into his right mind, or that he became less touched up thereso, but that all at once the village was too small for him. He started wandering beyond Watersgate and into the town square, begging, telling bigger stories to stranger people, teasing dogs, making himself more than just a mild nuisance; trying hard, it seemed, to become a great disaster. Some would say he succeeded because one day Zero wandered straight out of Watersgate and onto the front page of the *Jamaica Gleaner*. The alliterative headline read: St Mary Mad Man Held For Mayor's Murder.

To this day, no one could tell you exactly what happened, not even Zero. People made all kinds of guesses and conjectures, the most convincing of which went like this: Zero, that day, must have wandered up into the hills behind Alexander Town Square, into the slightly better-off community where people like the mayor and the principal of the high school and the postmistress lived. When Zero passed the mayor's house he found the gates open – not that they were tall or imposing gates, but what would have seemed particularly welcoming to Zero were the three big German Shepherds who were lying down, useless, in the front yard, panting, their eyes wide open, their mouths agape and their tongues lolling. He would not have been able to tell that the dogs had been drugged but still would have had great fun making funny faces at them, pulling their tails, pulling their fur, drawing down his pants and putting his bottom right up to their noses.

Then he would have heard a sudden noise – something to suggest that things inside the house were not as they should be. He would have got up from the dogs and gone over to one of the

French windows, pressing his pointy nose against the pane and peering through the glass. And what was it that he saw? More than likely – the mayor and his wife bound up in fishing rope, pleading for their lives. He would have seen the thieves point the gun at the mayor's temple and pull the trigger, that big balding mayoral head exploding all over his frizzy-haired wife who then became nothing more than a scream. He would have heard the thieves telling her to *shut up bitch! shut up! Don't make we have to shut you up too!* before they finally did, a bullet to her chest. If it didn't happen exactly like that, it must have been something close, and whatever little intelligence was in the boy's head would have flown out right then, like a flock of birds lifting off as one from a tree, so that the sum of all he knew was his name: Zero. Nothing. Zilch.

He went into the house after the men had left, and this is where Zero was found, sprawled over the two bodies. When Superintendent Carmichael arrived, his kerchief over his mouth, and stepped carefully into the house, he called to Zero.

'You there ! You, stand up.'

Zero turned and pointed at the superintendent with his index and middle fingers as if they were a gun.

'Bang bang!' It was all he would say from then on. 'Bang bang.'

'*Zero, do you remember me?*'

'*Bang bang.*'

'*Zero, are you all right? How are you doing?*'

'*Bang bang.*'

'*Do you remember anything that happened that day?*'

'*Bang bang.*'

Of course they had to hold him for questioning – no one could argue with that. But a few months later police raided a house in St Ann and it was full of things taken from the Mayor's house. They found the gun that did the killing and two men were arrested and charged for murder, one of them even confessing that it was not he who had pulled the trigger, he had only tied them up with the rope. All that time no one seemed to remember Zero, who was still being held for questioning for a crime that had now been solved. Zero just stayed in the corner of his cell, pointing his gun fingers at the wall.

'Bang bang. Bang bang.'

It was Tessa who remembered her son – for that is the lot of mothers, to keep their children alive and safe by the sheer power of their thoughts. She went to the lock-up every day to bring him food and listen to him say the only word he could. She suffered his vacant eyes and still she went. When they caught the actual criminals she started asking, *Why in God's green earth mi son still being held? Why you don't let him out now?* But to ask such questions was to enter a strange and complicated maze – Third World Bureaucracy – or maybe not so much a maze as a never-ending relay where batons are constantly being passed but a finish-line is never reached, so the only thing one can look forward to is death by exhaustion.

The sergeant at the desk only shrugged at Tessa's questions. When he was tired of them he suggested she take up her case at the superintendent's office across town. The secretary at the superintendent's office refused to let Tessa even see the super-intendent, saying he was a busy man, and in any case could not get involved in situations like Tessa's. *Police only lock up people, my dear. We don't release them. That is the job of the court. If you want your boy to be released you will have to go to the magistrate's court.* The bored secretary at the court immediately sent Tessa back to the police, who sent her back to the court, who sent her all the way to the Police Commissioner's office in Kingston who in turn sent Tessa back to the court. Tessa decided then that she would speak to no one but the judge. The magistrate was no longer the man Tessa had washed clothes for and returned money to, but she believed instinctively in his fairness and sense of justice. She was wrong. For four days she sat in the galleys, waiting to get his attention; for four days she failed. On the fifth day, frustrated and desperate, in the space between one case closing and another one opening, Tessa just stood up and spoke.

'Yu Honor, please, my son is in jail for something he never even do, and he still in there now and they say only you can let him out, Yu Honor, and I is coming here every day to ask you humbly, sir, just to do this small thing because him is a good boy, and him don't harm nobody, and him need to be home with him own mother right now because jail not good for him, Yu Honour, so I am here to humbly beseech you.'

The magistrate looked down at Tessa. Her speech did not move him; he had heard it a hundred times. She was one of several mothers who had come to his court to demand the release of their criminal sons, as if the mere fact of these truants having a mother who came to plead for them and to assure him that they were good boys exonerated them from their crimes.

'Madam, your son will be released when the due process of law has been done.' He hit his gavel on the desk, calling for the next case to begin.

Poor Tessa. She ran out of the courtroom excited, for all she had heard was, *Your son will be released* . . . That evening she bought a new broom on the way home and swept every room with an even greater ferocity than she did each time Harry came back. She swept away the dirt, the bad feelings, the bad spirits, anything that might have been lurking in corners. In their stead she placed bundles of lime grass and bougainvillea flowers. She hung up clean curtains in every window and spread clean sheets on the beds and then she waited. The waiting was a week, and then two, and then three. The lime grass and bougainvillea withered and lost their scent after a month. The dust crept back slowly.

Tessa returned to the magistrate's court. She waited again through dreary case after dreary case until a small moment of pause and then she stood up in that space.

'Yu Honour, my son is still in jail . . .'

'Madam!' he snapped, 'I believe I told you already your son will be released when he has served his time! Now do not disturb my chambers again! Your behaviour is simply outrageous.'

She was back again two months later to ask, what exactly was the time Zero was supposed to serve? But she had only managed to say 'Yu Honour' before the judge exploded.

'NOT YOU AGAIN! Listen here, if you dare interrupt my court one more time I swear to God I will throw you in jail alongside your son. Would you like that?'

'No, Yu Honour.'

In Jamaica there are no real seasons to speak of, so what is a year but mangoes and guineps, avocados and tiny yellow butterflies – the turning, falling and rotting of the first three, the sudden fluttering swarm of the latter until their deaths, everyone walking nonchalantly alongs roads covered with yellow wings. And so the time of mangoes and the time of guineps and the time of avocados and the time of tiny yellow butterflies had come and gone twice while Zero was in jail.

Tessa learned once again, as every human will learn a hundred times during his or her lifetime, about the many chambers of the heart where things too awful to touch or utter or look at can be stored. It is not that she forgot about Zero, but that she took her grief and folded it neatly like a tablecloth, placed it in a drawer and closed it. When she was alone at nights, she would sometimes open that drawer and put her hands in, run her palms across the fabric of her grief. But she did not take it outside any more. Her grief was her own, and she thought it would be hers through the coming and going of many mangoes and avocados and winged creatures and hurricanes and poinsettias and all those other things that come and go to mark the passing of a year.

But some years bring unexpected seasons, and 1979 brought with it The Time of Return. Maas Jeffrey who had, over the past five years, written sixty-seven letters of complaint to the government for things ranging from his arthritic knees to his neighbour's dog who was, to his great annoyance and dis-pleasure, also called Maas Jeffrey, had all of them returned to him at once – *Sendee: Address Unknown* for indeed he had simply posted them all to THE GOVAMENT OF JAMAICA. The postmistress, reasonably considering herself to be a paid representative of said *govament*, had opened all sixty-seven envelopes and read their contents with much amusement until she decided in 1979 that it was her duty to return them. And all over Watersgate, inexplicably, neighbours who had borrowed things and had kept them in their own houses till they almost believed the items were their own, had the sudden urge to return them. In all, fifty-three pens, forty-seven pencils, twenty-five LPs, eight dutch pots, four Bibles, three chairs, one table and a great variety of clothes and bedlinen were returned to their surprised, and sometimes weeping, owners.

And some returns were sad. It was in this year that Teacher Sarah Richardson was returning home alone one night when her heart stopped working. When she didn't arrive at her usual time Desmond went out to look for her. He discovered her body on the road and cried out once. People who heard the sound weren't sure if it had been made by man or bird or beast, but it was a sound full of loss, and everyone's hearts broke as one. People came out with lamps to look for the hurting animal and found both Desmond and Sarah lying on the road, and seeing them like this, their bodies curled together, no one was sure who was dead and who was alive.

One return lead to another; because Sarah returned to heaven, Imelda returned to Watersgate. Then one day, as Tessa returned from the river, she stopped at this first house and called:

'Imelda-oooooh!'

'Auntie Tessa? G-good to see you. We haven't even had a chance to talk p-properly since the funeral. Would you l-like a glass of water?'

'Childe, that would be exactly what I needing.'

Imelda returned with a tall glass of water which Tessa drank in one long draw. She rubbed the middle of her chest vigorously and belched. 'De gas, de gas.'

'How are the b-boys? I don't see any of them.'

Tessa told Imelda about The Fifth, who could not seem to get married. Then she told lies about Four, Three, Two and One, saying that they wrote to her constantly and she knew for a fact that they were doing well. She ended like that – no mention of her last son – so Imelda had to search for the hidden drawer.

'And what of Zero?'

Tessa shook her head from side to side.

'Auntie T-Tessa? Something wrong? What happened t-to Zero?'

'Lord, child, don't ask me. The Lord sees and the Lord knows . . .'

Imelda put her hands around Tessa's huge body. 'T-tell me. What happened to Zero?'

Tessa shook her head again but slowly opened the hidden drawer; she took out the broad sheet of her grief, held it by one end and threw it out so it could unfold in the air and cover them. Her weight resting in Imelda's arms became tears, and the tears falling onto Imelda's arm became anger.

'I los' my son. And my son done los' his mind. Two years now he in jail. Two years. Oh, Imelda, I call his name plenty night. I call his name when I think nobody listening, thinking maybe if I call enough, him will just open the door like that. But the jail strong, Imelda. It stronger than God. I call and I call, and I keep looking up but all I see is the same door closed onto me. Zero lock up for something he never do. Imagine that, Imelda. They catch the real criminals, the murdering brutes, and my son still in jail for nothing at all.'

'B-but you m-must go to the court!' Imelda protested.

Tessa wailed. 'I done gone. I done gone too many times already. I go to the magistrate as a broken woman but all he do is throw me out. Him say next time him will throw me in jail. Oh, Imelda, Zero is lost. Him is lost to me for ever.'

Big tears fell from Tessa's eyes and splashed onto Imelda's arm.

All the younger woman said was, 'We're going to get him out of jail today.'

It was the sound of Tessa's weeping all the way along the road that brought the villagers out. They ran up to ask What was going on? Where were they going? Tessa told them, 'We is going

161

for Zero.' So the two women became a small crowd, and the small crowd became half of Watersgate, and the march to the courthouse became all of history – it became every reason every man or woman had ever taken to the streets: to reclaim children, lost wages, a whole country, or their very selves. They poured into the courtroom and Imelda held Tessa, who, in the face of the judge, lost a little of her confidence. They did not wait for the case that was under way to pause.

'Sir. W-we are here to s-secure the release of Nathaniel Walcott, otherwise known as Zero, from unl-lawful imprisonment.'

'Now look here! You and this ... this,' the magistrate looked fearfully at the crowd, 'rabble will get out my courtroom this instant!'

The magistrate's gavel and Imelda's fist fell at the same time, but it was the sound of Imelda's fist that won. It hit the table in front of her and the audacity of the sound caused the people behind to jump.

'Fucking hell!'

And in telling the story after, this is the only part everyone would agree on – that curse which exploded into the courtroom, but which also sounded so proper and English on Imelda's lips, as if it had in it all the strength and indignation of the mother country. In truth, she had only said it so that her next words would come out steady.

'You look here. My client [a careful lie, for she had not sat any bar exam in Jamaica and was not yet allowed to practise law on the island], my client has been held for two years without a single charge being pressed. This woman,' on cue Tessa began to bawl, 'has repeatedly brought the matter to your attention and all you did was threaten her with imprisonment. So you listen to me, if my client is not released today, so help me God ...'

The magistrate looked down from his bench at Imelda and the village of Watersgate behind her glaring up at him. He knew they were more than ready to burn down the courthouse and him with it. He turned meekly to a constable in the courtroom.

'Is there a ...'

'N-nathaniel Walcott. Otherwise known as Z-Zero.' Imelda repeated.

'. . . a Nathaniel Walcott otherwise known as Zero being held in the lock-up?'

'I believe so, Your Honour.'

'Has he been charged with any crime?'

'No, Your Honour. But him is not well in the head.'

The magistrate nodded. 'Is he likely to be charged with any crime any time soon?'

'No, Your Honour. I would not think it likely.'

The magistrate nodded again. 'You will go and tell the sergeant to arrange for his immediate release.'

If the march to the courthouse was like all of history, then the march back to Watersgate was like its end. This is the heart of every celebration – a conviction that history is no more, that the world as it existed has now changed and the earth is no longer the same. So it was joy, and it was Carnival, and it was August Morning, and Jonkoonoo. At times Tessa just marched in front, holding Zero to her breasts, and at other times she broke away, dancing on her thin ankles. Zero smiled broadly and blankly, his hand shaken over and over by a hundred persons. He pointed at everyone and everything and said, simply, *Bang bang*. Then someone got a drum, and another person got a fife, and people broke branches off trees and waved them like flags, and they sang:

> A come we just-a come
> A come we just-a come
> We nuh want nuh boderation-ooooh!
> A come we diss-a come
> A come we diss-a come
> We nuh want nuh boderation-oooooh!

When they crossed the bridge and went back into Watersgate the story travelled faster than the procession, and all who hadn't been there were told how Imelda had gone before the magistrate, like Moses before Pharaoh, and said 'LET MY ZERO GO!' It made women cry – to see Zero among them, being hugged by his mother, saying 'Bang bang'. The people said, 'That Imelda, she was always a good person. I know. I always see it. Thank the Lord she has returned onto us!'

And perhaps it is true that a small kernel of resentment is at the heart of every compliment and every bit of praise – but in one man this kernel was especially large. Pastor Douglas Braithwaite despised Imelda's success – despised the confidence with which she had walked to Alexander Town Square and done what he himself had not cared to do. He despised what happened after-wards – how everyone in Watersgate who had any kind of problem would now go to Miss Imelda, *for she would know. She is knowledgeable into these things.* They asked her advice about getting birth certificates, land titles, loans from the bank, getting their children into a good high school in Kingston. They asked her to read letters sent to them. They asked her to write letters on their behalf. So Pastor Braithwaite began to preach from Psalms One – *Blessed is the man that walketh not in the counsel of the ungodly.* He told them how dangerous it was to take advice from people who did not go to church themselves. He preached from Psalm Five – *There is nothing reliable in what they say; Their inward part is destruction itself. Their throat is an open grave.* He preached from Proverbs 4. *Do not enter the path of the wicked, and do not proceed in the way of evil men.* When a few of the children began saying '*fucking hell*', he preached a great sermon about the dangers of Foreign Lands, and how it was Certain-and-certain people were coming in and setting bad examples for the children. The villagers hesitated, but over the years they still went to Imelda for legal advice; they still asked her to read their letters; they still asked her to write letters on their behalf.

Then there was the Neighbourhood Watch.

The Strange and Various Dreams of Imelda Agnes Richardson (JP)

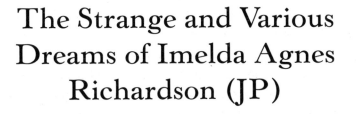

The first dream Imelda had, having returned to Watersgate, was about going out in search of bush medicine. In the dream her skin was itching and she knew, of course, that the thing to cure such an ailment was cerasee tea. She went into the yard looking for the vine which mostly grew over short trees, covering them like a spring jacket. But all the trees boasted only their own leaves; none had the vine that could relieve her itching. So Imelda thought she would search for the cerasee by its scent – a strong, pungent green which was also its taste. She closed her eyes and followed her nose, but the smell of cerasee was nowhere. She smelled pine; she smelled mint; she smelled ginger lilies. She smelled bamboo; she smelled the earth; she smelled lime-grass. When she opened her eyes she was almost all the way out of Watersgate.

'There is no cerasee!' she sighed. Then, all at once, she was standing in the village shop.

'What happen to you, Imelda?' asked Mr Edwards, the shop-keeper.

'I cannot find cerasee, and my skin is itching.'

'Cerasee don't grow here no more. But look, we have Earl Grey tea.'

'Earl Grey tea?'

And Imelda looked around the shop to see that it was packed to the ceiling with boxes and boxes of Earl Grey tea.

'Yes,' beamed the shopkeeper. 'De women dese days say cerasee too harsh. So we chop and bum all of it. But now we have de lovely Earl Grey tea and all de women say it settle de movement under dere skin just like cerasee, but widout being so bitter.'

'It is the same,' Imelda muttered.

'Yes. Is basically de same t'ing. Only more smooth.'

But it was not tea that Imelda was comparing.

In her first year back she dreamed mostly about her mother, except it never occurred to her that this was who she was dreaming about. Her mother never appeared in these dreams, so Imelda might have told you it was a dream of Purletta, or a dream of Ozzie, or maybe even the dream of bowing cows. And always it was the dream of walking on water. It would start in Purletta's living room, or in Ozzie's apartment and then all of a sudden the carpeted floor would become the widest water. The walls would dissolve into sky, the light bulbs into seagulls, and she knew she was supposed to walk across this ocean. Purletta and Ozzie and the cows wearing tiaras would wave adieu. She walked and walked, unafraid of whales or sharks. She walked until the ocean became a river — a river that she knew. She stepped off its bank and climbed up the steps to the one house she could never forget. Then the dream would end, but with a voice.

'My darling, my love, my dear, finally you are home.'

She often dreamed of frogs. This was to be expected. Living so close to the river it was their lullabies that sang her to sleep, so the frogs demanded space in the first part of her dreams. Sometimes in the middle and the last parts as well. She dreamed at times that she was a frog in a storybook waiting to be kissed. She dreamed of having a tongue so long she could throw it out like a rope, or wrap it around her own body. And this dream was a nightmare, because a tongue so long made her stutter even more. She could

166

not control it and would keep quiet because to say anything was to have it unroll and she would spend all day winding it back up again, putting it back in its place.

She dreamed of eating cooked flies. Boiled flies. Roasted flies. She once dreamed of a fly so big it had more meat on its bones than a chicken.

On one occasion she dreamed a very strange dream that she was not a frog, but the sound of a frog. How frustrating that was – to be a complete and utter slave, subject to the will of an ignorant amphibian. She tried to tell her owner the sound she really wanted to be – a deeper, higher, broader, more intricate sound – but the frog would not listen.

In her second year she dreamed mostly of him. She dreamed of him raising himself off her his body hovering in the air, but his head still bowed as if he were praying. In this position, he was still touching her; his long dreadlocks would fall onto her body and if he moved his face at all, the dreadlocks would stroke her nakedness. She wanted to be touched like this always, by the soft brush of Joseph's hair.

She dreamed that Pastor Braithwaite was running up and down the length of Watersgate with half an orange in his hand, its face purple with ink. He was screaming, 'My stamp does not work! My stamp does not work!'

One by one, villagers arrived at Imelda's house with the same complaint – *Pastor's stamp does not work. Just look here. The old fool has stamped my letter with orange juice! Please, do you have the right stamp?*

Imelda told them she did not have the right stamp, but the villagers insisted that she did. She looked around her kitchen and found half a pomegranate, half a grapefruit, half a lime, half a guava, but none of these could stamp the villagers' documents, and the documents were now stained with all kinds of fruit. Rude children began to steal their parents' important papers and drink the juice from them.

The villagers insisted again. *Surely you must have the right stamp. You have misplaced it.*

And at last Imelda remembered – she did indeed have the right stamp. The same magistrate she had stood in front of two years before to demand the release of Zero had called her back to his court.

'Miss Richardson, I am to appoint a new Justice of the Peace in St Mary and I can think of no one better qualified than you. Will you accept?'

So she had become Imelda Agnes Richardson, JP. She found the stamp in her pocket and started stamping people's documents correctly. But Pastor Braithwaite came to shout at her gate. *You harlot! You thief! You Jezebel! Judas! Betrayer! You have stolen my stamp. You have stolen it from me. Woe be unto you.*

Sometimes she dreamed that she could fly. She would jump into the wideness of the sky and fly across many horizons. But no matter how far she flew, every time she looked down she still saw Watersgate. In this dream she was always happy.

She dreamed of things that had actually happened and conversations she had had:

'I wonder if I and I is enough for you?'

'How you mean?'

'I just get worried because you is more than you pretend to be. You pretend to be less than you is because you don't want I and I to see it – but I see it. That's why I and I care for you so much. Because you is so much. But sometimes that also make me worried.'

'Joseph, I am with you because you're the k-kind of man who can never really be worried.'

'Maybe I and I asking another thing then. I just struggling with the words. Maybe I wonder if this place is enough for you. You could go anywhere you want. You could be a big-shot lawyer and have the world.'

'But I've seen the world and I d-didn't like it. I didn't want it.'

Imelda, I ever tell you that I and I come back to Watersgate to wait on you? When I go to Kingston and see the world, I and I never want it either. I only wanted you.'

'You tell me that every single day.'

'Not every single day.'

'Almost.'

'I and I only tell you because it is true.'

She dreamed that she had been under the river for days, searching for something. Finally she found it − a great stack of golden combs, glittering deep beneath the river, as bright as the sun that didn't touch it. She grabbed the stack of combs, stumbled out of the river and into the village shouting.

'*Look! Look everyone at what I have found. We are going to be rich.*'

But everyone who saw her pointed at her legs and ran away − even Tessa. She looked down at herself and understood. She did not have legs but scales, and a tail like a mighty fish fluttering back and forth. The people were shouting, *River Muma! River Muma has come out of the river!* And Imelda realised that she could not breathe − that she needed to be in water.

Her waking dream was simply that she should matter − that she should earn her place in the small world that she belonged to. She had felt that she mattered when she got Zero out of jail, but over time that feeling faded. She wanted to know that she was still important to the place and its people. When all the villagers came to her for advice, she listened. When she did not know the answer, she went out to find it. And it was this dream − this desire to matter, that made her read their letters when they could not read. It was this dream that made her accept the JP stamp and stamp their documents. But sometimes she thought that if she had not been there to give advice or to read letters or to stamp documents, advice would still have been given, letters would still be read and documents would still be stamped by someone else. She felt jealous of the people in Watersgate − she begrudged

them their simplicity. They did the simple things peasants did –
raised crops, knitted, worshipped their God and that's all that
was important to them. In this small world, they had found a
small way to matter.

It was this waking dream, the desire to matter and make a
difference, and the theft of a few panties, that got Imelda thinking
of a Neighbourhood Watch.

One night she dreamed that she was in the middle of a large
bamboo forest, and all the bamboo stalks that grew there were
red, green or yellow. They broke off easily in her hands, and she
went around snapping hundreds of them until there was enough
bamboo to build a small kingdom.

Then Joseph appeared beside her, looking at all the bamboo
she had collected.

'For our family?' he asked.

'Exactly.'

And finally – this has been said already – on the night when the
river turned around, Imelda was dreaming of dirty water.

The Wise Advice That
Silly Mr Solomon Did Not Take

October 1983

'I'm quite glad of your company, Eulan, but listen to the advice of an old policeman: you should find a friend or two in that village.'

'No. I wouldn't torture myself like that.'

'And especially when you live in a house as big as yours, in a village as small as that.'

'Nothing is wrong with the size of my house!'

'But history, my dear boy. Poor people could see you as some kind of Buckra. They will want to burn down the house and not even know why.'

'Actually, I do know two people from the village.'

'Really?'

'And one of them is such a big gossip, she must count for the entire village. That woman doesn't seem the type to keep anything to herself. If I told her that I went to the bathroom and described the exact state, colour and texture of my morning shit, she'd be knocking on every gate to tell them.'

'Every village has one. Some have two You're lucky.'

'She is enough for three. I'm not lucky at all. I drive in late some nights and there she is, waiting with a bag of peas.'

'And who is the other person?'

'I think her name is Imelda Richardson.'

'Aah yes. The lawyer.'

'She's a lawyer? And she lives in that little village?'

'But so do you.'

'Yes. I suppose. But she seems to live among them.'

'She is wiser than you are.'

'And you say she's a lawyer?'

'I don't think she practises though. She's something of a local hero in these parts. You must ask your gossip woman to tell you the story of how that Imelda Richardson got a crazy boy out of my jail.'

'I almost killed her.'

'The village gossip?'

'No. Imelda Richardson. Last Sunday it looked as though we were going to have a hurricane. That's why I didn't come over here. And even on Monday morning it was still grey and wet. I was leaving for work and couldn't see anything at all, and she chose that exact moment to walk across my driveway, just as I was reversing. I had to slam on the brakes.'

'Good grief.'

'I will probably never see her again. Maybe she could have been a friend.'

'Why will you never see her again?'

'Imagine this . . . she was lugging a suitcase in all that rain. I put it in the car and ended up taking her all the way into Kingston.'

'But why will you never see her again?'

'I dropped her off at this fancy house in Gordon Town, and when I asked if she was coming back, she said . . . "*I'm afraid never!*"'

'Good grief.'

'Well, old man, if you don't want the people from the village to burn down my house over Christmas, you must keep an eye on it for me. I will leave you the keys.'

'Are you off somewhere?'

'Yes. Not sure where yet, but I've decided I need a vacation.'

'Good for you. You'll be far away from the enemy.'

'Far, far away.'

Blue Panty, Green Panty, Polka-dot Panty!

June 1979–September 1983

When Tessa realised that her three panties had gone missing, she could think of no one else to tell first but Imelda Richardson. She believed in Imelda and the power of the young woman to return lost things. So it had moved Tessa deeply, this formation of a Neighbourhood Watch. Imelda had told her that they would put a bright yellow sign at the bridge, right before you entered the village. On top there would be WATERSGATE in bold; below that, a huge eye, like the eye of God. And then below that, a message – WE ARE WATCHING YOU! Imelda had told her this sign would protect all her future pairs of panties, and she, Tessa Walcott, would never have to wear damp underwear again. That's what Tessa had come to. On the awful Sunday morning of 28 September 1983, for instance, it was a pair of peach panties that Tessa had worn to church and they were slightly wet. She had decided she could not afford for any more to go missing and had stopped hanging them outside on the line. They no longer knew sun or dryness. They became damp, clammy things to wear, and in church that morning she was uncomfortable. So she was not paying any attention to Pastor Braithwaite when he climbed up to the pulpit.

'Oh my people. Oh my people!'

Tessa was in her own world.

'Oh my people! Lift up yourn eyes. Look to the heavens.'

And truth be told, she never did like Braithwaite.

'Who has created all these things?'

He wasn't like Old Parson from before, who had been a kind man . . .

'Do you not know? Have you not seen? Have you not heard?'

Who had made her Harry a deacon when he never even deserved it.

'The Looord our God is God and God alone!'

Pastor Braithwaite was a different creature altogether:

'In the book of Matthew, chapters 10 and verses 29 . . .'

He was selfish and arrogant and power-hungry. So she often tuned him out anyway.

'It says are two sparrows not sold for a mere farthing?'

She began to think about the Neighbourhood Watch instead.

'And yet not one of them shall fall on the ground without your father.'

What a glorious thing it would be when it got started . . .

'But the very hairs on your head is numbered!!'

Her panties would be dry again and comfortable.

'Fear ye not! Ye are of more value than many sparrows!'

And she would treat herself to some more slips and stockings.

'The songwriter says, his eye is on the sparrow, but he watches over me!'

Yes, she was going to buy herself some nice cotton panties.

'Our God is watching over us! My people . . . my people . . .'

In all colours and patterns. Red and purple and orange . . .

'Nobody cannot watch yu like Jesus.'

And she would replace the ones that were stolen.

'Yu mother cannot watch yu like Jesus.'

She would buy a buy herself a blue panty.

'Yu father cannot watch you like Jesus.'

A green panty.

'Yu boyfriend or yu husband or yu wife cannot watch you like Jesus . . .'

And a polka-dot panty!

'and no Neighbourhood Watch going to watch you like Jesus!'

Tessa jerked her head up. A sudden panic had filled her whole big body. She tried desperately to reconstruct the sermon she had been hearing, but not hearing.

'Oh yes,' Braithwaite had continued, 'I been hearing the talk. And the Lord wants to ask you today, who do you put your trust in?'

'In God!' Miss Millie shouted, and Tessa hated her. She wanted no part in this.

'I said, who do you put your trust in?'

Despite herself, Tessa had shouted with the rest of the church. 'In Jesus!' and her hands were raised, waving a salute to the Holy Father. It shamed her, this weakness, and she began to understand how they were all robots waiting to be commanded. In her declaration and in the waving of her hands she had forfeited the right to protest – to not be a part of the madness. She had not even spoken up after church when Miss Millie gathered all the women around her and spoke to them.

'We not going to that evil meeting tonight! You hear me, people? We not supporting any Neighbourhood Watch, because we is people of faith. We put our trust in God. And you know, people, that is what I was telling her the other day. I tell Imelda 'You can't escape from God!' Straight to her face I tell her. I look at her and I say, 'Imelda, you can't escape from God.' But you all know how she is; her mouth is very foul, and her heart is very hard. Mmm. I pray for that child every night.'

Tessa did not go to the Neighbourhood Watch meeting, for she knew the whole village would be watching. Instead she tried to sleep, but she thrashed about in the bed and had nightmares. At around ten o'clock she got up with a start and decided she didn't care how late it was – she was going over to Imelda's. She would tell her everything, and she would ask Imelda to forgive her for her weakness. But when Tessa got up she heard the rain. It surprised her that she hadn't been conscious of it before. It was rain like they were in the middle of a hurricane and she could hear the river roaring. She fell back down on her bed and curled up, afraid. Soon she fell asleep again, and this time slept peacefully.

It was anger, more than anything, that had led Imelda back to Watersgate. It was anger that made her impatient, and resource-ful; it was anger coursing through her body that made her stand up so straight, that made her words sharp, that made her seem like someone to be reckoned with.

The anger was born in her the day, back in England, when she had come home to find out her mother had died.

'A telegram come for you today,' was what Purletta had announced.

Imelda trembled because she had imagined this moment before. She had dreamed it in detail – this receiving of a telegram. She had imagined it in a way that she had not imagined her mother or her father actually dying – just the awful fact of a telegram was enough, as if on that small piece of paper existed all tragedy and all grief.

The night before she had come in, run upstairs, almost stum-bling over her own feet, with a sudden and incredible impulse to bury her hand in the potted plant she kept in her bedroom. A strange compulsion, this. But sitting through the last lecture of the evening, what she ended up daydreaming about was not mushrooms and chicken gravy and pasta – the dinner she would make for herself that evening – but the rosemary bush that stood by her window. When she finally reached home she sunk her hand into the dirt and something like an electric shock had entered her body. In a flash she saw her mother and her father and all of Watersgate, and she felt an awful premonition settle beneath her ribcage.

So the fact of the telegram didn't really surprise her. She walked over to the couch and sat down. Purletta took hold of Imelda's hand.

'You want me to read it to you?'

Imelda nodded. Purletta read: **So sorry   your mother just dead your father sick bad   don't look like he going to make it   come home.**

Imelda did not weep immediately. She stood up. Sat down. Stood up. Sat down. Went through the strange catatonic moments of grief. And then she burst. She wept into Purletta's arms. She wept all the way up to her bedroom. And she was still weeping later that night when she went over to tell Ozzie.

She should have understood Ozzie's reaction. She had known him long enough. She knew how arrogant he was, how proud, but how all of that stood shakily on a vast platform of loneliness which he had only admitted to that one time in the park. He had never tried to show her the emptiness again, but having caught that one glimpse, she had always been aware of it, and had always tried to fill it. When she told him that her mama was dead and she was going back to Jamaica to bury her, she probably shouldn't have expected him to act reasonably. But this time she was the one grieving; she was the one who needed him.

All Ozzie felt was an incredible, irrational wave of jealousy and panic. He was going to lose Imelda. He was going to be stuck in this country alone. He couldn't trust that without him by her side, without his constant cynicism, she would remember what an awful place the Caribbean was. He was afraid she was going to go back and fall in love with the place all over again. No. He could not afford for that to happen, so he reacted – ensuring in that reaction the very thing he was trying to prevent.

'Let the dead bury the dead,' he told her.

And those words had lit a fuse. And that fuse had lit an anger. And the anger had exploded.

'Y-y-you know what, Ozzie? Goodbye! I leaving and I n-never coming back to this fucking country!'

Though perhaps all it was was the final realisation that while Ozzie loved her, she did not love him. She could never love a man like him. And perhaps it was also a waking up from the dream that had been England. For if you asked Imelda, years later, what was it like living there, she might have told you *wonderful; it meant so much; it m-made who I am.* But she would have said this only because it is what you might want or expect to hear. If you probed a little deeper you would not have come up with much. What did she remember about her classes, her fellow students, her lecturers? What did she remember about the rituals of each day? What had it all meant? Her declaration was just a way of guaranteeing that she would not return to this dream – to this life that had passed through her like an amnesia. She had always wanted to go back. She had been waiting patiently for the day and the excuse. But how could Imelda confess to such a longing, for she would then have to confront the part of her that rejoiced that her mother was dead, because now she could go back home. No; it was anger that she felt, not epiphany.

So, like Tessa, Imelda also slept through the thunder and the rain. She did not hear it. She did not hear it in the way a sleeping man is not conscious of his own snoring. How could she have heard all that thunder, how could she have heard the river churning, when it was the same thing as her anger? And when she did wake up, splashing into the water that now flowed through her house, she had no clue that it was she who had called the river unto herself.

The Silly Way Imelda
Thought She Would Die

Every step Imelda took out of Watersgate was painful because it felt as if the place itself was pushing her out. The very earth which she had known all her life was now rejecting her – imagine that! It was supposed to be the other way around; people rejected Watersgate and every other village on the island. After that they rejected the island itself. It was as if they were saying this soil wasn't deep enough for their dreams to take root. People ran away all the time, and so had Imelda, but then she had chosen to come back. And as a young woman at that, not even thirty! She had chosen Watersgate over England, so as she walked out, she felt a strong sense of injustice. And this feeling hurt her twice, as Imelda was forced now to recognise in herself an arrogance the villagers might always have accused her of, but which she had always denied having – the arrogance of the returned who want to be congratulated and eternally honoured for this decision to come back, as if this were their Calvary, the ultimate self-sacrifice. They were the ones who had mastered the contemptuous frown, and who, whenever they did not get their own way, would remark, 'But this would never happen in New Yark!' or London, or Miami, or wherever it was they had been. Foreign had made masters out of them, for wasn't this what they now had in common with Buckra — contact with a far-off mystical land that made them superior?

Imelda had not intended to become this person, but as she walked out of the village it struck her that she had become it all the same.

The morning was still grey and the rain was still falling. Imelda sighed heavily and continued walking, straight into a sudden screech of tyres – the blue BMW belonging to Mr Solomon. Now, Imelda had in fact seen this car. She had acknowledged it and its speed and its trajectory and the destruction that it would certainly cause if she didn't do something like stop or jump out of the way. But something strange had begun to happen in her mind. The anger and injustice expanding inside her felt physical. She thought of her life, from birth to the present moment, all twenty-eight years of it, and a premonition took root in her. She was certain, and resigned to it, that if these seconds were to be her last, then she should not resist.

House at the End of the Hill

September 1983

Eulan Solomon learned something important on the morning of 29 September 1983 – that he was not alone on this earth, and therefore he should look where he was driving. It was a Monday and it was raining. The previous morning had been dark as well, and full of thunder. He had buried himself under a quilt and two pillows, hoping that this, along with the thunder, would drown out the sounds of the church he usually avoided on a Sunday. Snatches of Braithwaite's sermon still reached his ears: *His eye is on the sparrow . . . who can watch you like Jesus? . . . No Neighbourhood Watch going to watch you like Jesus!*

It was a bad Sunday; in the morning he had suffered the sermon and that night he suffered the river. It was roaring so loud Eulan hardly got any sleep. On Monday he woke up miserable and uninspired. It took him a whole hour to get ready. He tried on five ties with seven shirts before finding a combination that worked. He walked out of the house wearing one brown shoe and one black, and so had to turn back again. Eulan took it for granted that he was the only unfortunate person in Watersgate to be up and about in this weather. Finally ready and reversing his car, he was thinking to himself: *What I need is a vacation.* In his rear-view mirror he caught a glimpse of something out there in the grey, moving behind his car. He slammed on the brakes so hard his head almost hit against the windscreen. The woman passing did not stop, though she must have noticed the car that nearly hit her. She was soaking wet and dragging a suitcase. Eulan got out of the car.

'Please, ma'am. Let me offer you a ride.'

He opened his book and went to take the suitcase. She did not protest. But almost immediately Eulan regretted his kindness. He thought of the whole car ride ahead – the relentless small talk, the unrequested biography and the thinly veiled questions about him and who he was and what he did.

But Imelda surprised him by remaining silent. And Eulan surprised himself by being annoyed at discovering that he actually wanted to hear her story – at least the bones of it. It was Eulan, not Imelda, who tried to engage in small talk. It was he who asked her name, how she was doing, what she did. But none of the answers she gave provided him with the real information he wanted: who was she, exactly? Why was she so angry this morning? Why had she been walking in the rain? So he asked her when she might be coming back, and she answered politely, 'I'm afraid n-never.'

She just couldn't bring herself to say much. She was thinking all at once that she didn't want to leave, but she was going anyway. And then she hoped, more than anything else, that Joseph would come looking for her. She would always remember the night in Watersgate when she had met him again. She had been back for three months, and was sitting on her patio one night, feeling what she thought at the time was empty, when the air around her changed and she smelled kerosene oil. A tall presence materialised out of the darkness, climbed up the steps and stood there in front of her.

'Shit, Joseph,' she exclaimed, catching her breath. 'You scared me!'

'What happen? Yu heart get weak over there in England? I tell people all the while, England not good for black people. Anyway,

I heard that you was back so I come to say hello. And I bring you some oil for the lamps.'

He sat down and placed a plastic bottle on the floor between them.

'I b-been back three months now, Joseph, and is only n-now you come to look for me? I heard you w-was around. But I don't see anything of you. L-like you been avoiding me.'

'You know what they say, everything in its own season.'

'Well, I happy to see you. I guess you never forget about this p-place after all.' She paused, You look so different, Joseph.'

She was contemplating his dreadlocks and his beard. Beneath all that hair he seemed suddenly self-conscious.

'Is not me alone look different,' he snapped.

He didn't mean his words to sound harsh, but they hurt her. He tried to take them back.

'No, no. Is only natural. We grow up, that's all. I think you look beautiful still. Even more than before.'

'I like you with the dreadlocks,' she returned, and reached out her hands to touch them. It felt strangely intimate, as if she were touching his skin, even his manhood.

Someone coughed inside the house behind them.

'Is your old man that?'

Imelda nodded. 'From Mama died he not doing so well. We thought he would have gone already, but him hanging on. Just barely. Him not as strong as him used to be. He been in that bed for a m-month now.'

'Well if he have the strength to take howdies, tell him howdy for me. Miss Sarah and Mister Desmond was always good people. It sad to see them go.'

Joseph stood up then.

'We will see each other from now on, I hope?'

'I hope,' Imelda agreed. She watched him leave, something newly awakened fluttering in her chest.

So as she sat in Eulan Solomon's car, trying to make space in her heart to accommodate her newly flooded house, the love that she was leaving and this unknown that she was headed towards, she could find little space for talk.

Mr Solomon drove Imelda all the way to an old house in the hills of Gordon Town. There were roses in the front garden and hummingbirds in the roses. Anyone observing the cut-stone architecture partially hidden behind tall green hedges would know that they had arrived in the part of Jamaica where the rich live. This wasn't Norbrook or Jackshill, where the houses were five storeys high and the gates were black and tall and fat Dobermann pinschers growled between bars. This was quieter, older money. The lawns here were perfect and green, and in the centre of them were fountains, or sundials, or even polished black cannons, as if the ghost of some ancestor were still protecting the property from invaders.

The house, like all the others on that road, had a name. In 1978 the local government council whose business it was to establish order and coordination in the city and its suburbs had put up a green sign at the beginning of the road which gave its name as Starline Crescent. Each lot of land was also assigned a number. The sign disappeared quickly and mysteriously, and none of the houses ever acknowledged that their road had a name and that their house had a number. They continued to give their addresses as: Whithington Hall, Gordon Town, Jamaica. Or Bougainvillea Lodge, Gordon Town, Jamaica. Or in the case of the house at which Imelda arrived: Hillend, Gordon Town, Jamaica. The seemingly posh name had quite a literal meaning: it was the last house on Starline Crescent; it was the house at the end of the hill.

'Who lives here?' Mr Solomon asked.

Imelda realised her answer would give Mr Solomon the wrong impression of how and where she had grown up. Still, she answered simply:

'My father.'

*

When Imelda had returned from England to bury her mother, Desmond was not doing well. 'They was true lovebirds,' people said mournfully. 'The real thing.' Imelda understood. Sarah and Desmond had been the kind of people who live their lives so much with each other that when one dies, the other one is sure to follow soon. They live and die together. So Desmond's health deteriorated fast. He was in and out of hospital; caught every infection possible and his bones became weak. He was suddenly hard of hearing. Couldn't see properly. No longer went outside to care for the plants he used to love so much. Desmond simply waited in bed for death to come. But after a year he was still alive. Then one day it was as if he had decided to carry on. Just like that. Imelda came home to find him outside, planting seeds again. He stopped asking her to repeat everything she said, and all of a sudden he could see fine. Just like before.

Imelda could not fully explain the relationship he struck up with Mrs Johnson. Purletta had flown down for the funeral. Even now Imelda could remember how surprised she was to see her friend in Jamaica. She was a different Purletta altogether. Imelda had expected black sequins and loud bawling, for although Purletta didn't know Sarah Richardson from Adam, it was just the way with some Jamaican women to fall down in the aisle, hold on to a coffin and shout, *Mi want mi modder! Mi want mi modder!* whether they knew the deceased or not. Imelda had expected Purletta to be like this, but Purletta arrived in a smart, navy-blue linen dress, her hair pulled back in a severe bun. She walked slowly, and Imelda thought she had never seen this side of her friend – almost aristocratic.

At the graveside, Purletta inched up to Imelda and whispered to her.

'Lawdgod, mi dear, close yu mouth whenever you look at me. Yu don't expect mi to go on with mi hooligan ways in front of mi poor modder, eh?'

Imelda noticed the old, white woman standing a short way behind her friend.

'Because,' Purletta continued, 'you'd have to make space in

185

that grave to fling her in too. Old people's heart give out very easy.'

Imelda had to stifle a laugh. Later that evening she was introduced to the mother, Mrs Johnson, and the two fast became friends. From then on, whenever Imelda went into Kingston, she would visit the house in Gordon Town, Hillend, the architecture hidden behind green hedges, roses in the front garden and hummingbirds in the roses.

It seemed completely natural that Mrs Johnson always asked about her father.

'How is that nice gentleman, your father? Is he well?'

Imelda would give a full report on Desmond's health.

It never struck her as odd that, back home in Watersgate, her father would ask the same question.

'How is that nice woman? Your friend's mother, Mrs Johnson?'

Again she would give a full report. It seemed to Imelda that all communication between the two of them happened with her in the middle. But one evening, as she sat on the veranda reading, Desmond stepped outside and cleared his throat. Imelda looked up, waited a while, but her father just stood there, looking sheepish.

'Papa, if you have something to say is best you just say it.'

'Oh, yes. Yes. Uhm,' Desmond scratched his head. 'Well . . . is just that I can't live here no more.'

'What?'

'This house, man. I can't live here no more. I can't live in this village without her. We talk it over last night, and she said it was all right. She said every place has its season, and I said, Yes, Sarah, you are so right about that. So I know I can leave now, because she told me it was OK. But she said is only OK if you say is OK.'

'Papa, you not m-making any sense.'

'Leaving, Imelda. I talking about leaving. I need to leave this house. I need to move out.'

'But-but we can't just make a d-decision like that, P-Papa. We can't just g-get up and move. Where would we g-go?'

'Just me for now. I leaving. I not asking you to go anywhere just yet. But I need to go.'

Raas! Imelda laughed nervously. So this was it – the moment people said would happen eventually, the day a parent goes senile.

'Papa. B-be serious now. Where you g-going to? You going to look a job somewhere? You feel like young b-boy again?'

'I moving into Mrs Johnson's house.'

'M-Mrs Johnson?' Imelda asked. She didn't have two and two to put together, didn't know what he was talking about.

'Yes,' Desmond continued. 'Is she suggested it first, and I think is a good idea. We is both old. We could both do with the company. And she live alone in that big house and she have a real nice garden, I hear. And your mother say is OK. Is not any 'man and woman' story this now, Imelda. You mustn't think that. I not courting her. But . . .'

'M-Mrs Johnson?' Imelda asked again, as it suddenly dawned on her.

'Yes. That's what I said. She's a nice woman and is she first who make . . .'

'Mrs Johnson? When you and M-Mrs Johnson have time to p-plan all of this raas nonsense? When you ever s-speak to Mrs Johnson?'

'Now, now Imelda. I don't want you to get upset. But . . .' he swallowed, 'I need you to tell me is OK. Sarah tell me last night. So I need you to say that. Because . . . I can't live here any more. I don't want to.'

Of course it was OK. *You are my father. You don't need to be asking me for permission.* She finally gave him her blessing and Desmond moved to Kingston, to the house at the end of the hill. His relationship with Mrs Johnson was strange. They were, both of them, in their late eighties and seemed to have given up the part of their being that was sexual. Desmond and Mrs Johnson lived instead as if they were the sole residents of their very own senior citizens' house – that is to say, they passed each day on the cool patio with long glasses of lemonade provided by the

187

maid, and they argued with each other. Sometimes when their arguments peaked, he would call her a show-off, uptown, hoity-toity bitch and she would called him a little country bumpkin without a lick of sense. Sometimes he called her ma'am or Buckra and asked if she or her family had a whip outside to beat him. She retorted, 'You senile, old fool. Sometimes I think you should be whipped.' He called her 'Mrs Johnson' (never Patricia), and she called him 'Mr Richardson' (never Desmond). But when their arguments became intense, and they stammered over sentences and got confused, in these moments he would mistakenly call her Mrs Richardson, and she would call him Mr Johnson. The two never seemed to realise these slips of the tongue, but Imelda heard them and laughed to herself. It was in this accidental way, ascribing their names to each other, that the two at times seemed to be married.

Three Proposals for Imelda Richardson

On the day that Pastor Braithwaite threw Joseph's drum out of the church and tried to cast demons out of him, Deaconess Jennifer had stood at the back with her eyes down, shaking her head as if her sorrow would never end. She walked down to the river after church, dipped her hands in the water and wrung them.

'See here,' she said to the river and to the trees, 'I wash my hands clean of that boy. If he was younger I would take him home and give him a good beating, but he too big for my hands now. The Lord knows, I did everything I could for him.'

That evening when Joseph informed her that he was going to Kingston to make a life for himself, she walked through his words as if they had never been spoken. He left without either her blessing or her curse. Joseph lived in Kingston for six years, and when he returned to Watersgate with his new locks, he did not return to her house. For a month he slept on the bare earth and bathed in the river. Night and day he cut down bamboo and dragged it up the hill where he built his own small hut, the bamboo painted red, green and yellow.

Few people called him 'Joseph' again. It was as if that boy was a completely different person, lost to them for ever. As if the adult Joseph had no history with them – was not the same boy who used to play drums in church or who had stolen sugar from

Mr Edwards's shop. The people who trekked up to his house to buy kerosene stood at the window and called out 'Ras!' or 'Dread!' or 'Bhinghi Man!' He did not mind this. He lived his new life in Watersgate with a kind of resignation. He was waiting for Imelda.

He figured she would finally be coming back when Teacher Sarah died suddenly. So one night he approached the house but stayed back, hidden in the darkness. When he saw her it was as if the earth he had known for all his life became different. As if that hot country, which did not know seasons, suddenly went through winter one minute and spring the next. It was as if all the colours shifted on him, and the trees became yellow, then orange, then red, then green again. As if the temperature fell and the river froze over, but then it melted immediately into summer. He knew he was in love.

There is a kind of love so intense it will cause men to kill dragons, to risk their lives on the edge of precipices. To wage war. But there is a kind of love, even more intense, that will cause a man to do absolutely nothing. It will sit on his shoulders like twenty sacks of bricks, and render him utterly immobile. Days turned into weeks and then they turned into months, and Joseph could not work up the courage to speak to Imelda. She was right. He had been avoiding her. He continued to hide himself in the darkness near her house and just stand there. Some nights she sat outside on the patio, waiting for her father to cough or to make any noise so that she could go back in and attend to him. Joseph would keep very still on these nights, and it hurt him how uncomfortable she seemed, as if she didn't belong here any more. As if she wanted to leave. And this made his sudden love seem stupid to him – a thing that should never be uttered, that should stay still in the darkness and only watch. But one night, he could see that her face was trembling, and he knew he could not bear her tears, so he finally came and climbed up the steps to stand in front of her.

'O shit, Joseph! You scared me,' she had said.

'I brought kerosene oil for you.'

He didn't stay long that night. Her father made a sound and he knew she would want to go inside. He asked if they would see each other again and she said, 'I hope so.' So he left happy, his heart going faster than any rhythm he had ever beaten.

The night in Watersgate is full of frogs and crickets and fire-flies. Joseph made his way through the noise and the bugs lighting up their abdomens like it was Christmas. He walked along a bob-wire fence and reached the point where he could slip a loop of the wire off a wooden post – a makeshift gate. This was the path that led uphill to his bamboo house. He slipped the loop off, but then replaced it without going through. It was almost nine o'clock. The village was asleep. He turned around and walked up towards Miss Millie's house, and went in under the Sex Tree. He was only there for a few minutes when he heard the dry, fallen leaves being crushed and the small twigs breaking under her feet. He closed his eyes and opened his arms, and waited for Imelda to fit herself in his embrace.

'We too old for this,' she said.

'I know.'

He took her by the arm and led her out from beneath the tree, down the road and through the bob-wire fence, then up the hill which led to his house. It was here, hours later, that he asked, 'Do you miss England?'

'Sometimes,' she said. 'But not in this m-moment right now. It's all the same, you know. Whether it is Watersgate, or Kingston, or M-Manchester, or London, it don't make a difference if you're getting by, and you're happy.'

She had made him happy, but he was no longer convinced he had done the same for her. He blamed himself for this. Women wanted something tangible, a commitment, but he had been enjoying himself too much. He had taken things for granted. Three years had gone by just like that, and it was true, he would have let three more go by just the same. He had been content. But he woke up on 29 September 1983 and looked down to see the river larger than he had ever seen it before, with Imelda's

191

house right in the middle of it. He ran out of his hut and the ground beneath his feet was so muddy that he half slid, half ran all the way downhill. He raced towards the river and when he reached the neighbour, whose house was still on dry land, he called out.

'Miss Imelda is gone. She pack up her things from early morning and leave,' the neighbour told him.

He went back to his hut, the weight of love like twenty sacks of bricks on his shoulders, the weight of sadness like twenty more. He said to himself, *She is going to come back soon.* She had to, and when she did he would propose to her immediately. But after a month she still wasn't back. Two months and still no sign. He decided he would go to her, but it took him a long time to find out where she was. Then the love and the sadness weighed him down once more and he didn't do anything. In January he finally got up and walked down from his house and then up to the bridge and over to the house of Eulan Solomon. He knocked on the grill, rehearsing in his mind what he would say when the man came down: *Sir, my future queen is in Kingston and tomorrow I and I going to beg her to marry I. I don't want to do it in any fool-foolway, 'cause I and I fail her once already, and I want to do this thing proper. Please don't laugh at me now; I know they say Rasta-man don't wear suit, but I would like to borrow one from you. I see you all the while, dressed real sharp in nice suits. The kind of suit I cannot afford. And me and you is about the same height. The same body. I only borrowing it for one day, sir. Then I will take it back to you. Please. I know it must sound like a strange thing to ask, but I begging you. Man to man.*

Joseph knocked and knocked and he shouted. Mr Solomon was supposed to be there. According to a rumour, according to the Thing That Miss Millie Saw, a report that had rocked the village, according to that, Eulan Solomon was supposed to be there, at the house. But Mr Solomon wasn't there; he had gone on a vacation weeks ago. So Joseph had to go to Kingston to propose without a suit.

*

Mrs Johnson had been married three times and all three husbands had moved into her house, into her space. When the last one left some twenty years ago he had shouted at her.

'The problem with this marriage is that you are the husband, not me!'

She was a woman used to making decisions on her own. For instance, she decided it was best not to tell Imelda about the Rastaman who came to the gate early one morning asking for her. Mrs Johnson had been ambling through her front garden, looking at the roses and working herself up into a temper. The small and sporadic blooms were evidence enough for her that the gardener whom she paid to come on Saturdays was not doing his job. The grass, too, was a little high and so she planned to have a serious word with him. She was already in a foul mood when a Rastaman knocked on her gate. She looked up and frowned at the sight.

'I'm sorry, young man, I have nothing to give you today.'

He looked on her, confused. 'Ma'am . . .'

'Nothing today!' she snapped.

'I don't want nothing from you. I come to see Imelda. Imelda Richardson.' He said this very quickly before she could interrupt.

'No one by that name lives here.'

Mrs Johnson was surprised and relieved that the lie had come out so quickly, almost instinctively. The man in front of her looked confused. Even sad. She did not feel sorry for him – he was a Rastaman. She had once read that these scruffy fellows, with their unkempt beards and long matted hair, called themselves 'Dread' because that was their intention – to be dreadful, to stand outside the system and inspire dread in the hearts of all decent people. Well, she thought, it had worked. She did not like the sight of them, and most of them, she was certain, carried a smell. Even now she was holding her breath, not wishing to confirm her suspicions and upset her delicate stomach. She was curious, though, as to why he had come.

'What do you want with this Imelda person anyway?'

Hope flashed in the dirty man's eyes. 'I come to ask her to marry me, ma'am.'

'Imelda does not live here!' Mrs Johnson said it too quickly and haughtily. She ambled back inside. No, no, no ! The nerve of the ragamuffin ! Marriage? Sure, Imelda was from the country and sure, she was black. But such things should not be held against the child. She had gone to England and improved herself. She had done a degree in law. She had lived with her own daughter for years, and by all accounts they had been like sisters. But she knew that it was a truth everywhere – men kept their women down. In the poorer classes they did it in crass but effective ways. If a woman was getting too much education or having too much success in her business, her boyfriend would suggest they have a child. And for all of her new brains the young woman would not think it through properly; she would see the child as a way of tying the boyfriend down and not a way of him tying her down, the weight of her pregnant stomach slowing her, anchoring her, stopping her from rising. Mrs Johnson decided that Imelda's rise would not be stopped. Her wings would not be clipped. She decided Imelda would not be told about the Rastaman who had come to the house to propose. She decided also that Imelda would make Hillend her permanent home. She decided that Imelda would sit the Jamaican bar exam and become a proper lawyer. She knew, of course, that all of this would have to seem like Imelda's own choice. So Mrs Johnson schemed, and went to Imelda the next day with a proposal.

'I am old,' she said to Imelda, 'and my only child doesn't even live here. What is going to happen when I die? What will happen to this house? I need you to help me, Imelda. I trust you. You must be the executor of my estate. You must keep things going for Purletta. I will write in my will that you must continue to live here and keep up the house. But my dear, you will have to do the bar exam. It is time to finish your studies and practise law like you were meant to.'

*

194

Desmond was in his room talking to Sarah. Anyone passing and overhearing the conversation would think he was talking to himself. He himself would not dismiss the possibility. In these conversations it was his voice that spoke for both parties. He wasn't sure about the dynamics of this: was it Sarah's ghost that possessed him each time it was her turn to speak, or was it simply that he knew her so well that he could conjure up her opinions and thoughts? The answer didn't really matter to him – these conversations brought clarity and he was not going to stop himself from having them.

He had first told her about a recent happening, The Thing That Miss Millie Saw, for that rumour had reached all the way to Kingston. But Sarah hadn't wanted to discuss that, and she said she was deeply suspicious about any report that could only be verified by Miss Millie. Desmond then moved on to what he really wanted to discuss.

'Our daughter was crying again last night. I walk by her room and I hear her in there, sniffling.'

'Oh my poor darling. My poor dear. Is she still sad about Miss Jennifer's son?'

'Yes, I imagine it must be that. I not sure what she see in that fellow at all, at all.'

'He is a good boy. You always liked him.'

'Yes. But that was then. He rub me the wrong way now. Imagine three years that boy was going out with our little girl. Three years, and he never come to talk to me man to man. He never even think it might be right to ask me for her hand in marriage? And look at that . . . she been here four months now, and he don't even show his face. What kind of man is that? Him forget about her already?'

'It is odd. I admit. But we don't know what is what. We are not God . . .'

'I been telling her, Sarah . . . I been telling her what you told me. That every place have its season. I tell her that her time in Watersgate is done, and it is time to move on.'

'Desmond! How you could tell her stupidness like that?'

195

'What bout it is stupidness? That's what you told me!'

'Yes, I told you that every place has its season, but you can only know that for yourself . . .'

'Sarah, what is back there for her? Those people . . . I not going to say anything bad about them, they are my people too. But . . . but Imelda have nothing in common with them now. She is bigger than Watersgate.'

'No one is bigger than anywhere, my darling. And if she is different from them, it is all the more reason she might have to go back. But that is not my choice, and it is not your choice either. My darling, my love, we must let Imelda live her own life.'

'Believe me, that's what I want her to do. I tell you when that child was born I never bury her navel string in the yard. I throw it away. I tell you that already. I tell you a hundred times. I throw it away, because I want her to live her own life.'

'And still, all this time you been holding on.'

'No, Sarah ! That is not true. I have always let go.'

'You might be able to fool yourself, Desmond, but you can't fool me. You threw away that birth cord so the child could be free to leave Watersgate. But you never gave her the freedom to stay. You wanted her to be in England, so she went to England. Now you want her to stay in the city. Let the child go where she wants to go, my darling. And if that is back to Watersgate, then so be it.'

'But . . .' and now he was choked up, 'I want more for her than that.'

'Desmond, you want more for her than happiness?'

He did not answer.

'Desmond, my darling, my dear, my love. You must go to our daughter and you must make her a proposal. You must propose that she go back to Watersgate.'

'What? No, Sarah. I cannot do that.'

'You have to do it, Desmond. She might not go, but at least then you will know that if she decides to stay in Kingston, it's not because you were holding on.'

So Mrs Johnson proposed that Imelda stay, her father proposed that she go back, and Joseph didn't get the chance to propose at all. So weighing the only two proposals she could, Imelda decided to stay – to live permanently at Mrs Johnson's house. But in all, from the time that she arrived to the time that she left, Imelda spent only four months and three weeks at the house at the end of the hill. What happened to change things, not even she could explain to you fully. One night she went to bed as usual, but in the morning it was God who woke her up.

The Silly Thing Superintendent Carmichael Did

December 1983

The thing Travis Carmichael had always wanted to do was give a party. Not a polite dinner party with three or four polite guests having polite conversations. He wanted to throw a *party* party. With a dance floor and loud music and enough food to make you sick for a week, and a bar stocked with a never-ending supply of alcohol.

Of course such a thing was impossible for someone in his position. He was the Superintendent of Police in charge of the Parish of St Mary, and with the kind of guests he would have invited over . . . no. A great measure of propriety was required of him, and the idea of a party was something he only entertained idly.

But then one December his friend, Eulan Solomon, left him the key to his house and said he would be gone for a whole month. A vacation. With a giddy thoughtlessness the superintendent took out his collection, his brown leather-bound book full of names, and over the course of three days called everyone.

'My dears, I am going to have a New Year's Eve party. No, not at my house. At a marvellous venue in Watersgate. I will give you directions. It will be easy to find.'

The Thing That
Miss Millie Saw

January 1984

What was it that caused Tessa Walcott to go mad? Because this is what people said – that Tessa, widow to a deacon, mother of six sons, former owner of three pairs of panties now permanently lost to the Caribbean Sea, had gone stark raving mad. It was the only explanation people could come up with. How else to make sense of the events – how Tessa had stormed right up onto Miss Millie's veranda and jumped on her? Miss Millie screamed out only once under the sudden assault, but then fell uncharacteristically silent, as if she had quickly made peace with the possibility that this was how it all ended. That is dead she was going to dead.

But three men ran to her rescue, dragged all two hundred and seventy pounds, all fifty-nine years of Tessa Walcott, her grey hair undone, her fat arms flailing as if she was a schoolgirl, off poor Miss Millie. One of the men, Miss Millie's husband, in fact, took up his cutlass and made threatening motions towards Tessa. The two other men had to restrain him.

'But is how she so bright?' he was shouting at Tessa. 'How she so bright to come up in *my* house to manhandle *my* wife, eh? How she so bright?'

Tessa only stomped on the floor, going around in a circle, shaking her head as if she was trying to get something out of it, and muttering.

'It not true! It not true!'

And this temporarily froze Miss Millie and the three men, for each one was certain they had dreamed this moment before.

But what was it that caused this madness? Because that was only the climax of it. For the two weeks before Tessa had been acting quite strangely indeed. Almost every evening as the sun went down she would go outside and start walking up and down the road, the Bible in her hand turned somewhere to the middle, so it had to be a psalm she was looking at. *Yea though I walk through the valley* . . . Except she never was looking at it. Her eyes stared vacantly ahead and she just walked up and down, up and down, muttering. But nobody called it madness then – for the Spirit, when it wanted, could move strange in a person. Possess them. Could send a man out into the desert for forty days and forty nights and when he came back, starved, the whiteness of hunger caked up around his mouth, still that man would have something tall about him, something that made you humble and respectful because you knew he had been talking with God. So, at first, no one called Tessa's condition madness, for if it was the Spirit moving in her, then to call it madness would be blasphemy.

In these two weeks, in the silence of each early morning, Tessa's muttering would unravel. The sound would bounce off trees, climb up walls and slip through windows into a sleeping person's ear, and so all of a sudden, all over Watersgate, people were dreaming the three words. '*It not true! It not true!*'

Then one night, after the two weeks of walking, after her assault on Miss Millie, Tessa continued walking out of Watersgate to Alexander Town Square and then further across into the community of Durningham where her first son, The Fifth, lived. She walked right up to his gate but never opened it. Never went in. She called to him from the road, her voice loud but ghostlike. When he came out she demanded of him, the tears now falling down her face.

'Tell me it not true. Tell me that is not true.'

And he just stared and stared at her, even though she kept asking and asking.

Finally, Tessa dried her eyes and lifted herself up in the dignified way she had always been used to.

'I am going down to the river to wash my hands,' she said to him. 'You is no longer my firstborn. You was never born to me at all.'

And she walked through the night back to Watersgate. What was it that caused this strange sequence of events?

It was the Thing That Miss Millie Saw.

What was it that caused Pastor Braithwaite to order from Kingston three tall light poles and a piece of canvas that was almost as big as a field? Then came the speaker boxes, the kind they have at Reggae Sunsplash or one of those other big stage shows. And then he rented five hundred folding chairs, the letters BHCo painted in a sick orange on the back of each. The rickety truck that brought them announced that this stood for Benson's Hirage Company, though the orange letters did not keep them safe; whether out of criminal intent or just plain absent-mindedness, at least one BHCo chair ended up on every patio in Watersgate. Even the church held on to a couple.

But what was it that caused Pastor Braithwaite to undertake such an enterprise – to set up this massive tent, to send the choir into rehearsals every night, for he had announced it was time to have an open-air crusade? A month-long open-air crusade. Imagine that – right there in Watersgate! Not in the town square or anything. Who had ever heard of such a thing? Who would come?

But come they did, for Pastor B. would be screaming into the microphone each evening.

'REPENT!'

And the sound would carry over hills and valleys into distant communities and catch people unawares. A boy would have just jumped over into his neighbour's yard, for instance, climbing silently up the Julie mango tree to pick the fruit he saw hanging tempting and red up there at the top, and just as his fingers closed around the fruit . . .

'REPENT!'

An old man would be sitting on his porch as if half asleep, his sly eyes in truth observing the wonderful way the sixteen-year-old girl across the road was filling out in certain places. He would think how nice it would be to hold on to something like that, a piece of bottom that wanted to be held, unlike his wife's which, though broader than any other part of her body, still slipped out of his fingers. But oh to have that sixteen-year-old girl over . . .

'REPENT!'

From all around the parish people came. In Jamaica, church was a part of everything – the way people breathed, and the way they walked. People waited for the latest preacher in the way another might wait for the next big song – ears perked up for it, humming it when it arrives, feet and hands and neck moving to it for weeks. On almost every corner there was a pulpit, and every preacherman preached like he was trying to win votes. Trying to bring in the largest flock. Trying to outdo the last preacherman. Prove himself more powerful, more righteous. And so, on the island, it became easy to preach hate and call it love. Easy to tell people who they should spit on. Who they should turn their eyes away from. Who was not their neighbour instead of who was. Hate is easier than love. And Pastor Braithwaite was a preacherman like this, who would tell the congregation who and how they should hate, and the people would listen.

What was it that caused this fanaticism? The fervent preaching? And then the Sunday baptisms? After church each Sunday, Braithwaite would have the choir sing, 'We go down to the River Jordan to meet the Lord'. He would march down the aisle, and the choir would follow with their song, the rest of the church right behind them. Out the door and down to the river.

After so many months, Imelda's house still stood solid in the midst of all that water. The pastor would take off his shoes, roll up his trousers, walk into the swell, across to the house and up the stairs onto the veranda. He would look over to the crowd and they would in turn look up, spellbound. Up there on the flooded veranda, he reminded them of the saviour standing on water.

'It is not enough! It is not enough,' Pastor Braithwaite would cry, 'to sing songs on Sundays. It is not enough to call yourself a Christian. It is not enough ... You must be washed in the river. You must drown the old man and come up out of the water a new creation. Who wants to make a public declaration of their faith today?'

Without even taking off her heels, Miss Millie was always the first to lift up her hands and splash into the river.

'Me, Pastor! Me!'

Just how much sin she had to wash away, no one really understood. For wasn't baptism needed only once? But that's how it went each week. And each week everyone would be baptised all over again.

What was it that caused such a Pentecostal fervour to sweep over Watersgate?

It was the Thing That Miss Millie Saw.

What was it that caused Young Constable Brown to knock on the gate of Mr Eulan Solomon one evening? Mr Solomon opened the grill and stepped outside, his eyes raised in query.

'Yes, sir. Good evening, sir. Just want you to know I'm keeping an eye on things, sir.'

'Why ... why, thank you.'

Mr Solomon didn't know what to say next. Then it dawned on him, this must be something Superintendent Carmichael had told the officer to do – to keep a special eye on his house. He had only just, that afternoon, returned from his vacation. Thinking this, Mr Solomon offered the constable a drink.

'Would you like a drink of water? A beer?'

'Oh no, sir. Not at all, sir. I'm on the job.'

And the corporal adjusted his red-striped policeman's hat, tucked his shirt in further, and turned to walk back into the village where, truth be known, he was headed for the rum bar anyway.

Mr Solomon closed the grille behind him and went back into his house, a little bit confused but appreciating the simple courtesy of country life. He reflected that this was another reason why he had moved away from Kingston. The city could be so dangerous. People were out to steal from you. Harm you. Kill you. Kingston didn't seem to have officers of the law who would walk up one evening, just like that, and let you know they were about the place doing their job.

But Mr Solomon was not used to country ways, and he had read the policeman wrong. Young Constable Brown was not offering help; he was issuing a threat. And all over Watersgate there were other warnings being given, more stern than any Hurricane Watch. Parents were telling their children: *When you pass that big concrete house, don't linger! You hear me, child. Walk on the other side of the road. Make haste and pass it!*

What was it that caused such warnings? It was the Thing That Miss Millie saw.

What was it that caused Miss Millie to insist that her title was no longer 'Miss' or even 'Mrs', since she was in fact a married woman? Instead, she wanted to be called 'Evangelist'. Evangelist Millie. She said she was giving it all up, changing her profession. Miss Millie said the Lord had called her, that she was now working full-time in the Ministry of the Kingdom, amen! That she was called to intercession, and that her purpose here on earth, she finally realised, was to lift up people's problems and trials to the Lord.

To pass her days, Miss Millie was now calling at each and every house.

'Carol-oooohhh!' she would shout, for instance, and when Carol came outside Miss Millie would get to the point immediately. 'What is it you want prayer for?'

This directness might startle the owner of the house, and she might not have an immediate answer. But the initial shock always passed and old habits would kick in. In villages like Watersgate people share their problems the way other people talk about the weather – as small talk. Easy talk. And in the wider island there were radio shows competing all day for you to call in and cuss.

Cuss the cricket team, the water supply, the roads, the government who we need to vote out, whatever came to mind to cuss about, you could call in and cuss. So Carol or Jennifer or whoever would at last answer with a sigh.

'That boy Reggie. Him give us no end of trouble. I shouldn't be surprised, really. Is ten hours I lie on my back giving birth to him. Him was a pain then, him is a pain now. Miss Millie . . .'

'Evangelist Millie, please . . .'

'Sorry. Evangelist Millie, if you see the last report card him bring into the house! He almost pass no subject at all. And is not that him dunce or slow. The teachers don't know what to do. Me and him father don't know what to do. Lord knows Josiah give that boy more beating than would lick sense into any ordinary person.'

Miss Millie nodded, writing it all down in an exercise book she had brought with her.

'And the back, Miss Millie . . .'

'Evangelist . . .'

'Yes, yes. The back I was saying. It giving me a warm time, you see! Every time I bend over, from right here . . . you see? All the way up. I know I getting older, and the body not what it used to be . . . but!'

'Come,' Miss Millie would say, reaching into her pocket for a small bottle of olive oil she carried with her, 'we will pray for that one right now.'

And so it was, Evangelist Millie swept up and down Watersgate anointing aching backs and rashes and even a few calluses. Anointing fowl that didn't lay enough eggs and trees that didn't bear enough fruit. Anointing sick dog and puss and cow. Anointing doors that had swollen in the cool months of February, and roofs that leaked into rusty Berger-Paint tins. Anointing every godalmightything with her little bottle of olive oil that wasn't actually olive oil, but cheap coconut oil she topped up each night.

Every problem that was confided to Millie was written down in the pages of her exercise book. She said this was in order that she could remind herself of the various situations each night and continue praying; so, years later, a history student from the University of the West Indies would find that in Watersgate, in the year 1984, there was a book containing each household's trials and tribulations, dutifully recorded by one 'Evangelist Millie'. But what was it that caused the former-gossipmonger-now-turned-missionary to take on such a project? To go down on her knees every night and make petitions unto God?

It was the thing that she herself saw. The thing that made all of Watersgate tremble. The thing that Miss Millie said God had chosen her to see, because if anyone else had seen it they would not have known what to do. Or they would have turned into salt. Or something else really, really bad. But God had chosen Miss Millie to see it, because of all the people she was the one who could handle it, and because he was using it to lead her into this new ministry of intercession.

The Thing That Miss Millie Saw was dreadful, and the news of it moved from house to house like one of those August fires in Jacks Hill, where in no time at all the flames jump from hilltop to hilltop, the bamboo burning and bursting, and soon all of Kingston is gathered outside their houses watching and talking about the hills blazing orange around them.

The year 1984 had only just begun. In fact, it was hardly more than an hour old. Miss Millie was returning from Watch Night service in Alexander Town Square. She liked going there on New Year's Eve, to the old Anglican church, as seemed a more proper place to celebrate. Besides, Pastor B. didn't hold a Watch Night service, and if he had people would have gone to it in their usual ways – men in their old suits and women in cheap dresses, their heads tied with a matching piece of cloth. But at the Anglican church Miss Millie could put on her head a proper hat and look dignified. In the stone building she could light candles and receive the bread and the wine, kneeling down on red cushions placed by the altar. She could sing old-time hymns that had words like *yonder* and *thou* and *hadst* in them – words that seemed more biblical and therefore, in a way, more spiritual to Miss Millie. It was true, she would be the first to admit, that the Spirit didn't move in that church the way it moved in Watersgate. But didn't the Bible say there was a time and a season for everything? So New Year's was a time to worship God in dignity, without the clapping of hands or the stomping of feet, but in a proper, English, non-Pentecostal way.

And when the service was done, the congregation gathered in the church hall to have refreshments and 'hob-snob', as Millie would put it. She enjoyed this part of the night just as much, mingling with the wife of the local magistrate and high-society people who, out of politeness (what with the old woman in her ugly hat standing so close and straining her neck into their conversations), asked her what life was like in her little village – how quaint and wonderful it must be. Miss Millie happily obliged them, and at considerable length. She had a grand time of it all, sipping hot chocolate, eating 'hors devours', adjusting her hat this way and that, and hob-snobbing from little group to little group.

But The Thing Miss Millie Saw happened when all of this was over and she was on her way back home, humming 'How Great Thou Art'. As she neared the bridge, she noticed that the party Mr Solomon was having was now in full swing. The music from inside the house was loud, the beat insistent, and every now and then the back door would spit out two or three guests, laughing, their skin shiny with sweat. Millie sighed. She knew this was how the people of the world were. They would ring in the new year partying rather than praying. This didn't surprise her. Yet still, she stayed in the shadows across the road, watching. Something was strange about this party, and she couldn't tell what it was. So for many minutes she just stood there, the music playing, the backdoor spitting out people, the people laughing, she frowning.

She might never have realised what was strange about it but then out of the door came a face she knew well. The Fifth. She knew him even before he knew himself. She had tickled his little baby's feet, made faces and said goo-goo ga-ga to him. Harold Walcott the Fifth. Son of Tessa and Harold Walcott, who was a deacon – God knows how, for he was absent half the time. The Fifth came out of the door smiling, another man giggling into his shoulders. And that is what was so strange. All these men were so easy with each other. Too easy. Resting on each other's shoulders. Holding each other's hands. Yes! That was it. And where was The Fifth's nice new girlfriend, Sofia? Where was any woman, for that matter? That's the other thing that was strange. She had not realised before, because all these men had something so soft about them, so soft, the way they were laughing, it was just like the way women laughed. It made her think she had seen women, but in fact, she had seen none. And oh God. Could it be that? Oh God. Oh God. Could it really be that? Sodom and Gomorrah! Right here in Watersgate?

And it was at that precise moment that Miss Millie invented the most vicious rumour she would ever spread – not only about what she had seen, but also how she was sure, beyond a doubt, that it was Tessa Walcott's own son who had stolen his mother's polka-dot panties for whatever nasty game it was sodomites like him got up to.

Miss Millie looked up to the sky, wide-eyed. She forgot all about New Year's Eve and hymns and dignity. She started singing a sankey loud, loud. *Sweet Holy Spirit, Sweet Heavenly Ghost!* And as quickly as she could, she marched back to her house.

The guests of the New Year's Eve party held at Mr Solomon's house, reviewing the night with their friends, would tell of the strange incident at one-thirty in the morning, when there arose from out of the darkness a singing that, even as it started, began to fade into the distance. It was as if, for just one moment, one of those old-time country women had been praying for their souls. And though they told this story in jest, they were, of course, completely right.

The Silly Thing Joan Braithwaite Expected from Her Husband

February 1984

Being the pastor's wife and all, Joan Braithwaite had been to her fair share of church conferences, seminars, camps and the like, and had duly heard her fair share of church jokes. Even the naughty ones. Like the one about an old woman's dying request to have no male pallbearers, for since none of them had taken her out in life, she didn't want them to take her out in death. Or the one that said anyone who claimed they didn't struggle with sexual urges was either too young, too old, or too lie. But the one Joan Braithwaite loved the most was the story of a certain pastor who played a game with his congregation in which he would shout out a word, and they would sing the first song that came to mind. So the pastor shouted 'Love', and the congregation, almost as one, started singing 'Love, wonderful love, the love of Christ to me.' He shouted 'Peace', and they all sang zealously, 'when peace like a river attendeth my way.' He shouted 'Fire', and after only a moment's confusion, they all settled into singing 'Fire, fire, fire. Fire fall on me, on the day of Pentecost, fire fall on me'. But when the pastor shouted out 'Sex', the church fell into a deep silence, and only after many moments did an old woman from the back stand up and in her shaky voice raise the hymn *'O precious memories.'*

Joan Braithwaite loved this joke the most, for if she didn't laugh at it she would have cried. Because most times she felt that that old woman was her. She remembered when she first got married – Douglas was as fervent and dynamic in bed as he now was in the pulpit. Every night. Every single night. It always started the same – they would be lying down in bed together and she would hear his breathing shift. It took on a different quality, became hungrier. He would inch over slowly in the bed until his hand – just his hand – was touching hers. A tentative touch. Then slowly, slowly it would build into that great kaleidoscope of thrusts and mouths and legs and sweat and Oh Gods and even Hallelujahs! But it always started off with just that touch. Hand against hand. Now at fifty, Joan regretted how, some nights, she had been secretly annoyed. Some nights she had only wanted to sleep, or to cuddle with him without it becoming this enervating act of sex. When had things changed, she wondered? When did her prayers turn from *please don't let him bother me with anything tonight, to please, please, dear God, let him bother!* Sometimes she would think it was all her fault; that all that time Douglas was just trying to breed her. Produce a son. But for all his efforts, so much ploughing, it never broke up the barren land of her womb. Thirty years later they were still childless, Douglas Braithwaite was getting old, and Joan found it so sad – how a day could stretch into a week and then into a year, and how all of a sudden sex was something you just never bothered to do again. Oh Precious Memories.

Then, it was the last night of the grand crusade. Joan imagined counsellors were still in the tent talking to new converts while a faithful remnant of the choir, hoarse but determined, continued singing songs to themselves. She and Douglas had left a long time ago and were in bed. That's when it happened. His breathing changed. She heard it change, and her whole body became tense. He reached over and not only touched her hand, he held it softly – gently shaking it. Joan felt every part of her insides go weak. She bit her lips, rubbed her legs together, silently and profusely thanking the Lord. *Drought was about to done!*

Only after five minutes had elapsed and Douglas's hold on her hand had become weaker instead of stronger, she recognised that there was something strange in the way he was breathing. Finally she turned around. The moonlight from the window shone on his face, and she could see now that his eyes were flung open in terror, his other hand clutched to his chest, and what she took to be breathing was a desperate attempt to form the word 'Help'. Miraculously, it seemed, for a moment he was able to shout – and he was finally screaming this very word which had been stuck in his throat. But then she realised it was her own voice yelling, 'Help! Help!', loud, so someone would hear.

She put on her slippers and ran outside. She looked down the road to where Isaac, the taxi man, lived, but his car was gone. She started up the road and soon saw that Sophie's van wasn't there either. She didn't stop running. She continued straight up the hill and across the bridge to Mr Solomon's house. She banged a stone on his grille until he appeared, groggy, his face showing a mixture of confusion and annoyance, for he was sure it was Miss Millie with more peas. Joan started to weep.

'Please, sir! My husband, I need to take him to the hospital now!'

Maybe his teacher had been wrong after all because something melted inside Eulan Solomon. Something like his soul, something like his heart. He looked for the keys to his car while Joan ran back. He caught up with her, his headlights illuminating her back like the final scene of a sad movie, and he thought about the kind of tragedy it must take to make a middle-aged woman move so urgently. He went into Braithwaite's house, into the man's bedroom, lifted him up off the bed and took him out to the car where he laid him down on the back seat.

At the hospital the nurses whispered, *Yes, it seemed serious. Very serious. But don't worry, Mrs Braithwaite. Stay calm. The best thing you can do for yourself and your husband is to stay calm. Is this your son? Son, take your mother outside for a bit.* Eulan led Joan to the waiting room, holding her hands the whole time. It seemed like hours before a doctor finally came out to them. It was a stroke, the doctor said. Not a heart attack. But the pastor would have to be hospitalised. For how long he could not say. It was very serious indeed. He told Joan, *prepare yourself. He might never be the same again. Might be paralysed. Might not speak properly ever again.* She started to cry all over again. What kind of man would Douglas be without his sermons?

Poor Joan. That night she had expected sex, but this, she realised, was silly thinking. In all, Douglas Braithwaite spent four days and three hours in the hospital. What happened after that, of course, he could not tell you. One night he went to sleep as usual, but the next morning, God never bothered to wake him up.

The Evangelical and Pentecostal Work of Miss Millie

February 1984

They went to church out of habit, proving that it, this Sunday ritual, was bigger than any man or woman, bigger than any one pastor, and would survive its leader's death and move on regardless. What would they do without church? So the cock crowed, the villagers woke up, everyone, and the men put on their good trousers, their thin socks and their gentleman's shoes – wiping off any trace of mud, for these were the same shoes many of them wore to work. The women put on their floral dresses, and took off their gold chains and their gold rings and their earrings – it wasn't decent to wear jewellery to church. By seven a.m. they had opened their doors and marched out as families, leather Bibles tucked under their arms, and walked to the church without a thought of what would happen this Sunday, now that Pastor Braithwaite was gone. They knew simply, and they were right, that something would happen, because something had to. Because otherwise, they would unravel.

Miss Millie alone prepared with the diligence of a school teacher. From late into the night she had been breaking pencils in three and sharpening each piece. At the church she pulled out the large metal basin which they filled some Sundays when they were going to baptise a baby. She placed it in front of the altar. As she worked she tried not to think of Eulan

Solomon who should have been arrested but somehow hadn't been. She understood of course that Satan was strong. Very strong. And that goat-foot man would always try to thwart the plans of the righteous. She worked all the more diligently in light of this. Righteousness would prevail in Watersgate. She tore many sheets of paper into small squares, one for each person.

When the congregation had finally gathered together, Sister Carol and Brother Bruce led the church in worship. As one song ended a member of the congregation would raise another imme-diately – favourite hymns and choruses. They sang many more songs than they usually would have, trying to fill the time, and they would have sung on and on had Miss Millie not interrupted with a prayer.

'Oh Lord, thank yu for your songs and this time of worship. Hallelujah. Thank you that we can give you praise when times is good, and praise even when times is sad. We look forward now to yu message. Amen.'

The congregation became quiet.

Miss Millie passed around the offering basket and told them to take from it instead, as if this was, finally, the promised hun-dredfold return after years of giving – the measure, pressed down, shaken together and running over. The basket was filled with the paper and pencils Miss Millie had prepared the night before.

'Take one, everybody. Yes. There is enough. Pass it around. Good. You must be wondering what this for, but we will come to that in a minute.' She took a breath and looked out over the people. 'Who here today is righteous enough to meet the Saviour?'

A teenage boy in the front row was brave enough to answer. 'No one, Miss Millie.'

'Evangelist, please!'

'No one, Evangelist Millie.'

'That's exactly right. No one! Scripture say all have sinned and fallen short of the glory of our Lord God. Today I want you all to look into your wicked hearts as I have done. Ask God to shine a bright bright lamp in there for you.

Make him reveal to you how you displeased him this week, even this morning. Who was begging you to forgive them but your heart was too hard? Who you been malicing? Who you been chatting 'bout behind them backs? Who you steal from this week, eh? I want you to write down every deed on the piece of paper. Don't lie in the house of God. Don't add sin upon sin. Write down the things God show to you. No one will read it. But write it down same way. Admit your transgressions before the Lord God.'

The problem for some of the congregation, especially the older ones, was not that they didn't want to follow Miss Millie's instructions, but that they had never learned how to read or write. But eventually even these people wrote something down. Like slaves attaching their trembling non-signatures, they drew a big 'X' on the paper. They had given much thought to their deeds, however, and the X represented some of their deepest secrets.

When all the scribbling was done, Miss Millie stood before the iron basin.

'Today is going to be a day of burning and renewing! You must allow God to make you righteous again. Allow him to touch his fire to you sins. This here is an altar onto God. Come.'

One by one they came up and tossed their lists of sins into the basin, and when the procession was over Miss Millie struck a match and threw it in. The church watched in amazement as the orange flames circled the pan and before their very eyes their sins turned to ash.

'The day of the Lord's fire is coming! We must be ready for it. It going to burn up things you don't know could burn. All of the wickedness and sin in this community. We want it to spread and burn up all the sin in this country. The fire will be hot hot but we must be ready.'

'AMEN!'

Later that Sunday, Miss Millie and four men walked up the hill to the Rastaman's hut. The four men were sweating rivers in their long-sleeved shirts and jackets. They found Joseph sitting in a yard full of sawdust, the hollow stump of a breadfruit tree in his hand. With a chisel he was hollowing it out even more. Miss Millie spoke for the group.

'We come to buy as much kerosene oil as this money can buy.'

Joseph looked up, and then over to the two large barrels of oil sitting by the side of his house.

'You can have them for nothing.' He went back to his work.

Miss Millie shook her head.

'We will not accept favours from people of this world. Please, how much for the two barrels. We have our money. We take up a collection, this morning. We don't need no charity from you.'

'Whatever the good miss want to do,' Joseph said without looking up. 'I and I won't complain. Leave the money on the ground over there and take the two barrels.'

'Hmph.'

Miss Millie placed the collection money on the ground. It was hardly worth half a barrel, she knew, but maybe she could accept a little charity after all. God was on their side. She gave instructions and the men began to roll the barrels carefully down-hill.

'Thank you for your business.'

Joseph grunted.

Miss Millie looked back.

'What in the name of Jesus Christ our Heavenly Saviour is it that you doing anyway, young man?'

'I'm going to call her.' he said simply, losing himself again in the work.

That following week, several strange things happened, none of which were investigated because none of them had been reported. In fact, there was no one to report them to. Young Constable Brown had left suddenly. Supposedly, he had been reassigned. But he left without telling anyone and without making any arrests for the murder of Douglas Braithwaite which, rumour had it, he was about to do.

The strange incidents all involved fire. All kinds of burnt things were ending up in the rubbish. Burnt magazines. Burnt books. Burnt cassettes. A woman returned home to find that someone had set fire to two of her radios. They had melted into a strange black sculpture, permanently attached to the tables on which they been sitting.

The Sex Tree outside Miss Millie's house had become nothing more than a black stump. That fire had been seen as far away as the neighbouring communities but no fire truck had been called, for everyone in Watersgate seemed satisfied that it had burnt down.

Finally, the charred remains of a cat were found near the river. Around the same time, Mrs Joline Murdock who lived beside Miss Millie was seen walking up and down the road, whistling softly and calling for Sugar, a fat orange cat who was like a friend to her. When the villagers informed Joline, quite correctly in fact, that the charred body they had found by the river must have been Sugar, she started to hold her stomach and bawl. But people said weeping was like that, and it would last only for the night. Besides, Sugar had got her just rewards. Everyone knew that cat was a thief of no mean order, and not only a thief, but a glutton too. It had once crept into a neighbour's house and made off with a whole roast chicken. The fire which burnt it on its last day on earth was surely the first taste of the hell it had descended into.

And even as these fires burned, Evangelist Millie continued to preach each Sunday, 'The day of the Great Fire is still to come!'

The Silly Promotion of
Young Constable Brown

February 1984

It was true, Young Constable Brown believed all kinds of foolishness, and had the entire village believing the same foolishness right along with him. But the thing he believed which was not so silly after all was that the crowning moment of his career would be the arrest of Eulan Solomon. For murder.

Miss Millie had come all the way to the station to give a statement.

'Satan strong,' she had moaned and shook her head. She was sitting across from the constable who had his notepad and pen out, ready to take down the report. Miss Millie, however, was slow in getting to the point. She got up from her seat, jumped up and down on the balls of her feet, spread her hands wide and spun around, punching the air five times. She shook her head, sat down once more and repeated, 'Satan strong.'

Young Constable Brown was not alarmed by these theatrics. In fact, they impressed him, and he waited patiently for her to start.

'Young Constable Brown. Both of us knows Pastor Braithwaite was a good man . . .'

'My God! A better man than him you couldn't find.'

'You know he had an anointing.'

'Sent straight down from, heaven, Miss Millie.'

'Evangelist Millie, please.'

218

'Sorry. Yes, of course. Evangelist Millie.'

'You was at the crusade?'

'But of course. Everybody was there. I went in my official capacity 'cause you know we have to be where the crowds are. But I also went as a believer. You know I is a man who believe in God, Evangelist Millie.'

'Yes, I know. This is why I come to you especially. The Lord tell me to come to you. Because man can see and know with the Spirit things him can't see with his own eyes.'

'True words, true words.'

'You saw for yourself the powerful things Pastor B. was doing. How him was stepping on people's corns. How him was preaching the word without fear of neither man nor scorpion.'

'Oh yes. I see it with my own eyes, Miss . . . Evangelist Millie.'

Miss Millie started to weep.

'SATAN STRONG!'

'Take your time, dear. Take your time.'

The constable came around from his desk and held the old woman's hands.

'No way that man was ready to die. You saw him, Young Constable Brown. He look like a man who was ready to die?'

'Not at all. He was in his prime.'

'Young Constable Brown, listen to me.' She wiped away her tears and took a deep breath. 'It was bad magic that bring down Pastor Braithwaite. Is somebody work evil against him. An evil spirit! Someone was mixing up with the devil. Constable Brown, I is a spiritual woman, and I know you is a spiritual man. Can't you see it? Can't you see that this was the work of the devil?'

'But of course.'

Something flashed across Miss Millie's eyes then, and if the constable had been a wiser man he would have recognised it as lunacy.

'You know how, before he died, Pastor B. was calling us all to rise up against the evil in this world . . .'

'Yes. I remember the sermon, Miss Millie. I was even taking notes.'

'He say that these are the last days. And we, the people of God, need to do what is necessary.'

'Amen.'

'Constable Brown, I know who did do it. The Lord reveal it all to me in a vision. Who it was that burn bad candle against Pastor Braithwaite. I know who it is that kill him.'

The policeman's eyes widened. 'But who?'

'The man from the big house. It was him, Constable. Mr Solomon killed Pastor B.'

Miss Millie did not have to say another word. She did not need to furnish any kind of evidence or make her case, for it all made immediate and perfect sense to Young Constable Brown. He and everyone else knew about The Thing That Miss Millie Saw. That was what they called 'motive'. He had also heard that a few days before his death, Braithwaite had been driven somewhere in the blue motor car belonging to the same Mr Solomon. That was what they called 'opportunity'. Motive and opportunity. Brown was only upset that he had not seen the connection sooner.

'So you will arrest him?' Miss Millie asked, wiping away her tears.

'He will hang by the gallows! Leave it to me.'

When Miss Millie left he called the St Mary Police Headquarters.

'Yes, yes. This is Constable Brown from the Eastern division. Very, very urgent matters. Urgent matters indeed! I would like to speak to the Superintendent at once!'

On the other end of the line Travis Carmichael was sighing. Urgent matters? These kinds of things were happening more and more in the country. Murder; double murders; triple murders; suicide and murders; butchering. Rural officers, he had to confess, were less well equipped to handle such matters, but it seemed he was getting a call like this almost once a month now.

'Yes. Carry on,' he told the constable.

So Brown told the Superintendent about the Thing That Miss Millie Saw – a New Year's Eve party which had become a grand display of lewdness, moral decay and corruption – things which were foreign to the goodly village of Watersgate. He told him about the righteous Pastor Braithwaite who had been a man in his prime and who, it was confirmed, had been driven in a blue vehicle belonging to the wretched Eulan Solomon some days before he died. The evidence was circumstantial but nonetheless substantial, and so Constable Brown was requesting a warrant to arrest the man immediately.

In that long moment of panic it seemed to Travis Carmichael that his heart was racing inside his mouth, causing his every attempt at speech to come out as a stammer. In point of fact, when he answered Young Constable Brown, his tone was even.

'Well done. Well done, Constable. I've been hearing much about your work and today you have confirmed what everyone has been saying.'

The constable was staggered. His work had never been complimented before, and for good reason.

'Yes, yes,' Carmichael continued. 'Such sharp detective skills. Listen, you need to write a report on this incident and give it to me immediately so I can brief the next officer who takes over your post.'

'Sorry, sir?'

'We can't keep someone with talent like yours out there in the backwaters. Oh no! You are promoted to the rank of Sergeant with immediate effect. You must have been expecting this for some time now? You will come to Headquarters and do more important work as one of my assistants.'

Brown jumped out of his seat and stood erect. He clicked his heels and put his hand to his forehead in a salute; in doing this he let go of the phone and it clattered to the floor, but he bellowed with military fervour all the same, 'Yes, sir! Thank you, sir!'

So Young Constable Brown, now promoted to Sergeant, never wrote the report. He forgot all about arrests and murders. He packed up his things that very day. A third stripe upon his shoulders. *Sergeant Brown.* This time he would insist on the name.

And that is why the constable left — why there was no police presence near Watersgate in the week that the small fires started to burn, or on the morning that God woke Imelda up, the day when the big fire was about to begin.

The Same Earth

February 1984

On the morning that God wakes Imelda up, Joan is in her bed thinking of a parable. She has not been to church for two weeks. She is in mourning, and needs a break. She needs to think things through for herself. Slowly and carefully. And she needs God to tell her who exactly, is her neighbour.

From when she was young she has been hearing this parable. A Jew was walking on the road one day when a set of thieves and badmen attacked him. They took everything they could, but instead of just leaving him there like that, without money and without a cloak, they wanted to take his life as well. They took out long blades and slashed him, jooked him down to the floor and left him there in his blood.

A priest happened to be walking on the same road. The priest saw the man lying in his blood, but shook his head saying, 'No, no, no. I am on my way to church.' He had no time to stop the almost-dead from dying. Another man came along the same road – a Levite, the tribe of people who were supposed to take care of the Temple and minister to the people. But this Levite had no time for ministering. He crossed the road and walked on the other side. Finally there came a Samaritan. Everybody knew Samaritans and Jews were not friends. The division was deep – like men in Kingston who supported the colour red, and those who supported the colour blue. But this Samaritan man had heart and soul and something else. Something like compassion. He went over and helped the Jew, getting blood all over his clean white clothes in the process. He put the Jew on his donkey and took him to an inn where he paid the keeper to look after him.

When Jesus told this parable he tested his listeners with a question.

'Who was this man's neighbour?'

The listeners answered correctly, 'It was the one who showed mercy.'

'You are right. Go now and do the same.'

Since Douglas dead and gone, Joan has been thinking. Slowly and carefully. Sometimes Douglas used to preach a kind of sermon that made her nervous. Like after he was finished preaching, something evil was released. She wouldn't pretend to be a smart woman. She wouldn't pretend to understand theology and the deeper meaning of Scripture. She could not tell you what was wrong or unbiblical about the things he said, still something made her feel nervous.

She hasn't been to church for two weeks for an additional reason – she has been rearranging. She has taken down every single one of Douglas's black jackets, black vests, his black shirts, black undershirts, underwear and ties from the hangers. She has removed his black shoes from the closet as well, and she's hung up her own clothes instead. And this act has made her weepy for something she didn't know she had been mourning all along. She needs space to understand this.

And another thing – since Douglas passed, Miss Millie has been preaching the sermon, sermons full of wrath – *Let today be a day of fire!* – that seem to be getting the people more worked up than usual. Ready to turn on their own neighbours. Joan doesn't want to be a part of this any more.

The morning that God wakes Imelda up is the morning that Joseph finishes making a perfect drum. He has used the hollowed stump of a cedar tree, about two feet tall and the same wide.

Stretched over the whole thing so that you can almost see no stump at all is the dried and cured underside of a ramgoat's skin. The skin is secured to the base of the drum by four wooden pegs, and is so taut that Joseph needs only to put his little finger lightly on the surface and the whole thing begins to vibrate.

Two weeks earlier, when he went to propose to Imelda, he left the house at the end of the hill feeling angry and hurt. He had watched the old woman hurry into the house, and for a moment he thought he might jump over the gate, go into the yard shouting *Imelda! Imelda! Imelda!* over and over, scaring the hummingbirds away from their roses. He imagined Imelda would finally come out and find him on his knees, a ring in his outstretched hand – but he doubted himself for too long. What proof did he have that she really was inside? While he stood there contemplating, a police car approached slowly, patrolling the neighbourhood. The two policemen looked at him in a strange way, and he, remembering how dangerous these men were in the city, thought it best, and safest, to leave. He walked down the hill thinking about the system, about Babylon and about white women who could crush a big man's heart, making all the greatness of his love amount to nothing. The sadness settled into his shoulders and they drooped.

But that evening, when he returned to Watersgate, something happened – an idea that made his shoulders rise again. He jumped the fence into Miss Jennifer's farm and looked for the biggest goat. When he found the ram, a dangerous-looking beast with red eyes and long, sharp horns, he held its forelegs and its hind legs together and heaved it over his shoulders. He walked like this all the way up to his hut. He figured that if he was able to call down spirits from as far up as heaven or from as far across the oceans as Africa, then surely he could call one human being back from Kingston.

He sat down with the goat when he arrived at his hut and spoke to it.

'I and I sorry, but I have to kill you. I going to use your skin and make a drum. And I going to use it to call Imelda home.'

The goat nodded at this reasoning and lifted its head towards the knife.

So, on the morning that Joseph has finished making his most perfect drum, he starts to play a rhythm on it. When his hand falls on the drum it vibrates, the vibration enters him – violently – and to look at him you would think he was a man in the midst of a seizure. But somehow his hands continue to fall and lift from the drum. Joseph has never played this rhythm before – it is not Kumina, or Pocomania, or Gheri, or Dinki Mini, or anything else. It is more complex than them all. Perhaps you could call this rhythm Love.

On the morning that God wakes Imelda up; Miss Millie rises from her house and walks slowly towards the bridge, pushing against the air as if the strong winds of a hurricane were holding her back. With one hand she is holding the broad hat she is wearing firmly on her head, with the other she is clutching a Bible. The high heels she is wearing do not seem a sensible choice – but then, Miss Millie is not always a sensible woman. Her knees are wobbling but still she is pushing against the air with the determination of a lunatic. There is no wind blowing this morning but there is a drumbeat, a frantic drumbeat which started in the dark hours and seems to have made the air a wall she cannot pass through.

But Miss Millie pushes and pushes, and finally reaches her destination. She is a sight to behold – such a small woman appearing so big on the pulpit of the iron bridge. She is dressed all in white; a white hat, white shoes and a long white dress that falls all the way past her ankles. She opens her mouth now and shouts a prophecy down to the village. Hers is like the Old Testament prophecy *Repent!* Not a description of the future, but a call to action.

'Fire!' – Miss Millie shouts. 'Let today be the great day of fire!'

On the morning that God wakes Imelda up – you must not be scared – but the devil also wakes, which is another way of saying, evil stirred. For the devil is a creature of multiple shapes and genders and ages; sometimes the devil is you, and sometimes the devil is me. But on this morning the devil is Tessa Walcott and Zero; the devil is Miss Dorcas and little Jonathon who is no longer little; it is Mother Lynette, Maas Jethro, Deacon Rodney and the Seamstress Rose; it is Deaconess Jennifer, Sister Carol, Reggie, Isaac, Sophie. The devil is Watersgate, for it is the villagers who wake up, all at the same time, united in their hate.

And because, on this morning, the devil is plural, the devil thinks many thoughts. *He thinks: I have rice without meat; I have a doorframe without a door; I have a roof with holes; I have arthritis that hurts when the rain comes; I have cataracts that blur my vision; I have asthma and bad lungs; my kidneys are failing; my son has failed me; my four sons have left and haven't written a single letter; the job that took me so long to find and that I have been working at for the past two years has just been taken away from me; I have had no luck getting a visa but the embassy has had all the luck getting my money.*

The devil also thinks: *I am generally a good person. I must not be blamed for all the bad that has befallen me. It is all caused by something else – some other evil and wickedness and nastiness outside me. But wouldn't it be wonderful this morning, if I could find the root and cause of all this bad luck? If it is a man, I will take a knife and open his belly. I will open his neck. I will reach inside his ribcage, pull out his heart and stuff it in his mouth. Then I will set his body on fire. If he has a house, I will burn that to the ground as well. Fire upon all wickedness! Fire! Fire!*

Imelda wakes up laughing. To be more specific, it is her laughter that wakes her up. She had been dreaming the sound but now wakes to find it is her own self laughing. She doesn't know why, but she continues. The laughter is springing from something deep inside her, like joy. So she thinks, this must be God. Which is why in retelling the story she will always say: *That morning it was God who wake me up.*

She gets out of bed and the laughter becomes a song. She sings it as she walks out of her room, down the hallway and into the kitchen where Mrs Johnson and Desmond, early risers both of them, are making tea. Imelda says good morning. Desmond stares at her and Mrs Johnson takes a step back.

'Mr Richardson, what is wrong with Imelda?'

It doesn't seem odd to Imelda that this question is not directed to her, as if she were not capable of speaking for herself. Indeed, she does not think to answer. It is as if her father and Mrs Johnson are in another world. There, but not really there. She continues to sing.

'What is that she is saying, Mr Richardson?'

'I can't tell you. She is speaking in tongues.'

Desmond is calm. He has seen such things before.

'But it's as if she's possessed,' Mrs Johnson stammers.

'Yes,' Desmond agrees, 'she is possessed.'

Imelda thinks about the word. Is possession something like a conviction – that you needn't worry about paths diverging in the woods, because every road will come back to where you are supposed to be anyway? Is possession a foreboding – a sense that although a hurricane is coming, you need not fear it . . . you cannot fear it because to fear it is to fear yourself? You are a part of the hurricane. You are in the dead centre of it.

You are the eye and the calm; you are its howling and its violence. You are the wind that tears at the bridge, throws down the people. You are the rain that floods the field and puts out the fire. And is possession the same thing as being sure? For more than anything, that's how Imelda feels. She now knows what to do, and where to go. Knife and scissors. Yes. That's what she has come for. She takes them out of the drawer. And then her song becomes a dance. She dances back to her room.

'But it's as if she's possessed,' Mrs Johnson repeats, her voice full of worry.

'Yes,' Desmond agrees a second time, 'she is possessed.'

In her room Imelda opens the wardrobe, reaches up to the top shelf and pulls out the red cardigan she bought so many years ago. She cuts from it a long band of red and ties it around her head, like a warning. Her dance becomes an even bigger. She dances out of the room and out of the house, into the yard and onto the road. She is going back. All the way back to Watersgate. She isn't going to take a bus or a taxi. She is going to dance her way there, down into Papine, across Liguanea and Barbican, up Stony Hill then down again, pass Castleton. Towards Watersgate.

On the morning that the anger begins to recede in Imelda, the water surrounding her house likewise begins to recede. She cannot see it happening, but for every step she takes closer to the village, the river takes a step back. It is a strange dance between woman and water.

They emerge from their various houses – from the river to the bridge, they emerge. In dark trousers and white shirts and ties, in floral skirts and matching head-wraps, holding Bibles in one hand, bottles of kerosene in the other. They have to push hard at their doors to get out because the air is like a wall. And outside they have to listen to that rhythm – a drumbeat that is melting their hearts, a drumbeat that is filling the village, making them think complex thoughts, like who might be their neighbour, and who they might love, and who they might very well forgive. But then their prophetess is shouting something more simple. They take strength from her words and march slowly towards them, pushing against the air.

Come! Come!
Let today be the day of fire!
Let today be the day we learn to breathe in the midst of smoke.
Let we stand up for something today.
Come! Let we burn away the wickedness.

On the morning that Eulan Solomon sleeps and sleeps when, if anyone knew and loved him, they would be shouting – *wake up! wake up and run! Do you not see the people streaming into your yard? Do you not see them at each corner of your house anointing the walls with oil? Do you no feel the heat?* – the widow, Joan

Braithwaite, goes down on her knees to say a prayer. She knows who is her neighbour.

'Dear God,' she prays, 'bless Mr Solomon. Keep him safe from all pestilence that is coming his way. Send your angel quick quick. Protect him.'

On the morning that God wakes Imelda, God himself wakes up. For isn't it true, the belief in God is equally a belief in his deep slumber – a grudging acknowledgement that maybe this small earth is too big and too messed up, so that God, if he exists, is likely to be off somewhere else, fixing some other problem and greater than our own. But for those of us neglected, who live on an earth unvisited by God, isn't that the same thing as him sleeping?

But on this morning, God turns his face towards Watersgate; he has come to Imelda as laughter, and then becomes a song, and then becomes a dance. So look – there in the distance – isn't that God coming? She is dancing towards the village, a red band tied around her head like a warning. She is coming towards it all – dancing to the drum she can finally hear, dancing towards the smoke she can now smell, dancing towards the devil and towards love. On this morning, like every morning, everyone on the earth is on the same earth together – and in Watersgate, they shall understand this.